Judas

Judas

The Man From Kerioth

by
Zacarias Joel Olivarez

toExcel
San Jose   New York   Lincoln   Shanghai

Judas
The Man from Kerioth

This edition published by toExcel Press,
an imprint of iUniverse.com, Inc.

For information address:
iUniverse.com, Inc.
620 North 48th Street
Suite 201
Lincoln, NE 68504-3467
www.iUniverse.com

ISBN: 1-58348-732-8

Printed in the United States of America

I fondly dedicate this book to my loving wife, Dora and to my children, Joanie, Z. Joel Jr., James, Carol, and Lori. Also to my grandchildren Lyric, Z. Joel III, Colton, Justin, and to a grandson, for whom we will celebrate his birth in February, 2000.

Contents

Chapter 1
The Premonition

The sun warmed the cool winds of the early evening, as Sofia, a young Galilean girl, was at the village water well. Most of the women of Nain, a small village near Nazareth, drew water there for their daily needs during the early morning. But today, Sofia had been busy this morning helping her father and her two older brothers gather their flock. Their livestock had been scattered by the thunder and lightening that had accompanied the heavy rainstorm that had fallen on the countryside the night before. Therefore she had to wait until this early evening hour to draw the water for her family's need. As she pulled on the tattered rope attached to the well to raise the second of her three large water jars, she found herself in deep thought about a strange dream she remembered having during the height of the storm last night.

Was it a dream? It seemed so real. It was hard for Sofia to think of it as just a dream, and even harder for her to understand its meaning. It seemed to resemble more an omen, or a premonition of things to come than just a simple dream. But there were too many things to do at the present time and not any time to think about such things. The air seemed to smell extra fresh after a heavy rain. She raised her face to take a deep breath and inhaled deeply. She looked around and saw how beautiful the sparsely vegetated landscape with its mountain range at a distance seemed to be. As she worked and admired the countryside she thought about how much the God of

Abraham must love His Chosen People to have given them such splendor like these mountains and living deserts for their home land.

Sofia was a beautiful young girl with olive color skin, which despite the hot sun of the early summer month of Silvan still retained its youthful moisture and glow. The shape of her mouth and lips made it seem as if she had inherited a perpetual smile to go along with her dark brown hair that hung to her waist and her light brown eyes. She stood about five and a half feet tall and weighed about one hundred and twenty pounds. .

As long as she could remember, she had helped her father Ezra and her older brothers, Seth and Zev, with what many considered to be traditionally men's chores, but this did not prevent her from having to help her mother do the traditional female tasks as well. Sofia did not care though, on the contrary, she enjoyed the out-doors so much and she looked forward to tending the herd regardless of the weather conditions. Sometimes at night, when the moon was full, it seemed to light up the whole world as if it were daytime. The stars were so bright and shiny that she felt she could almost touch them from where she would sit watching the herd on the side of the hill. This extra busy schedule gave her a much firmer body then most girls her age, and the appearance of one a few years older than her actual fourteen years of age. Although her father Ezra never really said it, she felt very confident that she was his favorite sibling. He was a man of few words, but his family knew that he loved them all very much from his deeds. His eyes seemed to tell people what he could not or would not say. She was filling her last water jar, when she suddenly became aware of a Roman Legion marching, getting nearer and nearer to the water well. She could tell it was soldiers marching by the distinct sound of the soldiers' feet shuffling on the ground.

About sixty or sixty-five years prior, the Roman General Pompey had conquered Jerusalem and the Provinces of Palestine. They all became subject to Rome's rule including the countries of Judea, Galilee, Samaria and others surrounding the Sea of Galilee. King Herod, a Jew who liked to call himself Herod the Great was the Procurator, selected by Rome to insure peace and minimal rebellion. Sofia could only guess that this Legion of Roman soldiers were on their way back to Jerusalem from Cana. She had overheard her father and other neighbors' talking about a rebel leader named Tabor, who was refusing to accept Roman rule, and was attempting to rally support in Cana. He was recruiting additional young men for his army of Patriots to help overthrow the Romans.

She hurriedly finished her task and mounted the three large water jars onto her donkey's back and made her way down the worn pathway to her home not far from the outskirts of Nain. From a distance, she could still hear the Roman Centurion shouting orders to his commanders. He was ordering them to allow only a paltry drink of water to each soldier. It was evident that he was under some sort of timetable to return to Jerusalem and report his findings to King Herod, so time was of the essence. A frightening chill came over her entire body as all this commotion brought back the memory of the strange dream she had experienced last night.

In her dream, two men with glowing faces and dressed in white robes came to her. She could just vaguely remember their spoken words. They first said, "Sofia....do not be afraid. What your future holds, you will not be able to comprehend, nor will you be able to control. At first it will seem as if our God Jehovah has abandon you, but what will happen must happen if Scripture is to be fulfilled. But as with Jacob, son of Isaac, he will not condemn you or your offspring. Remember that although Jacob was a trickster and deceiver as his name implies, the Lord found favor with him; so much so that He even changed Jacob's name to Israel, which means 'Prince of God'. So it will be for you and your descendent to come."

In her dream she kept asking, "What Scripture? What will happen? What are you talking about?"

But the glowing figures only replied, "Do not fear for the Lord of Abraham has chosen you and your offspring to help fulfill the Scripture written in the Torah, and foretold by David and the Prophets Zacarias and Isaiah. Do not fear for yourself or your family or for your predecessors yet to come. It will be hard to understand but the Lord has found favor in you and your future offspring."

Was it a dream? How Sofia yearned to know for sure. It seemed so real! What could it mean? She prayed as she swiftly walked toward her home. "Yahweh, I am but Your humble servant. My family and I fervently keep all Your commandments and the Laws of Moses. Please take good care of all our family and relations. Do not let any harm come to us. I fully place my heart and soul in Your care, to do with me as You will."

She was nearing her home and could now hear Sarah, her mother, in a loud voice beckoning Seth and his brother Zev to check on their sister since the day was growing late and the evening shades had started to fall. As they left the house on their way to find Sofia, she waved to them from a distance, to let them know that she was just a few minutes from the house. They waited for her under a large fig tree that was by the small rock fence that surrounded their home. While they waited, they laughed and talked, and with their knife, they carved their names on the bark of the fig tree, occasionally turning to check on Sofia's progress. When she got to the fig tree, they walked with her and the donkey the rest of the way home.

That evening she helped her mother prepare the meal, which consisted of leaven bread, dry figs, cooked calf's meat, wild honey and wine. When supper had ended, she gathered the meal dishes and helped her mother clean the table and fireplace that served also as the stove. When she had finished, she set down near her father and conversed with him about the events of the day. She told him about seeing the Legion of Roman soldiers and how they had stopped at the water well to refresh themselves. She could not understand why the Centurion in charge did not allow the soldiers to drink all the water that she was sure they needed. After all, they had been on foot for several miles, eating each other's dust while marching. She was about to tell her father about her strange dream, when her mother came into the room and authoritatively announced that it was late and a long hard day awaited them tomorrow so it was time to go to bed.

Sofia kissed her father, said goodnight to her brothers and mother and went to her corner of the bedroom and laid down on the warm covers made of different animal skins. As she lay on the floor, she could see outside through a small crack on the window shutters just to the right side of where she lay. It was a beautiful night, all lit up with what she imagined to be at least a million bright-lit stars. As she lay there she prayed,

"Lord Yawah, keep all my family safe through this night and always. Continue to bless our home…and Lord, if another dream comes to me as the one I had last night, please give me the wisdom to interpret its meaning. Above it all, I am your faithful servant and always will be. Goodnight Lord." With that she yawned, turned to her side and soon fell asleep.

Dawn came early, arriving from the East. Sofia could hear her mother already busy by the fireplace, stirring up the ashes and fanning the small ambers that remained from the night that just ended. It was late in the month of Sivan, the ninth month of the Jewish civil year. Even though the days were bright and sunny, the nights had a chill to them and that made it hard to get out of the warm covers and begin a new day. She said her morning prayers as she picked up the skins where she had laid, and put them in a neat stack at the corner of the room. Today was not as hard to rise as other days. She was excited by the thought that today would be her turn to shepherd the flock. Her brothers Zev and Seth would be going to Nazareth with their father to barter some goats and sheep for some household needs. Therefore she would keep watch over the flock by the foot of the mountainside until their return. Last night had been Zev's turn to watch the flock and he had just come home from the hills where they pastured their flock.

The sun was rising higher and warming the air as the morning progressed. Sofia helped her mother with breakfast, and after thanksgiving prayers and eating, she walked with her brothers and father for a while until she reached the flock. While they were walking, Zev told Sofia that he thought he had heard the muffled sound of drums beating cadence much like a Roman Legion uses to maintain its step. They seemed to change directions constantly, at times seeming to come from the east then from the south until it seemed to be coming from all directions at one time or another. Ezra could only surmise that they must be after a band of freedom fighters that had been attacking some of the Roman garrisons at night. When they reached the side of Mount Tabor where the flock was grazing, Ezra kissed Sofia and implored her to be very careful and vigilant.

"Do not take any risks my child, "he said. "You are to keep watch over the flock strictly to protect them from preying animals scattering them. If you see any soldiers or any other strangers attempting to steal the animals, or harm the animals, I want you to leave at once and return home. You are more valuable then all the livestock in all of Galilee."

"Yes", chimed in Seth, "Let no harm come to you. If you cannot run for whatever reason, then hide in the cave near where some of the animals are grazing until danger passes."

She begged them not to worry since she had been taking care of the herd for quite sometime, even at night and the Lord God had always protected her. She waited and watched as her father and brothers went on their journey. They had a good ten miles to walk before they would reach the outskirts of Nazareth. She prayed for their safe journey as she watched them get smaller and smaller the farther away they got. Soon she ended her prayers and proceeded to the place where the flock was grazing. She looked for her favorite ewe and found her grazing on newly grown grasses by the foot of Mount Tabor. She set down by the ewe and gazed at the wonderful view.... the mountain, the valley, even the birds of the sea that had strayed about forty miles inland from the Mediterranean Sea. What a sight! Such splendor!

Sofia must have sat there for some time, almost in a daze, enjoying the majestic outdoors. Sofia was unaware that she was twirling her right index finger around an heirloom necklace that she was wearing that her mother had given her. Touching that necklace always seemed to give her a sense of peace. Her mother Sarah had gotten that necklace from her grandmother Anna Benjamin, her great-grandmother, whose ancestors had founded the village of Kiriath Jearim, now called Kerioth. Sofia had picked up the necklace this morning from the cupboard in the kitchen area, where she always kept it, and had decided to wear it today while she tended the sheep.

The whole family knew the story of how that necklace was given to Anna Benjamin's ancestral great-grandmother by her husband. It had come into his possession as spoils of war while he fought in the Maccabean Army under Eleazar just before he died at a place called Masada. Sofia made the tenth generation to own the necklace, so she was extra careful with it whenever she wore it. The chain was made of pure gold and was about sixteen to seventeen inches long. On it was a large round medallion about an inch in diameter made of gold containing a large topaz in the middle with silver inlay that looked like a spider's web around the topaz to hold it in place. This necklace was her most endeared possession.

The sun was almost at its mid-day spot when her serenity was disturbed by what she thought were sounds of muffled drums and faint sounds of scraping, much like the sound that soldiers feet make as they march in unison. She walked to the edge of the mountain and she could hear the sounds more clearly. She remembered the warnings that her father and brothers had given her but she felt that the soldiers where still too far away to do any harm. Besides, she enjoyed watching them marching. They seemed to be like a cloud of dust moving ever so slowly, being pulled along by what must be their leaders at the front of the formation on horses. She seemed to become hypnotized by the rhythmic booming sound of the drums and the sound of the soldier's feet rasping the ground as they marched. She becomes oblivious about time, and dazed as if in a trance. Little did she realize that what was to happen next would change her entire life.

Chapter 2
Conception of Judas

Sofia was startled back to reality by the sound of rocks sliding down the hill just behind her. She whirled around and looked up to see what had caused the rockslide. It was a soldier on horseback. He was leering down at her as he pulled the reins to keep his horse under control. The horse was white as a cloud, and it would stand on its hind legs, trying to keep from going over the edge of the hill. Sofia even thought she saw smoke coming from its nose as it snorted loud and often.

"Whoa you devil's horse," he shouted at the horse as it inched closer and closer to the hill's edge. It took some struggle, but he never lost control of his horse.

Sofia glared at him frightfully. She could see that he was wearing a short red tunic with leather straps and a saber on his side. He also wore leather sandals with straps up to the knee. He had a red cape tied to his neck and it was long enough to cover part of his horse's hip and haunch. He appeared to be in his mid to late twenties. From where she stood with her eyes fixated on him, he looked tall and intimidating. He yelled down to her as he struggled to control his horse.

"In the name of Caesar and the Roman Empire, I commend you to stay and hold your ground! Do not move from where you are or I will be forced to assume you are a rebel with intent to do me or my soldiers harm!"

Sofia looked at him in astonishment. She seemed to be frozen in her tracks momentarily. She quickly remembered the warnings and advice her father and brothers had given her. She quickly ran into the cave located to her right on the hill, as her father and brothers had suggested. She could hear the sliding of his horse's hoofs on the mountainside as he descended down, giving chase to her as she ran. Sofia entered the dim lit, cool and humid cave and hid behind a large boulder located almost at the back of the grotto. Her heart was pounding and her breathing was very rapid and irregular from fright. Suddenly she saw his silhouette at the cave's entrance. He drew his sword so very slowly that she could hear the rasping of the cold steel blade on the leather scabbard. While doing so he asked sheepishly,

"Woman, are you in this cave alone? Come out and show yourself. Is there someone else with you? Come out and I will be lenient with you. Come out I say," he demanded.

Sofia did not respond. She was terrified. "Oh God, please watch over me. Keep me safe from harm," she prayed to herself. The soldier began to walk into the cave slowly. As he walked his shadow behind him grew larger and larger, giving Sofia more reason to be frightened.

"I can hear you breathing," he said as he walked slowly towards her location.

Sofia could not contain herself anymore, so she blurted out, "Who are you? What do you want? I am not an enemy. I am of no consequence to you and do not pose a threat to you by any means. Please leave me alone and go away I pray"

"I am Captain Octavio Pantera, Commander of the Cavalry soldiers of the First Legion of Rome. I have come to scout ahead of my troops. Now show yourself. Let me see your pretty face."

He continued to walk slowly forward saying, "Do not make it hard on yourself, reveal you're hiding place."

She knew it was inevitable that he would find her. She thought it would be best if she voluntarily came out from behind the large boulder where he was almost standing. Slowly she rose to her feet.

Shaking like a scared little rabbit, Sofia uttered, "Please Captain Pantera, I am only a shepherd girl that does not pose any threat to you or your army. Be on your way and let me be I implore you."

He grabbed Sofia by her left arm and held her tightly as she struggled to get loose. He seemed to enjoy the fear exhibited by Sofia in the presence of the danger she felt. Her eyes were fixed on his, and resembled those of a scared rabbit.

"Aha," he sneered as she fought desperately to get away, "All of you young Galilean winches are full of spirit, just the way I like my women! Stop all this fighting and I might go easy on you girl." All the while that he was speaking, he was applying more and more pressure on her arm and to the back of her neck. The pain was becoming unbearable. All attempts to get away, by kicking, scratching, hitting and biting, failed to gain Sofia's release. She therefore stopped trying to gain her release for the time being. Suddenly Sofia looked into his eyes and she imagined him to be an incubus, descending upon her.

He put his face so close to hers that she could feel his hot breath. He said, "You and all who live in this land are no more then spoils of war. I can kill you, take you, or let you go."

"Then let me go I beg you in the name of our Lord God of Abraham! I am but a simple girl that has not caused you any harm." In an effort to sway his intentions Sofia added, "I am expecting my father and brothers to come here any moment."

"Good!" he replied, "Then I will have to kill them too. Killing one, two or three Jews, it's all the same to me. You have better do as I say and please me because if you do not, I will give you a fate worse then death. I will take you with me and make you a concubine for all my Cavalry soldiers, and I assure you that you will not value that very much."

With that, he released her momentarily and pushed her against the large boulder that she had been hiding behind. He stared at her bosom and looked at the necklace that she was wearing.

"Where did a poor shepherd girl like you get such an exquisite piece of jewelry," he asked?

"This is an heirloom sir, it belonged to my grandmother and to her grandmother, for many generations back. Please do not confiscate it I beg you."

He walked back towards his horse that was standing just inside the cave entrance. He reached into a bag tied to the back of his saddle and withdrew a canteen and a blanket. Leering at her, he spread the blanket on the ground inside the cave and knelt on it. He opened the canteen and took a large drink. When he finished that drink, he said, "The only thing I like about this forsaken place is its women and its wine. They are both intoxicating!"

Sofia tried to run past him as he knelt but he reached out and grabbed her by her leg and pulled her down on the blanket next to him. He gave a sinister laugh as if the more terrified Sofia became and the more she struggled, the more he enjoyed it.

"Come on, have a drink with me," he demanded of Sofia, "It is guaranteed to reduce any inhibitions that you might think you have; it will definitely make you less frightened of me. Who knows, you might even enjoy my company!" When she did not respond, he demanded in a loud commanding voice, "I said, have a drink."

When she refused to drink, he pinned her down and tried to force her to drink. He lifted the canteen and pour wine into her mouth. Since her mouth was closed, tightly, the wine spilled all over her upper body. He began to lick the wine off her breast cleavage as it ran down her cheeks, neck and upper body. One of the sharp edges of the necklace scratched his cheek. Enraged by it, he tore it off her neck, and flung it near the cave entrance. She squirmed and yelled, but he covered her mouth with his large hand. Even if he had not, here wasn't anyone around to hear her desperate cries. She gained temporary release when he positioned himself to take another large drink.

"Why are you doing this? Sofia asked almost in tears, "Is this what the great Roman army is all about? How can we accept Roman rule and government when this is the kind of treatment we can expect?"

"My father is the politician. He is a senior member of the noble Senate of Rome. I am a soldier, not a politician," he halfway shouted showing his frustration, "I don't care if you accept our rule or not." Pausing just a second he then added, "I am also a man who has been in the field of battle here in Galilee and Judea for more then six months." He continued to drink heavily as he spoke. Stroking her cheekbone lightly with his fingers be continued, "During all this time I have not bedded a woman." Sofia could see the lust in his eyes.

Blushing from what Pantera had just said, she responded, "What kind of man would take a woman by force? Only the most abominable human being would impose his will on a helpless young girl. No decent righteous man would ever consider, much less do this act against another human being and God's laws.

"I am a Captain in the service of Caesar, not a believer of you religious nonsense. I am also a man who has needs that must be satisfied. If I cannot be home in Rome enjoying myself with my lady friends, then I will take what I need to satisfy myself here and now." With that said, he took another huge drink of wine. Sofia attempted to get up, but he was too strong.

"Please, do not do this despicable thing, I beg of you," she implored as tears ran down her flushed cheeks. She was now in tears, and more scared then ever. "If you do this, and if people think I fornicated willingly with anyone other then a husband, I will be stoned to death for being an unclean woman. And if by some chance I am not stoned to death, at very least, I could never face my family again. I would be scourged and cast out of my family and village, for so it is written in the Law of Moses."

For an instant she seemed to reach his conscience as he set silently for just a brief moment; but the wine and his sexual desire and lustful appetite were too strong, thereby ending that remorseful feeling immediately. He pushed her back down onto the blanket and began to strip her clothing. She fought him in every way she could, but he was too strong. Eventually she fainted and was totally helpless. She was unconscious by the time he mounted her, penetrated, raped, and forever took away her virginity and innocence. The last thing Sofia remembered was fighting to get away and the thunder and lightning storm that had suddenly came up during this despicable ordeal.

It was difficult to tell how long Sofia had been unconscious. When she regained her mental faculties, she was laying totally nude on the blanket except for her tattered dress that had been tossed over her naked body. She must have been in this state for sometime since the early evening shadows had already started to appear inside the mouth of the cave. The thunder and lightning were still audible but had moved away toward the southeast. Captain Pantera was fully clothed except for his sword and scabbard, which were still on the ground where she vaguely remembered he had dropped them. He was sitting on a rock that was by the cave entrance, his head bent down and supported by his hands at his face. She jerked herself into a sitting position, clutching her dress in front of her in an effort to cover herself. He turned and looked at her as she sat on the blanket. She still was not quite sure of what had just happened and for what length of time. It did not take long however, for her memory to return to the events just prior to passing out. Remembering, she began to cry softly, almost within herself.

"I see you are awake and all right", he said as he turned to look at her. "I did not want to leave before you regained your wits about you."

She sprang to her feet; still covering herself with her dress that had been torn in the process. She quickly picked up her loincloth she used as her under garments and dashed behind the boulder that she had hidden behind earlier that day. There she began to dress as her crying became somewhat louder. She felt filthy, and violated. A thousand thoughts raced through her mind as she was dressing, all the while sobbing. Why did this happen? How was she going to get out of this cave? What was she going to tell her father and mother? More importantly, what were they going to do to her? Captain Pantera stepped out of the cave with his horse and adjusted the terrets and checkhooks girded under the belly of his horse. He also replaced the empty canteen into his bag behind his saddle. After a few minutes he returned into the cave to find Sofia fully dressed in her tattered dress and sitting by the boulder crying.

"Why do you cry? It wasn't all that bad," Pantera asked, "What is done is done, and nothing is going to change it."

"What is going to happen to me?" sobbed Sofia, "I will be banished from my family, if not stoned to death!"

"How will they know what has happened to you if you do not tell it yourself? No one need know, and they won't if you don't tell them yourself."

"How can I keep it from them? I am not a virgin any longer. How can I be pure now when I am chosen as a wife? A husband must have an unspoiled virtuous woman. I can not lie to my father and future husband when the time comes. Any man should have trust in his betroth's chastity."

"That is pure religious nonsense. I cannot concern myself with your problems now," he said as he walked out of the cave and took the reins to his horse. Climbing on his steed's back he continued, "I have an army to worry about right now. I must catch up with them before they run into rebel forces and I'm not there to lead them into battle."

As he readied to ride away, he reached into the same bag where he kept the canteen. He pulled out a small pouch made out of goatskin and threw it at her feet "Whatever happens to you now, you will have to deal with it. This will help you should you need to leave this area." Having said that, he galloped away towards the southeast.

She picked up the bag and examined it, and discovered that it contained several pieces of silver. There appeared to be about twenty or thirty pieces in the bag. She gave chase to him crying and yelling, "I don't need your filthy money." Without checking to see how many pieces of silver there were, she heaved the coins at him as he rode away. The coins scattered in all directions making dinging noises as they bounced on the rocks down the hillside.

As she went back into the cave she saw the necklace lying under a clump of weeds. She picked it up, clutched it to her sore bosom and set near the entrance to collect her thoughts and to get a grasp of her feelings once again. She could not believe what had happened to her. It felt like a dream....like she could just tell herself, "Okay, it is time to wake up", and all of this would be gone. But looking at herself, the bruises she got from God knows where or how, and looking at her torn dress, brought her to the reality of the event that had occurred. She set there for a while and sobbed while she fixed the clasp of the chain on her necklace.

"What am I going to do now? How am I to face my family? What is going to happen to me?" These were the questions that she agonized over for a while before gathering the courage to go home and face her mother. She thought about not saying anything, but this violation against her body and the loss of her virtue was too huge to bear by herself. Besides, not telling would be tantamount to lying and that would be truly a transgression against the Laws of God.

By this time, the rain and thunder had stopped. She began her journey back to her home. While she walked she prayed that the Lord God forgive her of any sin or wrong doing that she might have committed, although she felt strongly that nothing about this assault was her fault. She prayed for guidance and direction and the words to tell her parents what had just happened. She also prayed for protection for her and her entire family, that they all be kept from harm. All of a sudden her thoughts went back to the dream she had a few nights before. Could this be what the two men in shining white robes meant? The more she thought, the more confused and scared she became.

After composing herself as much as she could, she began to walk home. It did not seem long before she could see her house up the winding trail. The closer she got, the more anxious she became to get home so she began to run faster and faster. Her mother was inside weaving some cloth from sheep's yarn, when she heard Sofia crying and calling to her in a hysterical fashion. Alarmed and shocked to hear Sofia's emotional calls, her mother jumped out of her chair and ran outside to see what was the happening.

"Here I am child, pray tell me what is the matter?" Her arms were stretched out and open as she ran towards Sofia. As they met a few cubits from the house, Sofia and her mother fell on the ground as Sofia cried, and her mother tried desperately to comfort her.

"Oh mother!" she sobbed, "I am so ashamed!"

"Please Sofia, tell me what has happened to you", her mother asked as she looked at her tattered dress and the bruises on her arms. "What has happened to you?" she repeated in a very emotional tone of voice.

"I was raped by a Roman soldier," she replied in an emotive state.

"Where and when did this take place?"

"At the cave near the north ridge. I was watching the herd when he appeared on a horse from nowhere. I swear on my honor, and on this necklace, mother, that I did nothing to provoke him, I swear." She then went on to relate the events as they happened. When she was finished, she asked her mother, "What will happen to me? What will become of me? Will I be put to death?"

"No child, the Law of Moses are very precise in these matters, but let us not talk about that now. Let us go into the house. I will draw you water so you can bath and clean yourself. You will feel better after you have bathed and changed your clothes."

After they had both stood up, Sofia uttered, "I am so scared mother." They walked toward the house, all the while her mother was trying desperately to console her as she leaned on her mother, her head at her mother's bosom. When they reached the house, Sofia laid down on her mother's bed and tried to sleep, but to no avail. After some time had passed, her mother came and told her that her bath water was ready. She got up and washed herself. She prayed as she bath, again asking God to cleanse her of any transgressions that she might have committed on her part.

When she had finished, she put on clean clothes and set at her mother's feet while her mother dried and combed her hair. "I wish this had never happened to me," she said, "I am very fearful of what will happen to me now."

"Let's not think about that now. It won't be long now and your father and brothers will be home. They will know the right thing to do. Just relax and try to forget everything that has happened today." Her mother continued to calm her by humming a soothing lullaby and by stroking her hair with her hands and comb.

But things were not as tranquil and secure as Sofia's mother thought. Neither Sofia nor her mother had been aware of Delilah, the town gossip standing out of sight behind the large fig tree. She had overheard their conversation about what had happened in the cave. After they had entered the house, Delilah came out of hiding from behind the large fig tree that was on the edge of path and their home walkway. She hurriedly returned to Nain to tell other gossip mongrel friends of hers, what she had overheard. As the story got repeated, second and third hand, the episode got worse and worse. One version had Sofia enticing the soldier into the cave, and being a willing participant. Unknown to Sofia and her mother, this hideous event was the talk of the town within a few hours.

It was well after dark when the dogs' barking announced that someone was approaching the house. Sarah quickly extinguished the oil lamp and peered through the window to see who was coming. She could make out that the three men walking down the path near the house were Ezra and their two sons, Seth and Zev. Sarah relit the lamp, and stood by the doorway. By now she could hear them talking about how glad they were to be home, safe and sound, after the almost five-hour long walk from Jerusalem. Their trip, although hard and tedious, had been successful. They all carried a sack on their back containing the household items they had obtained by barter. It was a lot more then they had initially thought.

As Ezra entered the house, Sofia ran to him crying and set on the floor clutching his leg. Amazed and bewildered by this act he asked rather impatiently, "What is the matter girl? What has happened here while we were gone?" Ezra looked intently at Sofia, then at Sarah.

Sarah quickly interjected, "Ezra, Sofia has been violated!"

Falling on a nearby chair from shock he sighed, "Pray God, what do you mean woman? How did it happen?"

In a tearful voice Sarah answered, "She has been soiled....raped by a Roman soldier who came upon her on horseback near a cave."

"Oh father," uttered Sofia still sobbing, "I was surprised by him, and I ran to the cave to hid; but he followed and attack me. I tried to fight him off, I swear to you I did, but I passed out from the fear and terror I felt.

Ezra asked to have the story retold to him from the beginning, and Sofia recounted the incident to him and her brothers in gory detail. When she had finished telling all the shuddering details, her father set at the table with his head in his hands. Time went by without anyone saying anything. Finally the silence was broken by Zev who proclaimed in an enraged voice that he was going to go looking for Captain Pantera and revenge his sister's honor.

Quickly raising to his feet Ezra directed, "You'll do no such thing!" Swallowing hard, he added, "One transgression will not be paid by another. This is not the way of Yahweh. Let us all sleep on this and ask God to show us the best thing to do. Whatever He wants, let His will and not our will be done."

They prepared for bed, and prayed for divine guidance in the important decisions that had to be made in the morning. When the lamp was extinguished, not a sound was made by anyone, yet they all were in deep thought and meditation until the early hours of the morning. The last sounds Sofia heard before falling asleep were the outside night sounds of the various wild creatures and livestock in the yard. It was strange, but she seemed to feel that they were telling her that all would be well, and in time she would be back to normal.

Dawn came early the next day.

Chapter 3
Comdemnation of Sofia

That morning began like the night had ended, very quiet. There was hardly any conversation at all as each went about doing their morning house chores. They ate breakfast and afterwards they prepared for their day's labors. It was not until after the kitchen utensils had been cleaned that the silence was broken by a commotion outside the house. Sarah looked out through the door and noticed a horde of town's people walking down the pathway towards their home. They were all murmuring and conversing with each other as they walked. The Rabbi from Nain was leading them. Sarah alerted Ezra, and he peered out the door to see.

"Please be quiet," said Ezra as he looked at his family standing there in astonishment, "Let me do all the talking. We do not know what they are here for, so lets just listen. If there is any conversing to be done, I will do it." He then stepped out onto the small porch, and received and returned salutations to the Rabbi and some of the crowd that followed. The rest of the family followed him out on the porch also.

"Our Lord Yahweh be with you and your family Ezra,"

"And also with you and those that are following you," responded Ezra. "To what do I and my family owe the honor of your presence and good company?"

Looking around to each of Ezra's family members and then back to the crowd that followed him, the Rabbi told Ezra, "It is with a heavy heart that I come here today to discuss a very grievous situation with you that has come to my attention."

"Pray tell me Rabbi, what could be so important that it calls for this type of public pronouncement and discussion?" He waved his hand outwardly and motioned to the hoard of people standing behind and to the sides of the Rabbi.

Looking around again, as if following Ezra's hand motion, he said, "It has come to my attention that your daughter Sofia is no longer a virtuous woman. Ezra was about to rebuttal prematurely but the Rabbi holding his hands out in front of him continued, "Now Ezra, the whole village is speaking about his thing that happened yesterday. There is nothing to be gained by denying it, except eternal damnation."

"How do you know of this matter?" demanded Ezra.

"It has been the talk of the village since yesterday in the late afternoon. Your wife Sarah and daughter Sofia were overheard speaking of this matter, almost on this very spot, right here where we are standing." After a slight pause, he continued, "It is a simple thing that I wish to know, and Sofia could clear this up by a simple statement, and that is, was she a willing participant of this act or not?"

At that, Sofia could not contain herself and against her father's wishes moved in front of her father and blurted out, "I was raped.... ravaged...violated," she cried louder and louder with her hands down by her sides, clinched into fists as she glared at the crowd with her eyes as she talked. "How can anyone ever think that I was a willing participant? I have always been a righteous woman. Does anyone here know me to stand for something other then a virtuous woman?" She waited a few seconds for any reply but none came from the crowd. Turning back to face the Rabbi she continued, but in a somewhat calmer, almost pleading voice, "I have always kept all the commandments of God and His Laws that he gave to us through Moses. How can anyone dare think I would defile myself as well as my family?"

Ezra, motivated by Sofia's challenge to the crowd, spoke angrily, "Who would spread such hideous lies about anyone, especially someone as reverent as my daughter Sofia? Who? Speak up! Do it now in front of her and her family," he continued to demand in a raging voice.

"It does not matter, at this point, who spread the truth or who spread evil lies," replied Jacob the Rabbi. "My purpose here today is to find the truth, and I believe that I have found it in Sofia's words. But Ezra, I must also insure that the Laws of Moses are followed."

"What does the sacred Torah mandate us to do?" asked Ezra anxiously yet in a much calmer tone.

"It requires different actions for different situations. As example, if a man takes a wife and after lying with her, dislikes her and slanders her and gives her a bad name, saying, 'I married this woman, but when I approached her, I did not find proof of her virginity', then the girl's father and mother shall bring proof that she was a virgin to the town elders at the gate of the village. The girl's father must say to the elders, "I gave my daughter in marriage to this man, but he dislikes her. Now he has slandered her and said he did not find her a virgin, but here is proof of my daughter's virginity." Then the parents must display the cloth before the elders of the town and the elders shall take the man and punish him."

"What does that have to do with Sofia? She is not even pledged to marry much less married, "said Ezra, "This does not apply to her."

"I am well aware of that, Ezra, I was just giving you an example to show that the truth must be told about what happened. The Torah goes on to say that if the husband's charges are proven to be true, and no proof of the girl's virginity can be found, she shall be brought to the door of her father's house and there the men of the town shall stone her to death! Death, Ezra, would be the penalty because she would have done a disgraceful thing in Israel by being promiscuous while still in her father's house. The Torah commands that we must purge that evil from among us."

"My daughter was not promiscuous," ranted Ezra, "She was raped by a Roman soldier! Don't you understand that?

"Yes, I have heard Sofia state that, and I believe her. In cases like that, the Torah points out that if a man happens to meet a virgin who is not pledged to be married and rapes her and they are discovered, he shall pay the girl's father fifty shekels of silver. He must also marry the girl, for he has violated her. He can never divorce her as long as he lives."

"I do not want his money!" God forgive me, I want his life!, shouted Ezra. He surprised everyone with his statement for all that knew him were well aware that he was a peaceable, religious, and an honorable man.

In shock at what he heard Ezra say, the Rabbi averred, "That is blasphemy Ezra. God will hand out the appropriate punishment, not you. He has also made it quite clear that if we tolerated the taking of human life for reasons of anger and hate, or for other reasons not provided for in the Torah, the entire community must then share the guilt and all will be punished by God."

"Sofia can not marry this heathen! The Torah states that we are not to make treaties with our enemies. We are not to intermarry with them. It specifically says that we are not to give our daughters to their sons or our sons to their daughters for they will turn our sons away from following the God of Abraham to serve other gods. This will anger Yahweh and His anger will burn against us and will quickly destroy us," quoted Ezra.

Upon hearing this dialogue between them, the crowd began to talk amongst themselves and things could be heard like, "Take that evil from our midst" and "Exile her now before it's too late." The Rabbi turned to the crowd, raised his hands and began to talk to them.

"Hold your tongues. Do not rush to judgment. God's law tells us not to pervert justice. We are not to show partiality to the poor, or favoritism to the great, but we are to judge our neighbor fairly." He turned to Ezra who by that time was holding Sofia in his embrace, and continued, "I know this is not an easy thing that you must do, but the Laws of Yahweh require that what must be done, must be done."

"What if I chose to disobey these Laws, asked Ezra defiantly.

"Yahweh has said that if you do not listen to Him and carry out all of His commandments, and if you reject His decrees and abhor His laws, and fail to carry out all of His commands, and by doing so violate His covenant, then He will bring upon you sudden terror, wasting diseases and fever that will destroy your sight and drain away your life. You will plant seed in vain, because you enemies will eat it. He will set His face against you so that you will be defeated by your enemies, and those who hate you will rule over you and you will flee even when no one is pursuing you. He will punish you for your sins seven times over."

Ezra's head was bowed down; taking in all that the Rabbi was saying, and deeply thinking about his options. Jacob the Rabbi stopped just a moment so that what he had said had time to sink in, then he continued. "If you remain hostile toward Yahweh, and refuse to listen to him still, He says that He will multiply your afflictions. He will send wild animals against you and they will rob you of your children, destroy your livestock, and make you and your descendants so few that your roads will be deserted."

"Enough," acquiesced Ezra shaking his hands above his head, "I know well enough that I must comply with his Laws.... just, please allow me some time to do what must be done."

"I understand. It is not an easy thing that you must do, so I will allow you three days for Sofia to leave our midst. She must never return to this village again." Turning to the crowd again, Rabbi Jacob addressed them saying, "Let us leave this family alone now. They have suffered enough, and I know in my heart that Ezra will do what he must for we all know that he is an honorable and righteous man." Stepping down from the small porch where he had stood with Ezra, the crowd followed him as he walked down the pathway back towards the village.

When they all had left, the entire family went inside the house to ponder on what course of action to take. It was decided and agreed by all to spend the rest of the day in group prayer as well as individual solitary meditation for God's guidance, direction, and divine intervention.

The next day after the morning chores, Ezra gathered his family around the kitchen table and began a discussion about what needed to be done. Sofia's mother Sarah began by sharing a dream she had that night. In that dream, a stranger had told her that if Sofia stayed, the town's people would stone her to death. She also saw in the dream that the family had lost everything that they owned due to pestilence and afflictions sent God for their disobedience. She related how real and frightening the dream seemed, yet a man she did not know or recognize, dressed in white, had reassured her that Sofia had been chosen to help in fulfilling a prophecy. He stated that God would favor Sofia and her descendants. Sofia listened intently in amazement since this sounded almost identical to the dream she had a few days earlier, which she never had a change to share with anyone.

Her brothers spoke up next. They both agreed that if it was allowable, either one of them would gladly take her place, however, this was not what needed to be done. In discussions they had together and with Sofia that night, they had agreed that it would be in the best interest of Sofia if she would leave Nain and travel to Kerioth, a town near Bethlehem and Jerusalem in the Providence of Judah. There she could live with her Aunt Leah, who was Sarah's sister, and her husband Reuben. He was not the kindest of men, on the contrary, he was known to have a short temper at times to the point of being rude. It was rumored that he, at times beat and physically abused Leah. Sofia had heard her mother and father talk about this from time to time and they both seemed to think it was because Leah was barren and childless. She was past her childbearing age, and Reuben had always wanted children.

"Are you in accord with this course of action?" asked Ezra.

"Yes father, I believe that would be the best for all our family. I know that Uncle Reuben is not the most benevolent relative, but Aunt Leah has enough kindness in her heart for both of them. Besides, I feel deep down inside me that she needs me to help her at home and to take care of her."

"Then this is your decision?"

"Yes. Something tells me that this is where I should go and what I should do. I also feel that it would be best if I leave for Kerioth in the morning. I don't want the family to get into any adversity with the synagogue for failure to do what must be done."

"So be it then," said Ezra. "I feel no need to tell you, because you know already how I feel." Although tears could not be seen on Ezra's face, you could hear them in his voice as he continued, "I would rather cut out my heart than to lose you, but it must be done as it is written in the Holy Scripture. It is out of our hands and it is in God's hands." He hugged her close to him as he spoke.

Sarah was so devastated at the thought of losing her only daughter that she could not stop crying. Throughout the day, while she helped Sofia gather her belongings and prepare for her departure, Sofia could hear her sobbing softly, lamenting her absence even before she was gone. She noticed that Sofia was wearing the necklace around her neck as she always did. Her mother spoke in a low crackling voice to her.

"This necklace belonged to my grandmother, and to her grandmother, and to hers, for many generations. When she passed it on to me when I was a little girl, she told me that when things were at their worst, for me to hold it close and it would release an enchanting power to please and attract good fortune. I don't know how true it is, but just the thought that I was holding something from past generations, that was soothing enough to calm me during troubled times."

She picked it up from around Sofia's neck, kissed it, and gently laid the front, which contained a precious topaz gem, back on her bosom. Sofia looked at her mother and when their eyes met, there was no need to speak. Their saddened eyes said more about how they felt at that moment then a thousand words could have ever revealed. They held each other in a warm embrace, and remained clutched together, softly swaying rhythmically from side to side for a long time. Neither of them could have ever imagined that this would to be the last time that they would hold each other again.

Chapter 4
Journey to Kerioth

Early next morning, with all her belongings on a donkey, Sofia waited to join a merchant from Nain named Simon who was on his way to Cyrene to trade for goods from
that area. Ezra knew Simon very well and for a long time. They had grown up together in the same village, and he knew that he could entrust Sofia to him. Ezra had seen
Simon in Nain the day before, and had made arrangements with Simon to take Sofia
with him and leave her with her aunt and uncle at Kerioth. Kerioth is approximately
eighty miles, as the crow flies, from Nain, however, actual travel distance, due to the
winding road that traverses several mountain ranges, it is more like one hundred
miles. It also passes over several mountain ranges including Mount Tabor, Carmel,
Gilboa, Ebal, and Gerizim.

   The village of Kerioth had been established by people belonging to the tribe of
Benjamin, one of the twelve tribes of Israelites. In olden times the first settlers in the
village named the town Kiriath Jearim. Several villages had grown within walking
distance of each other, and when they merged, the name was changed to Kerioth.

   The other original eleven tribes that were included in the division of land were
Simeon, Zevulun, Issachar, Asher, Naphtali, Dan, Reuben, Levi, Judah, Gad, and
Joseph. There were a total of twelve, including Benjamin. Within each tribe were
numerous clans. Benjamin's clans allotted territory given to them lay between the

tribes of Judah and Joseph. The southern side boundary began at the outskirts of
Kerioth, which as mentioned earlier, was first called Kiriath Jearim. The town origi-
nally belonged to the tribe of Judah, and is still in the Providence of Judah.

As Simon the wares trader was traveling to Ezra's place to pick up Sofia, some of
the town people joined him and walked behind him. They were there to insure that
Sofia left Nain as required by the Torah. All her family was gathered around her as
the caravan slowly approached. After a few courtesies and salutations between Simon
and the family were exchanged, they were ready to depart. Sarah cautioned her not to
wear the necklace that she had given her, or any other item that could draw maraud-
ers or vagabonds during their long trip.

Shortly, Simon suggested that it was time to leave before they lost the cool of the
morning. With that, the family hugged and kissed Sofia and wished her fare-thee-
well. She glanced back at her family as she walked alongside the cart full of wares
being pulled by an ox. She could see her father holding her mother in his arms while
she cried uncontrollably, unable to withstand the pain of loosing her only daughter.
Sofia walked faster and faster because she knew that the further she got, the less she
would be able to hear the agonizing sounds of her mother crying. She stumbled as she
walked on the bumpy and rocky road. She could not see her footing because of her
own tears that were welling up in her big brown eyes. She prayed in an attempt to
block the indelible picture in her heart of her tormented and loving mother grieving.
All at once, the thought came to her that she would never see her family again. It was
a dreadful feeling, which she tried to quickly wave off by praying harder.

"Into your hands, Almighty and Powerful God, I command my life and future.
Please keep my family safe. Comfort and protect them always." As she prayed she
remembered her favorite song of King David and she began to recite it.

"Give ear to my words, O Lord, consider my sighing. Listen to my cry for help,
my King, and my God for to You I pray. In the morning, O Lord, you hear my
voice, in the morning I lay my requests before you and wait in expectation."

"You are not a God who takes pleasure in evil; with you the wicked cannot
dwell. The arrogant cannot stand in your presence; You hate all who do wrong.
You destroy those who tell lies; bloodthirsty and deceitful men the Lord
abhors."

"But I by Your great mercy will come into your house; in reverence will I bow
down toward your holy temple. Lead me, O Lord, in Your righteousness, and
because of my enemies make straight Your way before me".

"Not a word from their mouth can be trusted; their heart is filled with destruc-
tion. Their throat is an open grave; with their tongue they speak deceit.

Declare them guilty, O God! Let their intrigues be their downfall. Banish them for their sins, for they have rebelled against you".

"But let all who take refuge in You be glad; let them ever sing for joy. Spread your protection over them; that those who love Your name may rejoice in You. For surely O Lord, you bless the righteous and You surround them with Your favor as with a shield."

By mid-day they were about five miles from Nain, near the border of Samaria on the Plain of Esdraelop. They stopped to rest, eat and to feed and water Sofia's donkey and the ox that was pulling the cart.

"We have a long way to go child," said Simon, "You must eat and drink something."

"I am not hungry," replied Sofia as she set her back up against the cart. She had picked some anise or dill; a weedy aromatic umbellifer with yellow flowers and was pulling and smelling the petals from it.

Seeing how depressed and sad Sofia looked, Simon spoke as he fed himself, "I heard the rumors in town about you and the reason you had to leave Nain. If it's any consolation to you, I would never believe the terrible lies they were saying about you. Why I have known you since your dear mother Sarah brought you into this world, and I have never seen you give anyone any reason to speak ill about you, child, much less to believe vicious lies told about you."

"Thank you Simon. I don't understand why this thing is happening to me. What have I done to displease God?"

"God works in mysterious ways child. It is not our will but His will that must be done." Wiping his mouth and whiskers with his sleeve, he looked at Sofia and asked, "You believe in the Torah don't you?"

"Yes I do."

"Then look at the story of poor Job. He was a man who lived in the village of Uz, east of Palestine. Satan accused Job of being good only for the good fortunes that he was receiving from God. Job told him no, that he really and truly loved God. God even gave permission to the devil to test Job's beliefs. He lost all of his possessions and all of his family died. He developed leprosy and elephantiasis and other painful and horrible diseases. He lost his wife, and still he never gave up his convictions in God. He knew that God does not ever forsake the righteous, and he was a righteous and pious man." Simon paused for a few seconds, then continued to explain his statement. "We see this all around us every day. Why do some wicked people live long lives while some holy people die young? Why has He sent strangers from Rome to enslave us again after He gave us our freedom and our own lands through Moses?

Why does He allow the Romans to kill the Jews, His Chosen People, as one would kill a dog or a wild animal? These are hard questions that no mortal can answer. Yet, God Has His reasons. Some times we think we understand His reasoning, but most of the time we are at a loss to know why He ordains things to happen as they do."

"Why do you think it's that way?" asked Sofia very inquisitively.

"What do you mean child?"

"Why can't we comprehend the reason that God does what He does?

If he loves us like the Torah says, and if we remain faithful to Him and abide by His will, then why won't God let us understand Him?"

"The answer is really very simple when you stop and think about it. God is Omnipotent, which means He has no beginning or no end. The Torah says it this way, He is the Alpha and the Omega. Now to understand anything you must first *comprehend* it. Don't you agree?

"Yes, but.."

"Well, just listen. To *comprehend* means to take in some thing or some idea, and completely embrace it. As humans, we reason and understand things with our brain, therefore, we must totally embrace things with our brain. Yet, our brains have limits, yes they do, contrary to popular thinking. If you don't believe me, just put your hands around the top of your head. Your brain is inside your skull, it can not be any bigger then that, so it has a limit. Now, answer me this…How can something that has a limited, like your brain, comprehend something that is limitless?"

There was a short moment of silence as Sofia thought about what Simon had just said. Shortly, he continued, "The point I am making is this; no one can second-guess why God does or does not do this or that. We just have to believe that He has a reason, a very good reason, why He ordains the things He does.

Sofia seemed to grasp the point that he was trying to make.

"One more thing. God knows all His people personally. He appoints people before they are born in the sense that he has a plan and a purpose for each of us. Look at what is written about Jeremiah. When he questioned why God had selected him to be a prophet, God told him that before Jeremiah was formed in the womb, God knew him. Even before he was born, God set Jeremiah apart and had already appointed or predestined him to be a prophet to the nations. Therefore, if you believe in the validity of the Laws of Moses, you must be willing to believe as I have told you, and continue to seek and discover the inner meaning of what God has ordained for you. Only a Sadducee would have views and practices opposed to these. They deny our oral traditions, even to the point of not believing in the final resurrection of the dead and in the existence of angels, who are the messengers of God.

"I am not a Sadducee, I am a Pharisee, and I do believe as you have said. I am frightened only at not knowing what my future has in store for me. I have never been away from the safety and comfort of my father's house." Pointing at the road ahead of them Sofia continued talking, "I go to an aunt that I have not seen since I was a small child. Her husband is rumored to be a supporter of the rebellious Zadokites so the Romans keep a close watch on him and his blacksmith shop."

"Do they have any children?" asked Simon curiously.

"No, my aunt has been unable to bare him any children. He longs for a boy child. I think that is the reason he beats her on occasion; at least that is what I hear my parents say."

"Well, I would not worry too much child. I have a good feeling that all will go well on our trip and with your stay with your aunt and uncle." As he talked, he was gathering his things used for lunch and was placing them back into the cart. "We have rested long enough. Let us be on our way. We must get as much travel in as we can before the sun retrieves its light. If you get hungry as we walk, just reach into the cart and get some melon, figs, bread, or whatever you fancy and eat. You must keep up your strength because we have a long ways to go. Okay?"

"Yes Simon, thank you very much. You have helped to ease my apprehensions some. Thanks again."

Their travel was tiresome and uneventful for the rest of that day, and the next. Except for her heart aching and longing to be home with her parents, the trip so far was satisfying because of Simon and his wealth of wisdom. He seemed to have the talent to say exactly what she needed to hear those times she became acutely melancholy. He had the uncanny ability to express things so simply that Sofia could not help but wonder why she did not think of that same thing in the first place.

The beginning of the third day started out much the same as the days before. After breakfast and morning prayers, they were on their way up the foot of Mount Gilboa, just passed the town of Seythopolis. Reaching a high peak, they could not believe what they saw in a small valley below. Sofia was stunned and frightened by what she saw. From the high mountaintop they had just climbed, they could see two smaller hilltops below that created a ravine between them. The ravine was a natural passageway, northwest toward the city of Seythopolis, and southeast to Ginae. Marching through the ravine were approximately one hundred and fifty Roman foot soldiers and fifty or so cavalry soldiers mounted on their horses. They had muffled their own feet and their horses' hoofs with cloth so as not to make any unnecessary sounds as they marched. That ploy was working, since neither Simon nor Sofia had heard, nor had been aware of them until they had reached the mountaintop. It was then that they saw the Roman army below. They seemed to be prepared to launch a surprise attack on an unsuspecting foe.

The trap was set, however, it was the Romans that were the prey about to be caught in the trap. Unknown to the Roman leaders, about fifty or so Zadokites were well hidden and camouflaged on both hillsides overlooking the ravine. Sofia could barely make out their spears since they had coated them with some kind of mud to prevent the sun's reflection giving away their position. They also had long bows and cross bows, all aimed at the Roman troops marching slowly through the ravine. Even though the Roman army had muffled their feet, they still created dust that tended to blow into their own faces and to the faces of the soldiers marching behind. This made it more difficult for them to see the Zadokites' position and what was actually happening.

"Get down child," said Simon, "Hold on to your donkey. Don't let him make any noises or stir up any dust."

"Oh my God! What is going on?" asked Sofia in a puzzled yet exited tone of voice.

"It appears that the Romans think they are going to trap this group of Zadokites, yet they are the ones walking into their trap. See the tall man with the long reddish hair and beard standing on the top of the hill to the right? That is Judas Zadok, the leader of an army of liberators called Zadokites. It is rumored that he belongs to the same family that controlled the office of High Priest in the Sanhedrin for many years. Not too long ago, he and his band of fighters raided the royal palace at Sepphoris and emptied their arsenal of all their weapons. They have been well equipped for battle ever since."

"Is this the only band of fighters fighting for political freedom?" asked Sofia.

"No" answered Simon, still looking with great anticipation at what was about to happen below. "There are several other groups, one lead by a man named Simon to the east in Perea past the Jordan River, and one lead by a man called Athronges who fights the Romans mostly in Galilee. Then there is Tabor, who fights around Galilee also. Judas Zadok is the one who has been trying to unite all freedom fighters into one concerted unit. May the Lord be with Judas Zadok and help him defeat our enemy."

The Zadokites waited until the Roman soldiers were well into the trap before Judas Zadok gave the order to attack. At first they concentrated mainly on the cavalry troops. Once it became clear to the cavalrymen that they were sitting targets on their horses, they dismounted and took cover behind rocks. Their horses began to run away through the ravine. That maneuver seemed to provide the best protection at the time, but it turned out to be the worst decision they could have made. The soldiers that took cover behind the rocks and the ledge on the left side of the ravine made excellent targets for the archers and spear throwers atop the hill to the right side of the ravine. Those that tried to hide behind the rocks on the right side of ravine were being wiped out by the Zadokites that were positioned on the left side of the hill. There really was not any save place for the Roman soldiers to hide or to run on foot.

Sofia could hear a lot of shouting and yelling and cursing by the Romans during the battle. The main leader ordered a squad of approximately ten soldiers, to rush up the hillside, but they were all slaughtered. He sent about four more squads, one right after the other, and they all met with the same disastrous end. After the fourth wave, some of the soldiers began to refuse to carry out orders. The whole battalion became undisciplined and confused. Bodies lay everywhere, and blood ran like a small tributary through the crevasses on each side of the ravine. Some soldiers tried to hide underneath the dead bodies, but they were found out and executed where they lay. It became obvious that once the leaders were slain, the rest were in complete disarray. There was not any safe haven or cover anywhere on the battlefield for the Romans. The battle raged on for better then three hours. When it was all over, only a handful of Roman soldiers managed to escape and the rest were killed. Losses were few for the Zadokites.

During the battle, Sofia's attention was focused mainly on three participants. The first was Judas Zadok, the rebel leader, and another was the Captain of the cavalry troops. He was one of the firsts to escape the trap by fighting his way out while still on horseback. Most of the Romans that escaped were the cavalrymen that stayed on their horses. They moved around too fast on their mounts for the lancers and the archers to have a good shot at them. Sofia never got a good look at the cavalry commander, so she could not tell if he was Captain Pantera or not. She had been wishing, as the battle raged, that he would suffer the same fate as his troops; but it was not to be. Her disappointment was tampered none the less by the admiration of Judas Zadok. What excellent leadership skill and command presence he displayed!

"How smart and cagey he must be," she told herself, "To set and execute such a trap that enabled him to defeat a battalion five to six times in number then his small band of Zadokites."

The third person that drew her attention was a young rebel with longer then usual dark brown hair, about five foot ten inches tall, who seemed to be one of Zadok's lieutenants. He stood on the opposite hill from where Zadok stood, and seemed to be receiving commands through hand signal and relaying them to the men under his command. She was impressed by his commitment to what he was doing, and his determination to win this battle.

After the battle had ended, the rebels came down from the hills to the ravine and scavenged through the dead soldiers' pockets and belongings. They took their weapons, horses, shoes, clothing, shields, and any thing of value they could use. When the Zadokites had finished, they took their dead comrades' bodies and buried them. They then heaped the Roman soldiers' bodies into large piles and burned them as in the times of Isaiah.

"For every warrior's sandal from the noisy battle, and garments rolled in blood, will be used for burning and fuel for fire." (Isaiah 9:5)

The smell of burning flesh made Sofia sick. When the Zadokites left, Simon urged, "Come on child, we must leave this place now! If there are anymore Roman Legionnaires within fifty miles from here, they will be able to smell the death fires, and will come to investigate. We cannot be caught any place near here."

Sofia was most happy to comply because of the shocking things she had seen below. Besides, the bittersweet smell of burning flesh was choking her and she was about to heave her insides out on top of that mountain if they did not leave soon. Simon kept urging, "We must hurry child. It is almost dark. We will have to travel at night for the next few days so that we are not seen."

They walked from dusk to dawn, about twelve hours. Although it was not quite a full moon, the cremation fires gave a haunting glow throughout the night for about seven or eight hours as they walked. The smell of burning flesh was not as noticeable at that distance. They stopped to rest and eat for a very short period of time during that night's travel. They also changed their direction of travel. They headed south, southwesterly to reduce the chance of being seen by any soldiers that might be coming from Caesarea, which was the Roman seat of government in Samaria.

Shortly after daybreak, they reached the small village of Salim, on the shores of the Jordan River. They were exhausted and tense from the fear of being seen during the night. When they reached the Jordan River, Simon suggested that they rest that day and the coming night in the beautiful small wooded dale that they had come to by the river. Sofia did not argue, she was so tired that she forgot how hungry she was at the time. It was funny, she seemed to be hungrier the past few days then ever before. She just rationalized that the long strenuous walking and all the excitement of the past few days were the cause of her hunger.

"You stay and rest here," said Simon, "You'll be safe here. I am going to Salim to see a friend of mine who will help us with some supplies. I need to know what kind of military activity has been happening around these parts so we can be more aware of what we can expect during the remainder of our journey. Okay?"

"Okay," she replied, "I'll be all right . I will keep out of sight and rest. You go do what you must do. Don't worry about me, I'll be okay."

Simon unpacked the donkey and placed Sofia's belongings that she carried on the donkey in the Ox drawn cart. He said goodbye and took the donkey with him. She sat under a small tree to rest awhile and enjoy the river as it flowed down stream. How peaceful and serene it seemed to be. The longer she watched the small ripples caused by the wind come to shore, the more relaxed she became. Listening to the soft splashing of the waves as they reached the shoreline made her mind relax, which was a welcomed relief after yesterday's ordeal. She thought of nothing except how peaceful and beautiful this spot and this moment seemed to be. She thought, that this must be what paradise is really like! The river and all the serenity reminded her of one of her favorite hymns in the book of Psalms, so she began to recite it to herself.

God is our refuge and strength, an ever-present help in trouble. Therefore we will not fear, though the earth give way and the mountains fall into the sea. Though its waters roar and foam and the mountains quake with their surging. There is a river whose streams make glad the city of God, the holy place where the Most High dwells. God is within her, she will not fall. He lifts His voice and the earth melts. The Lord Almighty is with us, the God of Jacob is our Fortress. Come and see the works of the Lord, the desolation's he has brought on the earth. He makes wars cease to the ends of the earth. He breaks the bow and shatters the spear. He burns the shields with fire. Be still and know that I am God. I will be exalted among the nations. I will be exalted in the earth. The Lord Almighty is with us, the God of Jacob is our fortress." Eventually her exhaustion overcame her and she fells asleep under the tree where she set. While she slept, she dreamed, and in her dream, the same two men dressed in white came to her again. Their faces glowed golden bright, and a subtle emanation came from them and surrounded their entire body. They shined as if the sun was their backdrop. One of them spoke to her. "The Lord is with you! He has truly found much favor in you. He had a seed planted into you that He will use to fulfill His word. Your are like Zion the Lord has said, you should not be afraid, for you shall not suffer shame. Do not fear disgrace for you will not be humiliated. You will forget any shame you may feel of your youth and will not remember any reproach you might have endured. The Lord will call you back to your heavenly home when your destiny is fulfilled. Thus sayth the Lord, "For a brief moment I abandoned you so your fate could be brought into being, but be assured that with deep compassion I bring you back to Me. In everlasting kindness, I have compassion in you. Therefore Sofia, do not be afraid, for I am with you and your descendents...always."

Sofia awoke shaking. Although the breeze from the river was cool, she was sweating profusely. "What a dream!" she thought to herself. "What did it mean? Was it a dream?" It all seemed so real; it was hard to imagine it as only a dream! How long had she been asleep? The shadows on the ground showed the time to be a few hours after noon. She decided to take this opportunity to get into the water of the Jordan River and bathe while she waited for Simon. The water was so refreshing. After a time she forgot about her dream, and enjoyed her swim. She felt her stomach spring as she entered the Jordan River. "It must be that I am feeling hungry," she thought, "What else could it be?"

It was past nightfall when Simon came into the camp. He had the donkey laden with wares and supplies.

"I am sorry I was gone so long," he said, "but there was much to do and so much to talk about with my friend Michael that I lost track of time. I also slept a few hours at his home. I was totally exhausted."

"That's all right, I was safe here," replied Sofia. "I slept for a few hours too, and washed myself in the Jordan. I have never felt so safe and secure in my entire life, as I did when I was in the Jordan. I felt that all had been lifted and washed away from me. I wish I could explain the feeling. It was as if I had experienced a rebirth! Isn't that silly?"

Simon did not answer her question, instead he asked, "Did you eat anything?"

"I ate from some fruits and bread that you had left behind. Just as you arrived, I was debating whether or not to light a camp fire."

"I'm sure a fire will be all right. Michael told me that there had not been any Roman soldiers in this village for about ten days now. I think we will be safe to continue our journey early in the morning."

They lid a fire, talked small talk, ate supper and relaxed watching the tranquil river flow on its way until it was time to bed down. When they had bedded down, Sofia asked, "Simon, have you ever had a dream that seemed so real that you were not sure if it was a dream or the real thing?"

"No, I can't say that I have. Why do you asked?"

"Oh, for no reason…I was just wondering. Goodnight Simon." With that, they went to sleep in anticipation of continuing their journey the next morning.

Early next morning, as dawn was breaking, they gathered their belongings and began their trip once again to Kerioth. They traveled for six more days, all without incident. In their travel they passed by or near the villages of Aenon, Sychar, Arimathea, and Gophna, where they spend their last night together. During these two weeks of traveling together, Sofia had grown very fond of Simon, and the feeling was mutual. During this time together, Simon had spoke to her about biblical accounts and about Jehovah, the God of Abraham. He always had the right words to say when she felt melancholy. That last night, before bedding down she spoke to Simon.

"I want you to know that my burden has been made much more bearable because of you. You have been more then just a travel companion and a guide. You have become a very close friend who I admire, respect and revere because of your gentle ways, your patience, and your kindness that exceeds what anyone could ever expect. I will miss you dearly when our journey together ends tomorrow." She could not help having tears pool up in her eyes as she spoke.

After a personal sniffle or two from Simon too, he managed to say, "Well child, I have known your father for many years. He is a good friend and an honorable man. I could do no less for him, and I am glad I did, for I would not have had this opportunity to meet you and to get to know you. There is something special about you, I can see it in the aura that you emit, and the way you relinquish bad feelings and accept what cannot be changed. It has been a pleasure for me indeed and an honor to travel with you. You won't forget me soon will you now?

"I could never forget you Simon, and all your wise teachings and advice. I will pray for you every day of my life."

"Thank you child. These old bones need a little praying for and divine intervention at my age!" As he got under the covers of his bedroll Simon said, "Goodnight Sofia."

She said goodnight too, and they both laid in their bed rolls staring at the many bright and shiny stars that glowed so bright that it seemed you could just reach up and grab a hand full for yourself. After her night prayers that she recited silently, and after some time spent watching the majesty of the sky, she heard Simon beginning to snore. Shortly after that, she fell sleep too.

The next day was the twenty-fourth day of the month of Tammuz, the tenth month of the civil year, and the fourth month of the sacred year. It was around four o'clock in the afternoon when the reached Kerioth. She could not help but wonder how she would be accepted by her Aunt and Uncle Leah and Reuben and what Kerioth had in store for her. She prayed silently as she came into Kerioth.

"Lord God, I am your unworthy servant who needs your comfort and protection. Please lead me in the path of righteousness and into a new and happy life with my relatives here in Kerioth. Soften their hearts and let them accept me as you have accepted your people who do not deserve your love, kindness and attention. Into your hands I command my future, Lord."

Chapter 5
Sofia's Arrival at Kerioth

Reuben was from the house of Gibeon, therefore, so was her Aunt Leah by marriage. There home and blacksmith shop were located inside the village, but outside the village walls. Their home was modest yet somewhat larger then most. It was attached to the blacksmith shop where Reuben made his living. There were two entrances to the house, one on the side of the structure used as the living quarters and the other through the blacksmith shop. It sat on approximately three acres, with most of the vacant land located on the side of the structure, and in the back of the house. In the backyard, Leah had planted a garden in which she grew most of her spices such as garlic, dill, sage, mint, and coriander. She also grew onions lentils and broad beans when in season. Leah's favorites were watermelons and muskmelons along with cucumbers.

Approaching the side of the building that served as the blacksmith shop, Sofia could see her Uncle Reuben hammering some red hot metal on an anvil. She could hear the sharp dinging sound as the hammer fell, giving shape to the metal. He wore a thick apron made of some kind of animal skin to protect his clothing. His face had traces of burnt charcoal where he had more then likely rubbed his face with his forearm. He was a solidly built, thick set and a strong man. He was about six feet tall, had an olive complexion and receding hairline. Sofia could see his profile as he stood sideways poking the metal into the hot fire once more. The sweat from his brow made a sizzling sound as it fell unto the hot furnace. His total attention was on his work, as he did not notice them approaching until they were almost upon him. Looking somewhat startled when be saw Sofia and Simon, he wiped his forehead with his right forearm again and called out for Leah.

"Leah. Leah, where are you woman? Come out here and see who has come to pay a visit."

Sofia smiled and said, "The Lord be with you Uncle Reuben. I bring you greetings and salutations from my family. They send their regards and sentiments of esteem and affection!" She reached out to embrace him but he shied away. Why he did was somewhat puzzling to her. She hoped it was nothing personal but rather due to his perspiration and his desire not to get smudges of coal all over her.

"What brings you to Kerioth girl?"

Sofia was trying to evade the question for as long as she could. She wanted to wait for an appropriate time to discuss the reason for her being here. She therefore replied, "Uncle Reuben, this is Simon, my friend the Merchant of Nain. He has brought me safely at my father's request, to visit you." Simon and Reuben acknowledged each other, then there was a brief tense silent pause for a few seconds. About that time, Leah came through the door. Sofia had never been so relieved to see someone at that moment.

"Hello Aunt Leah!"

"Well blessed be God! Sofia, what a wonderful surprise! Where are your parents?" She was looking around to see if she could see them.

"I came alone, Aunt Leah." Turning once again to Simon, she said, "This is Simon, a very good friend of my father. He is a Merchant at Nain. He is the one that my father asked to guide me here." After a few protocol niceties, Leah invited them into the house for some food and drink.

"You too Reuben, come along and eat so you can rest a while. We can visit with Sofia and find out all that is happening at Nain with Sarah and Ezra."

"You all go on in," he replied, "I will be along shortly. I have to finish forging this sickle while the iron is hot." He was steadily pumping the foot pedal that was attached to the bellows, creating a wind draft to fan the flame in the hearth.

"Can I be of some help to you," asked Simon?

"Oh no, thank you for offering, I am almost done here. Please…go on in and rest. You must be tired and hungry from your long journey. I'll be there in a few minutes after I finish and wash off."

They left Reuben in the shop, and they entered the house through the shop door. The first room served as a combination kitchen and dining room. In the middle of the room was a round pit used for fire and was made of flat stones. It functioned as the cooking furnace and table. It also provided heat for the house during the winter. It was about three long cubits (approximately five feet) in diameter and its outer boundaries or circumference was about two cubits thick. This thick circumference was also about two cubits in height. It was just high enough so that you could sit on the floor on pillows. The outer thick circumference served as a table. There were pillows made out of ostrich feathers on the floor around this outer boundary that they used for sitting. In the middle of the pit was a nice cozy fire. On the top of the fire in the pit was a griddle made out of some kind of steel mash where Leah had cooked some breads, quail and dove. They were still on the grill, but away from the direct fire, just to keep them hot. She had also prepared a plate full of pomegranate, olives, figs, and cucumbers, all basted with olive oil and spices.

"Come, sit down both of you and eat. Tell me all about my sister Sarah and the rest of the family. How are they doing?"

"They are all fine, and they send you their very best wishes."

Sofia did not wish to get into the main reason that she was there, not just yet. They made small talk while they ate. Soon Simon excused himself from the table, pulled a couple of pillows away and went to the corner of the room to get some much-needed rest. Leah and Sofia were still enjoying their visit when Reuben came into the house. He wiped his hands with a drying cloth, looked around and saw Simon napping in the corner of the room and then spoke.

"Poor fellow, he must be really tired."

"Yes he is. He has not slept well in the last six or seven nights, ever since we saw an armed band of Zadokites attack a Roman battalion."

"Are you sure it was Judas Zadok's men?"

While Reuben ate his sustenance he listened intently as Sofia proceeded to relate the whole story about what had happened that day near Mount Gilboa.

"Yes," Sofia answered, with an infatuating gaze on her face. "Judas Zadok was so magnificent in battle, so calm, so brave, and so smart too! He set such a good trap that the Roman soldiers could not escape. No matter where the soldiers tried to take cover, they were within the sights and range of the Zadokites. He stood like a rock though out the battle, giving orders to his leaders on both sides of the mountain through hand gestures, until the battle was won. I am so impressed by him, that I think that if I ever have a male child, I will name him Judas after him! Upon hearing Sofia's comment regarding children, Leah and Reuben's eyes turned towards one another, and the pleasant atmosphere turned somewhat cold and silent. Sofia could not help but notice the abrupt change that set in when she mentioned children. She was well aware from listening to her parents' talk, that Reuben and Leah's domestic problems stemmed from not being able to conceive a child. She had heard how Reuben had always been the perfect husband for Leah, always doing good things for her. She also heard he was always a very kind and considerate man with a big heart. His demeanor had changed slowly through the years when it became evident that they could not have a baby. Sofia always believed that deep down inside he still was a kind and gentleperson. He might be firm, strict and uncompromising at times, but Sofia was quite confident that was the way he was raised by his parents. He had always been very nice and kind to her and her brothers whenever they came to visit them in Nain, which was not very often. Sofia decided that it was time to tell them exactly why she was there. She had a personal letter from her father to give to Reuben explaining the situation in detail, yet she felt it best if she told them first, then let them read the letter.

"I have been waiting for a good time to tell you something very important. There is a reason why I am here." She tried to hold back her tears, but to no avail. She repeated the whole story of what happened to her about three weeks before. She did not leave out any gruesome details. It took close to two hours, and when she was finished telling them about being raped by a Roman Commander named Octavio Pantera, and the rumors and condemnation that followed, Reuben and Leah were totally bewildered and astounded.

"My poor child," sobbed Leah, "It must have been horrible! What a deplorable deed committed by an abominable human being. Are you all right now child?"

"Yes, physically I am. It will take some time however, for me to get over my hurt feeling over the way people treated me. My own town people!" As tears rolled down her beautiful cheeks she added, "It was not my fault, I did not ask for this to happen!" Giving a long sorrowful sigh she ended, "I miss my family so much."

Even Reuben was visible moved by the story he had just heard. He stated, "The Laws of Moses are very explicit. Sometimes what God Jehovah requires and especially what he denies some of us, it hard to understand." Looking at Leah he continued, "But I want you to know and fully understand that we welcome you into our home. It is not much, but we will share what we have with you as if you were our own daughter."

Leah turned and looked back at Reuben with amazement when he was through speaking. She had hoped with all her heart that he would respond just the way he did, but never in her wildest dreams did she expect it to happen. She could not help but wonder what had come over him. As of late, this was out of character for him. Just this morning he had been easily provoked over some insignificant thing that had happened. Whatever the reason for his response, Leah was extremely pleased.

Back at the corner of the room, Sofia's crying as she was telling what had happened had awakened Simon. He lay there acting as if he were still asleep, praying in his heart that Reuben would accept her as he did. When it became evident that he was, he gave a yawn and set up on the floor.

"Thank the Lord, and you good people, I sure needed that nap. Thank you for sharing your roof and your excellent cuisine madam with me. I will be forever grateful to both of you."

Reuben replied, "No Simon, it is us who owe you a debt of gratitude for bring Sofia safely to us. We could never repay you."

"You already have." He did not mention it but by their act of kindness toward Sofia, he felt more then adequately compensated. "Well, as much as I like it here, I must be on my way now. I have some ways to go before I get to Jerusalem"

He gathered his belongings and they all walked outside to his ox drawn cart. Reuben had taken the ox to a drinking trough and had placed some hay nearby for it to eat before he had come inside a few hours ago. Once again, Simon thanked them, and he hugged and kissed Sofia on her forehead. "I know the God of Jacob has blessed you and will keep you safe with these fine people," he told her. They embraced and then they said farewell. All three watched him as he went on his way.

Several weeks had passed since Sofia began her stay with Leah and Reuben. By now she had grasped the daily routine of living with them. Reuben always worked hard all day long as a smith except when he would have some sort of meetings in the back of his shop, each time with the same group of men. This did not happen often, only once in a while. Once, Sofia came into the shop during one of those meetings, but Leah quickly retrieved her away, back into the house. She sensed that she had intruded by the surprised looks on the faces of the people participating in the meeting.

"What kind of meeting does Uncle Reuben have in his shop," she once asked? "Who are those people Reuben meets with?"

"I don't know child. He has told me not to disturb him when these meetings are going on."

"Are they clients of Uncle Reuben?"

"I don't know that either. Some of the men I do know personally like Paul. He was the magistrate of the village before the Romans deposed him and put someone else in his place. Then there is Eber, he was the leader of the village militia group. Sidon was the chief Scribe and teacher. He interpreted the Jewish laws for our village until he had a misunderstanding with the Sanhedrin in Jerusalem. It is said that young Caiaphas himself ordered that he be ousted for not conforming to the constraints place by the Romans."

"Who is this Caiaphas," asked Sofia in her innocent way?

"Caiaphas is the newest and the youngest man ever to be selected to the Sanhedrin, and he already possesses great power. I heard say that he is married to the daughter of Annas, the High Priest and Leader of the Sanhedrin"

"What do you think they discuss at these meetings?"

"I would not dare ask, nor would I dare speculate," replied Leah, shaking as if a cold frigid northern wind had just touched her soul. "Whatever it is, I am sure it's for the best of all concerned."

"I thought that I recognized one of the man sitting directly across from Uncle Reuben. I know I have seen him somewhere before, but I do not remember where."

"It is best that you leave these things to the men. Now that we are through with our house chores, I have to go harvest the garden for some vegetables and fruits. Do you want to come and help me?"

"Yes, I love being outside! There is not any better feeling then being outside with the sun warming your very soul."

After they had been in the garden for a while, Sofia stated, "Aunt Leah, it is strange, but I have not had my lunar period."

"What did you say my dear?" she replied somewhat stunned, not quite believing what she thought she had heard.

"You know, my periodical cleansing by blood." Seeing a puzzled look on Leah's face, Sofia added, "You know, my monthly period."

"Are you sure child? Could you be mistaken? Are you sure you have calculated the days correctly?"

"Yes, I had my last period about ten days before the incident in the cave happened to me. Two days later, I left Nain, and my travel with Simon took another ten days. That is twenty-two days. Also, I have been here a little over three weeks, that makes it about forty-five days not counting today."

"No wonder you have been feeling poorly the past few mornings! Sofia…I believe you are with child," shouted Leah as she leaped to her feet and tenderly embraced Sofia!

"Oh God of Jacob! No, I can't be!"

"Yes," Leah responded in an excited voice. She felt alternatively happy and yet frightened. She was happy that at last God had brought a baby into her home, yet frightened at what Reuben and the village people were going to say. Grabbing Sofia's hands and holding them tightly between their bodies, Leah warned, "We must not say anything about this to anyone except Reuben. He will know what we are to do."

She saw the puzzled look on Sofia, so she reached out and hugged her to comfort her and reassure her that everything was going to be all right. They walked back into the house in a warm close embrace, and entered through the side entrance. Once inside the house, Leah peeked into the shop through the back entrance door. The meeting must have all ready concluded since Reuben was back at work, hammering and shaping some metal.

"Reuben, please come here, I need to talk to you." Leah waited a few seconds then again asked in a more pressing tone, "Reuben, come, it's important that we speak to you."

"I'm coming woman. I am taking some of the soot off of me." In a few seconds he was in the kitchen were both Leah and Sofia waited apprehensively. "What is so important that you call me from my work? I am running behind, as it is, due to the meeting that just ended." Looking suspiciously at both of them he asked, "What is it?"

"Reuben, you better sit down." After Reuben had reclined Leah continued, "The truth of the matter is that we are quite sure that Sofia is with child."

Looking totally flabbergasted at both of them and at what he though he had heard, he demanded, "What did you say again?"

"Sofia has missed her lunar period by a substantial amount of time, and I have no doubt in my mind that she is pregnant!"

"God of David! How can this be? How can you be so sure?" Reuben's head kept turning towards Sofia and then Leah and then back again, in total disbelief.

"For one reason, she has missed her period by almost two month, and for another, she has been experiencing morning sickness for the last two weeks. I should have known it by her morning illness, but I thought that it might have been caused by her traumatic encounter at Nain."

"Couldn't that still be the case?" inquired Reuben.

"No, no, no. There has been ample time for her to adjust and overcome that experience. Take my word for it, she is pregnant."

"Does anyone else know about this? Does anyone else suspect her, condition?" asked Reuben.

"No, no one," replied Leah. "The question is, how are we to protect her from the same thing that happened in Nain?"

"I don't know," he said looking more perplexed then ever. "I really do not know at the moment. But give me some time to think, and sleep on it, and I'll come up with a solution, you'll see." Looking at Sofia, he could see that her gladdened emotions had change to fear by the thought of being cast out of this village also. He put her hand in his and asserted, "Listen to me child, nothing bad is going to happen to you, not as long as you are under our roof. Don't you worry, I have many friends and know many people who will be more then happy to provide any help that we may need. Just don't you worry. Worrying is not good for that baby you are carrying. Okay?"

Sofia nodded her head in affirmation and all three of them stood up and embraced in a group hug. After a short while, Reuben went back into the blacksmith shop and in a little while they could hear the steady rhythmic bing...bing...bing of the hammer molding hot steel on the anvil. Leah and Sofia spoke for hours about her condition, and talked about all the preparations that were going to be necessary for the arrival of the baby. With this new pleasant conversation, all of the apprehension left Sofia, and her usual happy mood returned.

A few more weeks passed. In spite of the impending danger should the town people find out about Sofia's condition, Leah was delighted about her pregnancy. Most of the days were spent listening to Leah talk about what a joyous occasion this was going to be. Her enthusiasm was contagious. It made Sofia forget the violence of its conception, and actually made her feel at peace with her condition. They kept a low profile during the day, venturing outside of the house only in the late afternoon or after sunset. Reuben's behavior was more subdued during this time, more then his normal self-assured demeanor. For some reason, his moods and demeanor seemed to be changing for the better. Leah had started to notice this ever since Sofia came to live with them, but the change had accelerated since finding out about Sofia's condition.

On the afternoon of the fifteenth day of the month of Elul, about an hour or so after one of his usual meetings had ended, Reuben came into the house accompanied by a much younger man. He looked to be in his early to mid twenties, and about four cubits (5ft 10inches) tall, with long dark brown hair. His eyes were as reflecting pools, blue as refreshing oasis waters. His face seemed to disclose a life story filled with much more tragedy then the average twenty-something year old could or should have ever experienced. Still, it was characterized by the presence of kindness and deep respect. Sofia remembered having seen him twice before, once at the meeting she had inadvertently walked in on while still in progress, and the other time she could still not remember when or where. After a few salutations between Sofia, Leah and him, they all set by the fire pit table, and Reuben spoke.

"This is Simon Josiah Iscariot. (The name Iscariot means 'from Kerioth') He is from this village. He has agreed to share in our dilemma. He has accepted to enter into a marriage contract with Sofia."

"Is this true?" questioned Leah.

"Yes," Simon Josiah Iscariot replied.

"But why? What made you agree? You do not even know our niece Sofia."

Swallowing hard, he related, "My mother, rest her soul, was a jilted woman. She was from Kerioth. She became pregnant with me and was forced to relocate to Cana, where I was born out of wedlock. Most of my life I saw my mother's pain and suffering caused by personal attacks leveled at her by supposedly God fearing people."

"Don't you believe in the Laws of Moses?" Leah questioned.

"I believe that the God who made us did not intend for any of His children to suffer unjustly."

"What do you mean unjustly? Did she not give birth to you out of wedlock?"

"Yes she did." He paused briefly to gather the strength to continue. "Her betroth turned out to be an unkind, dishonorable, and impatient man. One night while she was asleep in her father's house, he sneaked into her bedroom and took her by force. A few weeks later, after he found out she was with child, he swore she was an unclean woman. He knew it was a lie, yet he used this as an excuse to unburden himself of my mother and me." He was noticeably emotional as he became teary eyed. "She died of a broken spirit and a broken heart." Pausing a brief moment as he looked around at the three, he added, "Now, you tell me how God can condone or approve any condemnation for something that is not your fault like that, and that is out of your control?"

As Sofia listened to his tragic story, she could not help but identify with what had happened to his mother. Although not exactly the same, their tragedy seemed to parallel each other. Simon Josiah turned to Sofia and continued speaking.

"I do not expect any rights or privileges of a husband, but I would be very proud to have you enter into a marriage contract with me and use my name, Simon Josiah Iscariot, as your husband."

Leah's face glowed with gladness as she uttered, "May God smile down on you and shower you with all good things that you truly deserve, Simon Josiah Iscariot! Isn't he the most remarkable man you have ever seen Sofia?"

"Yes... yes you are," she said, halfway turning towards him and curtsying. "Thank you Simon Josiah Iscariot. Your kindness is well noted by me and I am sure by God Almighty Himself."

"Do not thank me. It is the least that I can do to help you in the memory of my dearly beloved mother. As Reuben well knows, I am quite well known by many people around these parts as well as Judea, Samaria, and Galilee. No one will ever doubt you if you tell them that you are my wife, for I will so attest." Still looking intently, yet gently at Sofia, he continued, "Do not worry about anything that you cannot change or that could cause harm to you or the baby you carry inside of you. I promise I will come back from time to time to see how you are doing." Standing up from the table he said, "I must go now. I must get back to Ramah were my men are waiting for me near the mountains."

When he said that, she remembered where she had seen him before for the first time. He was one of the Zadokite leaders at the battle she had witnessed on Mount Gilboa, near Seythopolis. She distinctly remembered him getting commands through hand signals from Judas Zadok, which he then passed on to the men under his command on the top of the hill opposite the one where Zadok stood. As he whirled around to exit, Sofa spoke.

"I have seen you before. I could not remember at first where it was, but now I remember."

"Yes, I know," he said, "A few weeks ago you saw me when you came in unannounced into a meeting we were having back in the blacksmith shop."

"Yes, that is true, but I had seen you even before then."

Reuben and Simon Josiah looked at each other, then Simon Josiah inquired, "Where have you seen me before?"

"It was about two months ago, near Seythopolis."

"I do not remember being in Seythopolis about that time, you must be mistaken," he replied sheepishly.

"It was on Mount Gilboa. Simon, the merchant of Nain and I were on our way here to Kerioth and as we were crossing Mount Gilboa, we spotted Roman soldiers below, marching through a gully. You were one of the Zadokite leaders." The room became so quiet that you could hear a small housefly buzzing as it flew around'the kitchen trying to find a landing place on the fresh bread that Leah had just baked, and that was covered on the table. "Were you not there with Judas Zadok?"

After what seemed to be a long pause, he hesitantly replied, "Yes I was there. I fight for liberation of our lands from the oppression of Roman rule. This land was given to us by God Almighty Himself through Moses, so that we could be self-governing and fulfill our own destiny. We are the Chosen People, chosen to live in peace, and to serve only our God Jehovah, not to be slaves to the Romans."

"It is not my place to judge you or what you do Simon Josiah. I am only a girl that is with child and I do not know anything about politics. My concern is only for my unborn child. I feel nothing but gratitude towards you for what you have offered me here today. For that, and the kindness you have shown me today, I only wish good things for you and that our God Almighty watch over you in whatever you chose to do."

"Please, no one outside of us must know that I am a Zadokite, never."

"Go in the Lord's peace. Your secret is safe with me," said Sofia, "Go now in peace to serve the Lord the way you think best."

He then turned to Reuben and as they walked outside of the house he asserted, "Take care Reuben, stay vigilant with your ears to the ground. I will return soon to see what information you might have for us by then. Take care of Sofia. My prayers and thoughts will be with her."

"Watch yourself too, the Romans are everywhere," replied Reuben as Simon Josiah mounted his horse and rode slowly away.

As Simon Josiah rode, his thoughts were of Sofia and of the future battles he must still fight to gain their freedom from the Romans. These thoughts brought to mind Moses' final words to the Israelites before they entered the Promised Land.

> When you go to war against your enemies and see horses and chariots, and an army greater than yours, do not be afraid of them because the Lord is with you. When you are about to go to battle, do not be fainthearted or afraid. Do not be terrified or give way to panic before them, for the Lord your God goes with you to fight for you against your enemies and will give you victory.

After Simon Josiah had gone and they had walked back into the house, Sofia, Leah and Reuben began to discuss the event that had just happened.

"I will get Sidon to scribe a marriage contract. He will know how it is done. He was the Chief Scribe at one time. I know he will be glad to do this for me."

"Yes, you are right, and from now on we will have to call you Sofia, wife of Iscariot!"

Sofia seemed swept up by the excited emotions exhibited by Leah. She felt like a tree leaf in a strong breeze, being carried away, never knowing the reasons why, nor its final destiny. All she knew was that what was happening must be good, or else her uncle and aunt would not be so animated about it all.

Three weeks later Sidon came to the shop and gave Reuben the marriage scroll. At last all of it was final. He had backdated the document to the thirteenth day of the third month of the sacred year, which is Sivan. They both reviewed it and agreed that it was an excellent workable document. After he handed it to Reuben to pass on to Sofia, Sidon asked about Simon Josiah.

"I have not seen nor heard from him since he was here the last time," replied Reuben. "He usually sends word every two or three weeks, asking me to set up a meeting of the Resistance Planning Committee. I hope all is all right. I will let you know when we will have the next meeting."

"I hope it is soon because I have some information to pass on," added Sidon. "Two days ago I observed what had to be half a Legion of soldiers heading towards Jerusalem by way of Gibeon. I did not have much time to gather information as to their final destination since they did not stop at the usual watering hole. I only got a chance to speak very briefly to some of the soldiers lagging behind the formation pulling the carts that contained their supplies. They didn't know much at all."

When Sidon left, Reuben came into the house where Leah and Sofia were busy setting aside some fruits and vegetables they had harvested the evening before from the garden.

"Who was at the shop with you Uncle Reuben? asked Sofia in anticipation that it might have been Simon Josiah.

"It was Sidon the Scribe. He brought the marriage contract. All is in order and complete. You now belong to and have Simon Josiah as your husband!"

They all smiled with joy and quipped about it for a while. Then Sofia asked, "Have you heard any word about Simon Josiah?"

"No, no one has heard a word. I am sure everything is fine." He sensed some concern on the part of the women, so he quickly changed the subject.

"Tomorrow is the tenth day of the month Tishri, which is the Feast of Atonement."

Looking somewhat dispirited Sofia said, "I never have liked to attend this festival."

"Why child?" inquired Leah.

"Because I never did like to see any animal suffer by being put to death as a sacrifice. I can not help but feel like it's a betrayal of friendship and trust between the animal to be sacrificed and the owner of the animal."

"It was God Himself who told Moses that the tenth day of the seventh month was to be celebrated as the Day of Atonement. He commanded that we hold a sacred assembly and deny ourselves, and present offerings to the Lord by fire. He further commanded that we were not to work on that day because it is the Day of Atonement, when atonement is made for all of us before the Lord our God."

"I understand. My objection to this festival is the sacrificing and the rigid interpretation of the Law. For example, what if the house caught on fire, would you not 'work' to put out the fire?"

"The Lord said that anyone who does not deny himself on this day, must be cut off from his people, and that He would destroy from among His people anyone who does any work on that day," averred Reuben.

"But what about my question? What if your house was on fire?"

"I don't know the answer to that, and I doubt that any Rabbi or anyone else has the answer you seek."

"Well, I hope that someday someone will come along and interpret the Laws of Moses in a more kinder and gentler and loving way. It is hard for me to accept that our God, who made us in His own image, is such a vengeful, unforgiving God rather then a God of love and forgiveness. We are only human, just like He made us, not Gods like the Romans believe their royalty to be. We are fallible human beings that need forgiveness, not condemnation." She suddenly noticed how quiet the room had gotten. She seemed to astonish even herself by what she was saying. Why she said what she did, she had no idea, it just came from the heart as if it was beyond of her control.

Gazing at Sofia Reuben replied, "It is written in the Torah that when Moses freed our people from Egypt, God appeared to Moses on numerous occasions. Each time, the people saw the thunder and lightning and heard the trumpet and saw the mountain shake and smoke. They trembled with fear, so they stayed their distance from the mountain in fear. They even told Moses that they would much rather he speak to them rather then for God Himself to speak to them. They were afraid that if God Himself spoke to them, they would surely die, for they knew they had committed acts that went against God's commandments. God heard the fear of His people, so in the final years of Moses life, God promised that He would raise for us a prophet from among our people. He commanded for us to listen to Him when He comes, for this is what our ancestors asked of our Lord God at Mount Horeb." Reuben paused briefly because he saw the puzzled look on Sofia's face as if she did not understand why he was talking about this. Reuben continued, "I bring this up only to say that when this prophet or Messiah comes, I too pray that He will be as you describe, a kinder more gentle interpreter of the covenant . You may not agree with all that the Law of Moses demands, but until something better comes from God Himself, we have no choice but to do His will." He then turned to Leah and uttered, "We must prepare for tomorrow's feast of Atonement."

Sofia went to the required gatherings and ceremonies, and although she still felt the way she did, she never again questioned any religious practices in her uncle's presence out of esteem and respect for him.

Some time had passed since that celebration. It was now the first day of the month of Heshvan, and another celebration for the feast of the Tabernacles had also come and gone. For this feast, Sofia had actually enjoyed helping her uncle and aunt build the booth they were required to live in during this seven-day festival. They had made it out of tree branches. The feast of the tabernacle is intended to memorialize the journey of the Chosen People from Egypt to Canaan. It is also a celebration in thanksgiving for the rich harvest of the Promised Land. Except for the sacrifices by fire, it was a time of great joy for Sofia.

Chapter 6
The Gift of Love, Self-sacrifice

Now that things were pretty much in order, the only concern that Sofia had was that it had been too long since they last heard any word from Simon Josiah. It was the tenth day of the month of Heshvan around noon on the third day after the Sabbath. Reuben was working, as usual, in his blacksmith shop when a man approached his workshop. Reuben was busy repairing the outer steel rim around the perimeter of a wheel that had been brought to him by a nearby neighbor, so he did not notice him until he was at the entrance. Reuben was startled when he saw the man at the shop's door.

"Peace be with you Reuben," the man said as he came into the confines of the shop.

"And with you too Asa," replied Reuben as he rushed to him, embracing and kissing him on each cheek. Asa did the same.

Asa was of average stature with dark curly hair that had receded back passed the top of his head. His eyes were deep dark brown, and his complexion showed the signs of weathering exhibited by those that are constantly under the sun and weather elements. He was in his late twenties or early thirties, but he looked much older then his actual age. As he entered the shop, he went directly to the water bucket that was located next to the center post that supported the roof of the shop. After drinking his fill, he went to the large wooden keg filled with water that Reuben used to submerge hot metals for cooling them down. He emerged his head into the water, and when he came up, be combed and dried his wet hair with his hands.

While he was drinking his fill of the drinkable water, and immersing his head into the wash water, Reuben questioned him saying, "What has been happening Asa? I have not heard from Simon Josiah or from anyone in almost two months! I have been very worried. This is the longest the Resistance Planning Committee have ever gone without any communications."

"Much has been happening, and most of it, I fear, is bad news."

"What do you mean, Asa?"

Finding a place to sit, he gazed down on the water ripples in the large barrel. A blank and disturbing look came over him as he began to talk. "Where do I start? I guess about three weeks ago, we ran into what must have been a half Legion of Roman soldiers near the river that runs between Gibeon and Jerusalem. Since they surprised us, we were unprepared for battle, so we did the best thing we would have done under those circumstances. We fled north towards Ramah. This turned out to be our first mistake."

"Why? What happened then?" asked Reuben with a great deal of curiosity as he pulled a stool next to Asa and set next to him.

Looking down at the ground, and shaking his head slowly Asa said, "It wasn't pretty, because what must have been the other half of the Legion was coming south towards us from Bethel. They met us head on." Clasping his hands together and squeezing them tight, he added, "They had us squeezed between the both of them. We had no choice but to climb the mountain near Bethel, and try to hold our position. Several attempts were made by the Romans to ascent up after us and do battle, but we were able to ward them off for about ten days. After the tenth day or so, we began to run out of supplies and water. At night small parties of our men were sent out by Judas Zadok to gather water upriver from the place where the Romans were camped."

Still looking down at the ground, seeming to be reliving the events, Asa went on, "Well, it worked for a few days, but on the third or fourth nightly attempt, they ran into a Roman patrol and our men were captured." Closing his eyes so as to keep from crying he continued almost choking up, "They drowned them in the river. They took them in a small boat, one by one, out to the middle of the river, then tied their hands and feet and tied large stones, wrapped in a robe, around their necks, then they were thrown overboard ...screaming... to drown. We heard their screams most of the night!"

"What about Simon Josiah Iscariot? What news do you have about him?" questioned Reuben anxiously.

"That's why I am here. Those Roman barbarians murdered him.

"Oh God have Mercy!" gasped Reuben. How did this happen?"

"We believed that Centurion Tiberius Claudius himself was the Roman Commander of the Legion. He sent an Ambassador under a flag of friendship to demand our surrender. The Emissary stated that Tiberius Claudius promised that if we laid our weapons down, we would all be documented as enemies of Rome, our weapons confiscated, and that we would be allowed to return safely to our homes and families. Judas Zadok told the Emissary that he would have to meet with his commanders and discuss this matter, and that he would send Tiberius Claudius a reply the following day."

"So? What happened then?"

"After it was discussed, it was decided that we could not trust the Romans, especially after what they had done to our comrades at the river. Zadok asked for a volunteer from his commanders to take the message back to Claudius that under no circumstances would we surrender and that we were prepared to fight to the death. It was Simon Josiah who volunteered to take the message under a flag of friendship."

At this point, Asa became noticeably overcome by emotion, yet he continued with a crackling voice, "Simon Josiah left for their camp that mid morning. We heard nothing in return. It soon became dark, and we all thought that the Romans would release him the following morning to return to our camp as they should have done under the flag of friendship."

He paused momentarily as if to gather more courage and strength to continue. Shaking his head slowly from side to side, as if visualizing what he was about to say, he went on, "Later that night we could see a pole on fire, and could hear the agonizing screams of pain coming from it. With the light of day the next morning, we could tell that they had murdered Simon Josiah. Those savages had crucified and then made a Roman candle out of him."

There was a long pause and complete silence, and then Asa continued, "You see, the Romans believe, that the only death worse then being burned alive is crucifixion so they did both to him. Later that day, his clothes and steed were sent up the mountain by the devil Romans. His horse was intercepted by our sentry posted on the road leading up the mountain."

The silence that followed was deafening in the shop for what seemed a long time. Asa and Reuben just looked at each other for that time in disbelieve. Shortly, Reuben got up and retrieved a wineskin that was hanging on a peg near the house entrance door, and handed it to Asa. Finally, Reuben broke the silence as he cleared his throat then murmured, "What happened then? Please go on."

Taking a deep breath, and a long stiff drink, which seemed to provide the courage to mentally return to that place again, Asa continued. "We were all shocked at what we saw. Judas Zadok was outraged at what had happened. He gave the order that we would all fight to the death if need be, but none would ever surrender."

Asa took another drink of wine, wiped his lips with the back of his right hand and proceed, "Young Simon Zealotes, another one of Zadok's commanders, conceived the plan for escape, which was approved by Zadok."

"Pray tell, what was the plan?"

After another long drink he pushed on, "The plan was simple really. It was to divide our forces in to three parts. From observation, we knew that at night most of the Roman soldiers and their leaders drank heavily and frolicked from sundown until after midnight with their concubines that they had brought with them to the field. Our location on the mountain was directly north of their camp. The plan called for the three groups to scatter as quietly and as quickly as possible after midnight into the three remaining directions. Simon Zealotes felt that the greatest advantage we had was our personal knowledge of the terrain. Even if their sentries spotted us, we would have a good chance of some of us escaping.

"And so, what happened then?"

Asa tipped the wineskin up and after seeing that it was empty, laid it on his lap and stroke it as you would a puppy on your lap. After a short while, he rubbed his lips and the stubble that he had as a mustache and went on with the story. "Well, as we antic-ipated, that night the Romans drank too much again. Zadok took his group to the east, and Young Simon Zealotes took his group west towards the river, and Uris, the son of Eber, took the last group north towards Shiloh. The groups that survived the escape were to converge at our mountain hideout near Arimathea." Looking up at Reuben, Asa said, "It was a good plan. We had no choice but to take the chance. We would have died of thirst or we would have surely starved to death."

"So? Did the plan work well?" inquired Reuben with much anticipation.

"The problem was that unknown to us, Claudius had sent some of his men to the north of us to try to out flank us." He paused again for a moment looking down at the ground, containing his tears, then he uttered, "Most all of those men that went north with Uris were killed, including Uris. Claudius had also sent several platoons to the east of us. He must have though that since they had captured some of our men earlier getting water at the river west of our location, that we would not try to escape towards the river, but towards the east instead. So he had some of his troops ready on the east side of the mountain. When it was all said and done, less then half of our men survived."

This time he could not contain himself and he began to cry, barely audibly, mostly sniffles. Sobbingly and teary eyes he looked at Reuben and said, "Judas Zadok was one of those killed in that group."

"Oh God of Mercy," sighed Reuben, putting his hands over his mouth and face in disbelieve.

"The Lord was with those of us that went west towards the river with Simon Zealotes. We did not encounter any resistance at all. We muffled the feet of the few horses we had with us by binding cloth to their hoofs. We went slowly down towards the river, and when we got there, we crossed it as quiet as driftwood floating on the water. Seeing that we were a safe distance from their camp, and apparently we had gone unnoticed for the time being, we paused long enough to drink enough to quench our thirst, and to fill our canteens with water."

Asa stopped to take another drink of water. In the meantime he tossed the wineskin on to a worktable on his way to the water bucket. Wiping his mouth and beard with his outer garment sleeve, he said, "We were fortunate that it was a new moon, and the fog created by the warm river waters and the cool night air, gave us some cover during our retreat. By daybreak we were about thirty-five or so furlongs (approximately four miles) to the west of the Roman camp. Then we turned north towards Arimathea. It was almost a three day journey before we reached our hideout."

"How many men survived this ordeal?"

"By the grace of God, all of the men that went west with Simon Zealotes survived, and about fifteen or twenty of the others were able to get away."

"So how many are left to fight?"

"About sixty able body men and five or so that are recovering from wounds they sustained."

All at once Reuben, who had been caught up in hearing about what had happened, said in an awed voice, "Oh my God! Sofia! How do we tell Sofia?"

"Sofia? Who is Sofia?" asked Asa.

"She is my niece. She was married to Simon Josiah, and is carrying a child."

"Ah yes," remarked Asa, "He told us about her a few weeks before the attack. He was always anxious to come back here to see her."

After a few moments in deep thought, Reuben stated, "I don't think I will tell her exactly how he died, not just yet. It may bring harm to the baby she is carrying. I don't think it would be wise in her condition, but I have to tell her that he was slain. I pray

God will give me the strength and the proper words to tell her he is gone to heaven."
Turning to Asa, he said, "Tell me Asa, what do you need from me and the Resistance
Planning Committee?"

"Nothing at this moment. I am here only to tell you what has happened, and that
young Simon Zealotes has been chosen as our new leader. He is a very young man,
probably one of the youngest, but he has shown that he has an excellent military
mind. All of the elders and leaders chose him unanimously."

"So what are his initial plans?" asked Reuben.

"He wanted me to tell you that we plan to heal our wounds for a while. We will
probably send out small groups to all the villages in Judah, Samaria, and Galilee to
recruit and rebuild our forces. This is only the beginning, we now have a rallying cry,
Remember Bethel!

After a pause to reflect, Reuben asked, "How long will it be before the resistance
movement becomes viable again?"

"It may well take several months. We will be in touch with you in due time. For
now, I must go. While we plan to let the Romans think that they have crushed the
resistance, we will be letting our people know that we are still alive and well, and will
soon be more active then ever." With that said, Asa stood in preparation to leave.

"God be with you Asa," said Reuben as he hugged and kissed him on the cheeks.

"And with you too Reuben. Now comes the hard part of my journey. I must go tell
Eber Benjara that his only son Uris has been taken in battle. What a tragedy, he was
so happy a few months ago because his wife had given birth to their first child, a
daughter. I think he had named her after his dearly departed mother Cassandra, who
was killed by a drunk Roman Charioteer who was racing another Roman through the
street without regard for our people on foot. "

Reuben watched Asa for sometime as he walked down the road and turned
towards the Village Square. Reuben knew he had the hardest task ahead of him, to tell
Sofia and Leah about Simon Josiah. He went back inside the shop and set down on a
chair that was near the furnace. He sat there long enough to regain his composure, at
the same time thinking how he was going to break the news of Simon Josiah's demise
to Sofia and Leah.

Since Simon Josiah's kind gesture almost two months ago, he was all that they
seemed to talk about. They had really grown quite fond of him, even in his absence.
It was as if they had known him all along when in reality they had just met him. After
what seemed to be close to an hour of lamenting within himself over Simon Josiah's
death, Reuben was able to compose himself enough and had gathered the courage to
go inside the house to tell them the tragic news.

Entering the house, Reuben could see them busily washing and cleaning some fruits and vegetables that they had just picked from their garden. He could hear them talking and laughing about how Sofia's clothes were beginning to fit tightly. Her body was changing due to her pregnancy. Her stomach had started to protrude, and she was beginning to gain some weigh. Her appetite had increased and she seemed to always be eating or nibbling on something. It was hard for Reuben to remember when Leah laughed as much and acted so full of life as she had since Sofia came to live with them, especially since finding out that Sofia was with child. He had to admit to himself that this had also brought some changes in him for the better, in his attitude towards Leah. They seemed to be getting along better then ever in their married life. He gave thanks to Yahweh for this gift of newfound love in their relationship. Sofia's presence in their home had surely made a tremendous difference in their lives, all for the better.

When Leah saw him coming into the room, she said, "Oh, I'm glad you decided to come in and rest a while. You have been working too hard on that wheel and you need some cool herbal tea to relax you. You look so tense and worried, so you need to sit down and rest a spell." She handed him a cup of tea that had been boiling with some weedy herb and limes in it. As he took the cup and sipped his first drink, he began to speak in a low somber tone of voice. "I have just received word about Simon Josiah Iscariot."

"Thank God!" shouted Leah, "Is he well? Where is he now?"

After a moment of silence, Reuben continued, "It is not good news at all. Please sit down, both of you. What I have to tell you will not be pleasant for any of us."

They all sat down and taking Leah's hand into his left hand, and Sofia's hand into his right hand, he murmured, "Simon Josiah has been killed in action."

"Oh no!" they both sighed, looking with disbelieve at each other.

"How did this happen?" questioned Leah.

"When did it happen?" Sofia asked.

"Asa, the mason of Jericho, just left my shop. He brought me the news. It seems that the Zadokites were trapped on a mountain near Bethel. They would have all been killed if not for the unselfish brave acts of Simon Josiah and Judas Zadok. He was also killed in the same battle."

"Oh God of Mercy, "cried Leah, "Please grant them eternal peaceful rest!"

"But how was Simon Josiah killed?" Sofia continued questioning.

"He and Zadok used themselves as decoys to lead the Romans away so that the others could escape." He knew this was not what had really happened, but he could not bring himself to tell her the truth, not now, about how he was crucified and burned like a sacrificial lamb. He prayed that God would understand and forgive him for this falsehood.

"Please Uncle Reuben, please tell me again what happened," she asked once more, this time with such a tear filled voice, that it was hard to comprehend her utterance.

"Asa said that by some accidental chance the Zadokites ran into a Roman Army Legion. They were not prepared to fight them, so they fled up the mountain near Bethel. After a failed attempt to gain a truce, Simon Josiah and Zadok led a few volunteers one way off the mountain, and the Romans followed, and killed them in battle. The others escaped by going the opposite way." Reuben was able to suppress his emotions, but just barely. He knew that he had to be the strong support for both women.

"Simon Josiah was a strong brave man," he added, "he gave up his life so that others could live. There is no greater gift of love then that!"

Both women lamented deeply for Simon Josiah. They tore at their clothing in an outward sign of sorrow, and at the same time Sofia began an incantation that she had learned from reading the Torah as a child at her mother's side.

"My eyes will flow unceasingly without relief, until the Lord looks down from heaven and sees what is happening to me. Those who were my enemies without cause hunted me like a bird. They tried to end my life in a pit and threw stones at me; the waters closed over my head, and I thought I was about to be cut off. I called on Your name, O Lord, from the depths of the pit. You heard my plea not to close Your ears to my cry for relief. You came near when I called You and You told me not to fear. O Lord, You took up my case and redeemed my life. Now ease my sorrow, and give me the courage to continue through all of this lamentation."

Reuben took both women unto his arms and they grouped hugged for an extended period of time, crying, singing, and humming in honor and respect for Simon Josiah Iscariot.

Chapter 7
Covenent at Kerioth

Ever since the Roman General Pompey captured Jerusalem, the provinces of Palestine had become subject to Rome rule. Noblemen or sons of noblemen were appointed as procurators by Rome to govern the conquered. Herod the Great was one of those procurators, and he presently was the puppet Ruler of Palestine for the Romans. Even though Herod was the selected Procurator, he liked to call himself by various titles, among them, King Herod, Herod the Great, and the King of the Jews. In reality he was an insecure, savage tyrant who murdered many people, including his wife, mother-in-law, and three of his own sons. Because he was part Jew and part Gentile, the Roman Emperor felt that he was a good choice for Procurator with very limited authority to rule the Jews.

Since the Roman conquest, there had been splintered rebel groups of Jews from Galilee, Samaria, and Judah fighting to regain their freedom, but never as a cohesive group representing a united front. Young Simon Zealotes was the first to attempt, and succeed in creating such a union. There were plenty of reasons for animosity between the neighboring providence, but the loss of their freedom was the adhesive that Simon Zealotes hoped would bring them all together under one banner. There were not only nationality differences, but philosophical differences as well that had prevented their unity in the past.

There were basically four dominant groups within these provinces. The Pharisees was one of these groups. They believed in the validity of the oral law and in the free interpretation of the written law, always seeking to discover its inner meaning. They were the largest in membership with groups in most of the cities and villages in Palestine. However, they were the minority in the Sanhedrin, the Jewish religious governing body, but they yielded power out of proportion to their numbers because of their large following. Of the seventy members, only one-thirds were Pharisees. Each division had members from all economical levels, but the Pharisees had more from the middle and upper classes, and included mostly professionals and the well educated. Their distinguishing beliefs, as opposed to the other sects, were rigidly held observance of external forms of religion without genuine pity, to the point of hypocrisy.

Another division or sect was the Sadduccees. They made up about two-thirds of the Sanhedrin. Their philosophy, views and practices were opposed to those of the Pharisees. They denied the authority of oral tradition, the resurrection of the dead, and the existence of angels. Their name probably was based on the Hebrew language meaning "a righteous person with moral integrity." They believed that the religious edict was exactly what was written in the Laws of Moses, and, unlike the Pharisees, they did not believe in interpretations that tended to soften their requirements.

Next came the Essenes. They believed only in the inward nature of things. They believed that things were only what they are, and nothing more. They believed in the inward nature and in the true substance and constitution of things because a spiritual or immaterial entity made them so. No rules could change what is or isn't. They considered themselves the minority in Palestine. They were a sanctimonious group and as such, could not wait for the time to come for God Himself to intervene and wipe out everyone, including the other sects that did not keep His laws that He personally gave to Moses.

The last of the groups were the Nationalist or Zealots, as they now called themselves. They were the latest of the dominant groups to emerge. Its members were the most passionate and zealous patriots of Judaism. There had always been patriots fighting for "freedom and home rule" since long before the Maccabean era. Their philosophy can be found in the Torah were it states, "Be ye zealous for the law and give your lives for the covenant." They were the group involved in gorilla warfare against the Romans. Nationalist or Zealotes could be found in all sects, with their own leaders and agendas. These were the ones that Simon Zealotes wanted to unite.

Throughout their history there had always been constant strive between these Jewish groups or sects. They disagreed in their philosophical thinking and had many other differences, including their borders, possessions and their Godly ranking. Even so, there were plenty of freedom lovers that made excellent fighters in all of the various groups. The problem was that each band of rebels came with its own leaders and its own reasons for resisting Roman rule. To attempt to band all rebel groups together was a tremendous undertaking. There had not been any sort of joint venture between them, other then necessary but suspicious day to day trade.

In reverent respect for Judas Zadok, Simon Zealotes had taken the name Simon Judas Zealotes. It was commonplace for people to take on the name or names of past patriots that had similar beliefs and philosophies as their own. Simon's last name was first used by his great-grandfather who took the name from the Torah's reference to the Zealots. Three months had passed since the death of Zadok in the mountains near Bethel. Since that time, young Simon Judas Zealotes had sent almost all of his men back home to their respective villages to work underground, recruiting new freedom fighters. He had teamed up Galileans, Samarians, and Judeans as recruiting units to show that unity was imperative if they were to successfully fight off the shackles of bondage within their own Promised Land. Zealotes and his group of leaders also decided that Kerioth (previously known as Kiriath Jearim also Kirjath Jearim) would be their secret command post. Young Zealotes had a good reason for this decision.

As a child he admired and revered King David from the stories he heard told as a boy. He remembered sitting by the campfire with his mother and beseeching his uncles to recant the story of how David slew Goliath, the champion of the Philistines. Goliath was over nine feet tall and had a bronze helmet on his head and wore a coat of scale armor of bronze weighing five thousand shekels (approximately one hundred and twenty-five pounds). Young Simon Judas Zealotes eyes would be filled with awe when they would tell of how Goliath stood and shouted to the ranks of Israel.

"Why do you not come out and line up for battle? Am I not a Philistine, and are you not the servants of Saul? Choose a man and have him come down to me. If he is able to kill me, we will become your subjects; but if I overcome him and kill him, you will become our subjects and serve us. This day I defy the ranks of Israel! Give me a man and let us fight each other"

Of course everyone knows that the one who fought Goliath was a poor shepherd boy named David and he slew Goliath with a slingshot, and later became King. So it was that ever since Zealotes was a boy, he wanted to emulate the courage and cunning of King David. As David once united all of the Levant Coast into one Israel, he hoped that his recruiting effort would also have a unifying effect in their struggle for freedom.

He remembered that King David had relocated the Ark of the Covenant to Jerusalem from Kiriath Jearim when he proclaimed Jerusalem the Capitol of Israel. Therefore, Zealotes wanted the unification or covenant to fight as a united front to have oversight and coordination in Kerioth. Later, when the enemy would be overthrown and run out of Palestine, they could all rejoice together in Jerusalem. The Resistance Planning Committee that Reuben belonged to and that met periodically at the blacksmith shop was to be the coordinating body for this recruitment effort.

About fifty days had now past since Simon Josiah had been slain in the battle near Bethel. It was now the first day of the month of Tebeth, and while the unification effort was active, all rebel activity seemed to be at a stand still for now. Meanwhile, life went on as it did every day, without a hint that would alert the Romans that the revolutionists were rebuilding.

In the same village where Reuben and Leah resided, there lived a Jewish priest named Zacarias that Reuben and Leah knew well. His wife was named Elizabeth. Both were descendants of the lineage of Aaron. Both were upright and obedient to the Laws of Moses. They too did not have any children even though they had tried for many years much like Reuben and Leah. One day, while Sofia and Leah were in the village bartering for some necessary items for the household, they saw Elizabeth in the market place. To Leah's surprise, Elizabeth was with child. This was very strange, since like Leah, Elizabeth had long passed her childbearing years.

"The Lord be with you Elizabeth!" greeted Leah.

"And with you too, Leah!" responded Elizabeth. "Who is this lovely young woman with you?"

"This is Sofia, my niece, the daughter of my sister Sarah and her husband Ezra from Nain. You remember Sarah don't you?"

"Yes, I certainly do. It has been many years since I have seen her. How is she doing"

"She is in good health and with a joyous spirit. How are you? How have you been?" Trying not to sound too amazed Leah added, "I see your are with child! I am so glad for you!"

"During the warm friendly embrace, Elizabeth replied, "Thank you Leah. I am sure that the Lord God Himself blessed me with this child. I know I am past the age for conceiving. For the first two months I thought that something must be wrong, but about four months ago, I found out that I was truly pregnant. I am now six months along. How about you Sofia, how far along are you?"

"I too am about six months along. It appears like we will be having our babies about the same time!" Sofia reached and embraced Elizabeth in joy of their similar condition and good fortune. As they embraced, Sofia felt the child within her jump and kick more then she had ever felt it move before. It was an strange feeling. She did manage to mask her discomfort well as all three continued their conversation.

"What is your husband's name?" asked Elizabeth.

"Simon Josiah Iscariot", she meekly replied. "He was killed by the Romans about two month ago near Bethel."

"Oh yes, I heard about that. I heard that Uris, the son of Eber had also been slain." Shaking her head she murmured, "These are very painful times. We need someone to spread some good new for a change."

"Yes, replied Leah, "Good news like both of you having babies! I am so happy for you, both of you." They all three held hands and giggled happily.

After some more casual conversation had transpired, Leah inquired, "And how is you husband Zacarias? We have not seen him in about half a year. He has not presided over any religious rituals on the Sabbath as he use to do."

"Well, it's a strange thing that happened to him," replied Elizabeth with a mystified look on her face. "About seven months ago, his priestly division was on duty. He was chosen by luck, according to the custom of the priesthood, to go into the temple of the Lord and burn the incense. All the assembled worshipers were praying outside waiting for him. He stayed in the temple for a long time, so much so that the worshipers became worried. When he finally came out, he could not speak to them. They think that he must have had a vision in the temple, for he kept making signs to them. He has been unable to speak, even to this day."

"That is strange indeed," replied Leah. "I am sorry to hear this. Tell him that we will pray for him daily for his complete recovery. I'm sure he will be fine with time." Looking around and then turning towards Sofia, Leah said, "Well, it's getting late and Reuben is waiting for us at home. It was so good to see you Elizabeth."

"And it was so good to see you too Leah, and to meet you Sofia. Give my regards to Reuben. Shalom."

As Leah and Sofia walked home, Leah could not help thinking how impossible it was for a woman Elizabeth's age to be pregnant. However, she was still overjoyed for her.

It wasn't long before the entire community and surrounding area had heard about Elizabeth. Everyone seemed to be astonished that a woman passed childbearing age with a husband truly passed his prime would be with child. The consensus of opinion was that it had to be a miracle ordained by God.

Even stranger, a few months after their encounter with Elizabeth, it was also rumored that a cousin of Elizabeth's from Nazareth, named Mary, had come to visit and had stayed with her. The rumor was that Mary claimed to have had an angelic visitation. So the story went, Mary, a pledged woman to a carpenter from Nazareth had experienced a visit from angels. The carpenter whose name is Joseph is said to be a descendant of King David's lineage. As the story circulated, one night an angel appeared telling her that God had found favor with her and that she would be with child and give birth to a son. The angel also told her that she was to name Him Yeshua, (that is Jesus) meaning Yahweh is salvation. According to the story being told, it is said that Mary asked the angel how this could be, since she had not known any man, and was still a virgin. The angel was said to have replied that a Holy Spirit would come upon her and the power of the Most High would overshadow her. She was to have this child without union with man because with God all things are possible. The angel is quoted as saying to Mary that the Lord God would give her Son the throne of King David! Still, there were many that did not believe this story. Some even wondered why the carpenter stayed betrothed to her since she surely must have given up her virginity. Yet, some believed her since they know that God does work in mysterious ways.

The prophets of old, Isaiah, Ezekiel, and Hosea had prophesied that the Messiah or Deliverer of the chosen people would come from Nazareth and from the lineage of King David. Not one person dared to question her pregnancy without marriage. Besides, Joseph seemed to have chosen to keep Mary as his betrothed, and had never questioned or doubted her virginity. Strange things seemed to be happening now that defied reasonable explanations!

Chapter 8
The Birth of Judas

It was now the twentieth day of the month of Nisan. The time for replanting the vegetable garden had already come and gone. Both Sofia and Leah had planted most of the same fruits and vegetables as in previous years. The soil was good and the bounty was always plentiful. After sharing the harvest with friends and close neighbors, what was left on the vines and in the ground was plowed under and served as fertilizer for the following year's crops. Wintertime was upon them, but it was not yet as cold as it can normally get later during the year. Sofia had been extra careful in the performance of her chores and in helping Leah since her time for parturition was almost at hand. Leah kept insisting that Sofia stay in bed and rest during the day, but this was not, nor had it ever been in keeping with Sofia's ways. Leah had good reason to suggest that she rest. It appeared to her that Sofia was getting paler and weaker as her time approached. This did not seem normal to her. Leah did not mention it to Sofia for fear that she would cause unnecessary worry, which could have an adverse effect on the baby. She had mentioned it to Reuben about a month before, and he had suggested that she take her to Salome, the mid-wife and birthing practitioner in Kerioth. She had done as he suggested, but in her examination, Salome had found nothing conspicuously wrong. She did mention that it was hard for her to tell if the baby was in the position it should normally be, but she contributed that to it being her first child. As to her loss of appetite and paleness, Salome's only suggestions was that she partake several meals a day, and not restrict herself to the traditional meal times. It was Salome's opinion that it would not be much longer before this child would see the light of day.

One night, after repast and the evening thanksgiving prayers, Leah and Sofia sat by the fire and talk about what it would be like after the baby was born.

"I wonder if God is going to bless me with a boy or a girl?" asked Sofia.

"I don't know," answered Leah. "I have never been good at guessing the sex of an unborn child by looking at the growth pattern of the mother, not even by feeling the stomach. Since I have never been with child myself, I couldn't even tell you if it feels differently to be carrying a boy or a girl."

Lately Sofia would easily become very melancholy at times, because of their condition, and this was one of those times. She looked at her aunt and declared, "Aunt Leah, I have a confession to make to you"

"My dear, what could you possibly have to confess to me!"

"When this first happened to me nine months ago, I was terrified about what the future had in store for me"

Holding both of Sofia's hands in hers, Leah replied, "That is very understandable. I too would have been scared of being stoned to death or being exiled from my family."

"Yes, I was, but my biggest fear was coming here to Kerioth to live with you and Uncle Reuben."

Somewhat shocked at what she just heard Leah questioned, "Why Sofia? Have you not been happy here?"

Throwing both her arms around Leah's neck and embracing her, Sofia averred, "Oh yes Aunt Leah, that's the point, I did not know, nor did I believe that I could ever be as happy as I have been here with you. All I heard before was how unhappy you were with Uncle Reuben, and how he would abuse you for no reason at all. I didn't know if I could have been able to live here under those conditions at all." Letting go of Leah's neck, she continued, "The truth of the matter is, Uncle Reuben has been an altogether different man then what I expected. He is a kind, gentle and loving man and I have not seen him be mean or arbitrary to anyone during this time."

Looking down at the flickering flames that seemed to rejuvenate from the glowing cinders left in the fire, Leah uttered, "Yes, he abused me at times. I think it was because of the frustration and pain he felt at facing a childless future. I am not saying that there ever is a good reason or even any excuse for abuse. There is never any good reason for abuse even though, by the Law of Moses, we become our husband's property to do with as they please." Looking up at Sofia, and with a smile on her face, she continued, "But I agree, Reuben has changed since you came. He has noticed this change in himself, I know, because he tried to tell me that a few months ago, in his own repenting way. He has certainly been more understanding, patient, and gentle." Looking at Sofia, Leah continued, "All these changes I attribute to you being here and becoming the daughter that he thought he would never have. He loves you so much, and so do I. We would do anything for you. So you see, we all have benefited from you coming to live with us."

"I could never tell you how much I love you and Uncle Reuben. You have been more then an uncle and aunt to me. You have been like my father and mother, and for that, I will always be eternally grateful. I want you to know that if any thing should happen to me, there is no one else on earth that I would rather have, other then you and Uncle Reuben, to take care of my baby."

"Now now, Sofia, let's not talk about things happening. You are going to be fine, the baby is going to be fine, and we are going to be the happiest family in all Judah!"

Seeing that Sofia was about to shed some tears, Leah quickly changed the conversation to a happier subject. "Let's talk about what you want to name the baby when it is born, that's a much more cheerful subject to talk about."

"Well, I have been thinking a lot about that. I have come to the conclusion that if it's a girl, I want to name it Mary Elizabeth Iscariot. I like both of those names very much. And if it's a boy, well, I decided a long time ago to name him Judas,—Judas Iscariot."

"Those are excellent names. You have chosen well!"

"I chose the names Mary and Elizabeth for Elizabeth, the wife of Zacarias and for her relative Mary of Nazareth who is here in Kerioth visiting her. Their situations are very similar to mine."

"What do you mean?

"Well, I hear that Mary claims to have had an angelic visitation. An angel supposedly told her that she was to have a child."

"Yes, I have heard talk about that. I believe things like that can and do happen. Don't you?"

"That's just it Aunt Leah," replied Sofia. "There was something strange that happened to me too, a few days before I was violated. It happened again for the second time during my journey here to Kerioth from Nain."

"What was it child?" inquired Leah, her curiosity peaking.

"I had a same dream, twice, telling me that God had found favor in me. But the odd thing is that both times the dream was so real, that I can't actually say with any certainty that it was indeed a dream or if it actually happened and possibly I was in a trace when it happened."

"Who talked to you and what did they say?"

"Both times it was the same two manly figures. They were men dressed in shiny white tunics that seemed to shine like they were made out of sunbeams. They told me that my descendant had been chosen by God Almighty to help fulfill some prophecy. They said that God would take me to heaven when my part had been completed. I still don't really understand what it all meant." She went on to tell all of the details that she could possibly remember about the dream. This took the better part of an hour.

"Why didn't you tell me this before child?"

"I don't know. I tried to tell my father the night before I was raped, but I didn't get a change to tell him. I also tried to tell Simon the Merchant of Nain the night I had the second dream, but for some reason I couldn't"

"What was the reason you couldn't or wouldn't tell?"

"I don't know that either. I suppose it was because I did not want anyone thinking that I was crazy. These apparitions are not your natural every day occurrences you know!"

"Well, I am glad you told me. You know, you may have been touched by God and selected for something special. There is nothing odd about being chosen by God for any purpose he may have in store for you."

Letting out a small sigh of relief Sofia added, "You are probably right again. You are always right, and I love you very much." They hugged and kissed and held each other for a brief moment then Sofia continued, "I think I'll go lie down now. I am not feeling very well right now." Her voice connoted much discomfort and some pain. "I will see you tomorrow, with the grace of God."

Leah nodded her approval, and hugged and kissed her good night. While Sofia went to her bedroom, Leah went to her own room where Reuben had been working on some ledgers ever since he had eaten supper earlier. As Leah walked in, he looked up and asked, "How is Sofia feeling?"

"She's not feeling very well, I think that it is time now or past time for the baby to be born." As she sat on the bed, her back resting on the headboard she continued talking as she brushed her long black hair back away from her forehead with her hands. "God, I have a bad feeling about this, Reuben. I hope everything turns out fine."

"All we can do is pray that the Lord God Yahweh will take good care of her."

As she continued to run her hands through her hair, she spoke with a concerned tone of voice. "Sofia told me a curious thing tonight. She said that she has had a mysterious dream. She has had it twice already, once prior to her assault, and the other as she was traveling from Nain to Kerioth."

"What was odd about that?"

"Well, it's the content of the dream that is strange and the fact that she is not really sure if it was indeed a dream or if it was an actual apparition while she might have been in a state of rapture. She says that two male figures dressed in bright shiny white tunics came to her and told her that she had been chosen by God and that He had found favor in her. They told her that her descendant has been chosen by God to help fulfill prophecy, and that God promises to take her home as soon as she completes her destiny." They were both silent, and in deep meditation, for a while, at what Sofia had told Leah. Shortly Leah spoke again.

"What do you make out of that Reuben?"

"I don't know what to think about it. Maybe she has been touch by God Himself. We just have to wait and pray that His will be done...for all of us.

After another short period of silence, Leah asked Reuben what he was doing with those ledgers. He replied that it had to do with the Resistance Planning Committee of which he was a member. She had been aware of this committee meeting at the blacksmith shop for the past four or five years, and had never had the courage to ask Reuben the nature of their business. Tonight, she felt like she needed to know.

"It is nothing that I would want you to be involved with," he replied.

"Why?"she asked. "Anything that affects you also affect me."

"Yes, you are right, and maybe one of these days I will have to share with you what I am involved in, but not tonight." Feeling his voice rising in tone, Reuben took a deep breath to regain his composure. He then reached out to her and held her hands in his and said, "In the past, I didn't tell you because I didn't really care enough for you to tell you, but now, I only want to protect you from any possible harm. It is only because of my new found esteem, devotion and love for you that I do not want you to be in any danger by knowing about the committee and its business."

Leah did not quite accept his reasons, but she was elated at what she just heard him say about his newfound devotion and love for her. It had been a long long time since he had even hinted about his feelings for her. The delight she felt made her forget, for a moment, the pending predicament with Sofia. As she readied for bed, she kept thinking that tomorrow could possibly bring a better day.

That next morning was the day after the Sabbath and the twenty-first day of Nisan. Leah found it strange that Sofia was not up before Reuben and her as was normally the case. She got up and went to Sofia's room and found her still asleep but in an unconscience state and in a cold sweat. She had evidently been sweating profusely for some time since the bed and covers were soaking wet. Leah rightly assumed that she was in labor now, and must be having some problems with the baby.

"Reuben," cried out Leah, "Reuben, come quickly, its Sofia."

Reuben sprang out of bed and hurried to Sofia's room. "What is the matter?" Before Leah could answer, he saw Sofia and blurted out. "Oh God of Jacob! What is wrong with Sofia?"

"I'm not sure," replied Leah, "But I think that she has gone into labor, and is about to have the baby. This doesn't look like anything I have ever seen. She really doesn't look natural. I think that she is having a very difficult delivery. You hurry and get Salome and tell her that it is an emergency. I will get Sofia prepared for her. I don't think this is going to be an easy birth."

While Reuben went to get Salome, Leah placed pieces of linen cloth that had been soaked in cool water, on Sofia's forehead. She also took her nightclothes off, and pre- pared her for delivery. In doing so, Leah noticed that Sofia was clutching a necklace with her right hand, next to her bosom. After closer inspection of the necklace, to Leah's surprise, she recognized it as the one that had belonged to her grandmother and had been given to her sister Sarah. She assumed rightly that Sofia's mother must have passed it on to her for some reason.

Sofia became conscience for a little while and complained of severe pain in her lower abdomen area. Leah attempted to take the necklace away so that Sofia would not harm herself with it, but Sofia resisted. After a very short while the pain became so unbearable that she became unconscience again. About that time Reuben and Salome arrived. Leah was so scared and almost to the point of hysteria. She broke in to tears when she saw Salome, the midwife.

"How long has she been in this condition?" inquired Salome.

"I don't really know. She was this way when I found her this morning. She has regained her conscienceness once or twice in the last half hour."

Salome uncovered her body totally. In doing so, she noticed the necklace also, and tried to take it from her tight grasp, but she could not remove it from her hand. She inspected her stomach, the pupils of her eyes, and her vaginal area for what seemed to be a long time. After the examination she looked at Leah and Reuben and assert- ed, "This does not look good at all, not at all. She has entered labor, and the baby is not in the normal position for delivery."

"What do you mean?" said Leah, "What do you mean it is not in position?"

"From feeling the stomach, and from feeling inside her, I can tell that the baby is not in the normal birthing position, which is with its head down, and facing the moth- er's back. That is the normal way babies come into this world. This baby is positioned with its head up, and it is facing sideways. This is a very difficult and dangerous fetus position because the birth canal does not enlarge enough to allow the babies shoulders and head to come out freely, and the baby is more vulnerable to the pressure that is present in the canal. The only thing I can do is to try to manipulate the baby into the proper position, but there are dangers in doing so."

"What kinds of dangers?" asked Leah, who was reaching the point of a breakdown once more.

"For one, I may not be able to turn the baby into position. For another, I may lacerate the vaginal walls as I attempt to turn it, which might cause uncontrollable bleeding and she may bleed to death. Also, you never can tell were the umbilical cord is at this point. In turning the baby, you take a chance of getting the umbilical cord tangled around the babies neck, or squashing the cord, and cutting of the air and blood supply to the baby."

During the explanation, Sofia had regained conscienceness again and was listening to the assessment Salome was giving of the situation. She was about to speak when Salome continued her remarks.

"I don't want to alarm you, but I must tell you that in situations like this, when all is tried and all has failed, a choice has to be made whether to save the baby or the mother."

Hearing that, Leah gasped and clung to Reuben very tightly. She could not hold her emotions any more, and she began to cry. As she cried she was praying to God for His intervention. Reuben joined in after the first two sentences, and to their surprise, so did Sofia as she clung to the necklace and placed it on her lips.

"The Lord is my shepherd, I shall not want. He makes me lie down in green pastures. He leads me besides the still waters. He restores my soul. He leads me in the path of righteousness for His namesake. Yea though I walk through the valley of the shadow of death, I will fear no evil; for you are with me; Your rod and Your staff, they comfort me. You prepare a table before me in the presence of my enemies; You anoint my head with oil. My cup runs over. Surely goodness and mercy shall follow me all the days of my life; and I will dwell in the house of the Lord forever."

As their prayer was ending Salome was looking more perplexed then ever as she was attempting to turn the baby as she had explained. She gave out a low shout of bewilderment as a deep red stream of blood came gushing forth from Sofia's womb.

"Oh my God!" Salome said.

Some how Sofia knew that the baby was in trouble so she began to cry out, "Please save the baby, save the baby!" She reached and grabbed Leah's hand. "Don't worry about me, I'll be fine, just save the baby, please, oh please," she cried beggingly.

Reuben was every emotional and in tears also. He and Leah continued to comfort Sofia by holding on to her hands, praying some more and by assuring her that all would be all right. They could tell that she was getting weaker and weaker as the time past. The blood flow could not be stopped. Meanwhile Salome worked diligently in an effort to save both of them if possible. If it came to a choice, then she would attempt to save the baby. Over an hour passed and Sofia was still getting weaker and weaker. When it seemed that both would be lost, at that moment Salome lifted a baby by its feet and gave it a slap on the buttocks. The baby let out a cry, a good, healthy, strong cry!

"It's a boy!" she hollered. She cleaned it up a little with the few cloths that were still clean and not soaked with Sofia's blood. She laid the baby on Sofia's stomach, and she hugged it very gently with the hand that held the necklace and kissed his head while stroking him gently on his back with the other hand.

Salome had some trouble getting the remainder of the umbilical cord and the rest of the afterbirth. She had to yank and tug excessively, much more then normal. After she removed it, she gathered the dirty linen and wrapped the afterbirth in it and took it outside to dispose of it. While Salome was outside, Leah, Sofia and Reuben spoke together.

"Look, he is trying to lift his head to see you!" sobbed Leah.

"He is a strong handsome boy!" Cried Reuben wiping tears of joy from his eyes.

"Welcome to this world baby Judas Iscariot," said Sofia, a smile on her extremely paled face. "I know you will grow up to be a fine strong man, and I will be very proud of you. Maybe you will be famous one day and be known though out Judea. Just remember always, that your mother loves you very dearly. I would give my life for you many times over." As she was speaking, she looked up and said, "Aunt Leah, there they are!"

"Who is were child?"

"The two man that I told you about last night, dressed in white brilliant linen!"

"Where are they child, I can't see them, and neither can Reuben."

"There by the doorway."

Both of them looked, but still could not see anything. However, in their hearts, they knew that Sofia truly believed that she was seeing angels, so they knelt down and bowed their heads in reverence, praying all the while.

"Look! They are coming towards the bed. See how they are admiring Baby Judas." She began to talk as if she was having a conversation with someone in the room. Leah and Reuben could only hear Sofia's side of the conversation.

"Yes, oh yes, isn't he a lovely healthy child? Yes I remember seeing you before, and I remember all that you told me."

"Why must I go now? Why? "

"Yes, I understand, I love Him too with my whole heart and soul. I have always kept His commandments, and always did what I thought was His Will."

"Yes, I am very happy that He has found favor in me."

Finally, Reuben found the courage to look up and ask, "What are they saying now child?"

"They are saying, 'Do not be afraid. They say that I will not suffer shame or pain. That I should not fear disgrace, nor will I be humiliated." At this point, Sofia began to repeat, word for word what the angels were saying. "You will forget the shame of your youth and remember no more the reproach of your widowhood. The Lord God is calling you back to Him. For a brief moment He abandoned you, but with deep compassion He brings you back to Him.'"

"Now? Oh no, not my Sofia! Oh God please, not my Sofia!" cried Leah beseechingly.

"What about my baby?" asked Sofia,

Looking as if she did not understand something that was being told to her, she asked, "Whom did you say is going to teach him about God and being his own man?"

"Oh, that is good. They are the ones I would have chosen myself. They have been so kind to me. I love them so"

Stunned and overwhelmed with what was happening with Sofia, Reuben found the courage to ask, "What did they say about the baby, what did they say about him?"

Sofia replied in a soft weakened voice, "It is you and Leah who will raise my son Judas" As if something had gotten her attention again, Sofia looked up again and began to speak to whomever she was seeing, "Yes, Oh yes, I do want to see my mother and father!" After a very short pause Sofia then said, with a big smile, "There they are! Can they hear me? I love you mother! I love you father!"

"And there is Simon Josiah! He is waiting for me too. Look, he is smiling and waving at me! How handsome he looks!"

After listening intently Sofia said, "Really? We will all be together soon in paradise? Oh I can't wait!"

"Yes, oh yes, I do want to see paradise."

Gasping as if in disbelief Sofia uttered, "Oh my God how beautiful! I would have never imagined it to be so beautiful. This must be paradise!"

As she was speaking, she was reaching up with her hands as if to touch something up above her. The necklace her mother had given her was dangling in the air. She momentarily held her hand outreached upwards, with her bright shiny eyes wide open and her mouth gaped in total amazement. The most peaceful look of serenity that Reuben and Leah had ever seen on anyone or would ever again see came upon Sofia's face. After a few moments, Sofia let out a gasp, and her arms fell to her side, as she breathes her last. The necklace fell partly on baby Judas. As her last breath left her body, Baby Judas began to weep loudly and uncontrollably.

Chapter 9
Judas' Formative Years

Several weeks had past since the shocking death of Sofia. They had buried her near a grove of olive and fig trees that grew at the far end of their property. She had always loved that spot. She use to sit under those trees after she found out she was pregnant, and read the scriptures for hours and hours. Leah always knew she could find her there when she wasn't in the house or with her. Now, it was Leah and baby Judas who, for a long time after Sofia's death, spent most of their spare time sitting on the wooden bench that Reuben had build next to her grave, speaking to Sofia as if she was still alive. Even after baby Judas had grown into manhood and on his own, Judas would return to his uncle and aunt's home, the home where he was raised and would seek the solitude of this spot when he was troubled.

Reuben sent word to Ezra and his family, with some of the Zealots about Sofia, but he never heard anything in return from them. He did hear about a year later that Sarah had lost her senses a short time after Sofia had been banished. Reuben and Leah believed that her heartache was too much for her to bear, so she lost her mind and became an encumbrance to Ezra and his sons until the day she died. Ezra died a few days after Sarah's death. By the time Judas was five years old, both Sarah and Ezra had died. Zev and Seth remained at home in Nain for a time, but then they sold the place and moved. Some say they went to Rome, yet others claim they went to Greece. They were never heard from again.

Reuben missed Sofia more then he ever imagined possible. He had grown to love her as his very own daughter. He missed her gentle manner and loving and caring heart. For a long time he would still weep and lament for her. He tried to be strong in Leah's presence for her sake, but while he was working at the blacksmith shop his tears would make sizzling sounds for hours, as they would fall on the hot irons or the furnace.

In spite of the sorrow that Sofia's death brought, it also brought a bundle of joy that neither Leah nor Reuben thought they would ever experience. It brought baby Judas into their lives.

He was a wonderful, beautiful and happy baby boy. He was always alert and aware of what seemed to be going on. He seldom cried unless he was hungry or needed his loincloth changed. Leah would sing to him and rock him at her bosom and he would goo and made other verbal noises, as if he wanted to join in the singing. He was a big baby at birth, weighing over eight pounds and was about twenty-one inches long. He had a head full of thick and wavy hair for a baby. He also had a beautiful light tan color complexion and very light brown eyes that seemed to sparkle, highlighted by thick eye browse. He was perfectly shaped with nothing missing.

It seemed as if the first six months of his young life went by in a fleeting moment. It was even harder to believe that Sofia had been gone for that length of time. They both missed her so very much, but the delight that the baby brought each and every day seemed to ease the pain more and more as time went by. Leah was such a proud adoptive mother, that she would find any excuse to go into the village and the village market just to show off little Judas.

On one occasion she had a chance meeting with Elizabeth Zacarias once again. She also had her baby with her. Leah saw her first and spoke to her saying, "Peace be with you Elizabeth"

Looking around to see who was speaking to her, Elizabeth saw Leah. She smiled and responded, "And the Lord be with you too Leah. What a beautiful baby! Is he the one that was born to your niece, the lovely girl I met about six months ago?"

"Yes it is, and I see you had your baby also. I can tell he is a fine boy, just like my Judas, that's what we named him, Judas Iscariot. Tell me, what name did you give your baby?"

"Well, on the day of his circumcision the priests wanted to name him Zacarias after his father, but I insisted that he be named John."

"John, that's a wonderful name."

"Yes, but the priest did not want to dedicate him to God with that name because they assert that there was not any of our relatives named John. I kept insisting on the name John, so they made signs to Zacarias, since he still could not speak, so that he could tell them what name he wanted."

"So what happened then?"

"They gave him a paper and a quill and he wrote the name John." Touching Leah on her arm sleeve gently with her right hand she continued, "You won't believe what happened next!"

"What? What happened next?"

"Well, immediately upon writing the name John, he began to talk! It was as if his tongue had been loosened and he was given his speech back again. He is still praising Jehovah for returning his speech."

"Praise be to our Lord Jehovah!" shouted Leah.

"I am surprised you and Reuben have not heard about this happening, it seems all of the countryside is talking about it and calling it a miracle."

"We had heard something about it, but we didn't know the whole story. I am very happy for you and for Zacarias."

Suddenly a somber look came on Elizabeth's face as she said, "We also heard about your tragedy of loosing Sofia. She seemed to be such a wonderful girl when I met her before, so happy and full of life! But she left you a handsome son. I hope that he and my John can become friends when they grow up to be young men."

"I am sure they will be," replied Leah as she attempted to shake off the sad feeling that was about to overcome her. They held each other's babies for a short while then kissed each other's baby goodbye and parted ways.

Judas was not quite one year old when Herod the Great died. Upon his death, the Roman Emperor divided the conquered lands among Herod's three sons. Just prior to his death, he ordered the execution of another son, Antipater, who was next in line to his throne. He was one of three sons that he had executed, Antipater, Alexander, and Aristobulus.

The northern part of Palestine, which included Galilee, Nazareth and Nain, was given to his son Antipas. Of all the sons of Herod that survived him, Antipas' character was more like his father then were the rest. He did a lot to gain the favor of Rome. He even built a new city by Lake Galilee and named it Tiberius for Caesar Tiberius.

Another brother, Philip was given the north, northeast portion of Palestine. He too wanted to gain favor with the Roman elite, so he built a city at the foot of Mt. Hermon and named it Caearea Philippi. Of the three brothers, he was the most compassionate and benevolent of all, as witnessed by his longevity of rule.

Judea, better known as Judah, which included Kerioth, was given to his son Archelaus to rule. He lasted only a couple of years, then he was removed and replaced by a cavalry officer from the First Roman Legion who received the appointment because his father was a senior member of the Roman Senate. Judas was three years old by that time. The new Procurator reported directly to Caesar himself. His name was Octavio Pantera, who one rainy and thunder-filled day, four years before his appointment as Procurator, had assaulted Sofia in a cave near Nain.

Reuben loved and cherished baby Judas just as much a Leah did. Every chance he had he wanted to have him in the shop for company as he worked on projects that did not require extensive loud hammering. It seemed that the hammer sounds would startle him at times, and he would start crying. As he grew older, he outgrew the fear of loud noises. He must have gotten use to it since they could be heard coming from the shop almost any time of the day. It was inconceivable to Leah the change that had taken place in Reuben's character and personality. It was as if he was an altogether different man.

In addition to Reuben and Leah, every one of the Zealots that would come by to speak to Reuben, especially Simon Zealotes himself adored baby Judas. They all knew that Simon Josiah had been the husband of Sofia, and they just assumed that he was Simon Josiah's son. Simon Josiah had become somewhat of a martyred hero within the Zealot's movement, so his son was someone to revere. Some say that they would argue amongst them as to who would bring messages to Reuben, or who would be sent to represent the army of liberators at the committee meeting. They did this just to have a chance to see little Judas, since he was permitted to be present at the Resistance Planning Committee meeting. Everyone enjoyed having him around. He was developing a very gregarious personality. Needless to say, baby Judas did not lack for love and affection during his formative years.

As he grew into adolescence, both his physical and mental development was above normal. He learned to crawl, walk and talk at an early age. He also had all the typical childhood illnesses that most children have, and was able to overcome them without any problems. By the time that he was four years old, he really enjoyed being with his Popo, as he called Reuben. He enjoyed pumping the bellows for Popo and bringing him whatever tools he needed for whatever job he might be working on. He was quite a little helper. When he wasn't helping, he was hammering away on scrap pieces of metal with a small hammer that Popo had made just for him

Judas had many friends including John Barzacarias and Cassandra, the daughter of Uris who were about the same age as him. They would gather at Reuben's home and play outside around the garden area and in the blacksmith shop for hours. All three developed a very close friendship from the time they were three or four years old. Both Judas and John always felt that there was something that they were meant to, or had to do. They felt like something was missing in their lives. From the time Judas was four years old, Reuben noticed that at times, he was surprisingly quiet with an empty look or stare in his eyes. He would sit on the floor for long periods of time and gaze out into space as if he was a statue made of stone. If you let him, he would stay that way for such a long time that it would frighten Reuben and Leah. During these times Reuben would ask Judas what seemed to be the matter and he would always respond in the same manner.

"I don't know Popo, I feel like there is something for me to do, and I am trying to find out what it is, but I don't know what it is. Sometimes I think I am hearing voices telling me that I have been chosen, but for what, I don't know."

Troubled at hearing this and not understanding any of it himself, Reuben would attempt to change the subject by stating, "Well Judas, you can pump the bellows for me. You always like to do that."

"Okay," he would quickly reply, and with that, his eyes would light up again as if nothing had ever distressed him, and he was fine again for a while.

When he turned five years old, Reuben, with the assistance and intervention of Sidon, and some of Sidon's friends that were still priests, placed Judas in the Synagogue so that he could be taught and educated in the ways of Judaism and the Torah. . This Synagogue was one of the most coveted institutions for learning in all of Palestine. It had once been the resting-place of the Ark of the Covenant that contained the actual stone tablets on which God's Commandments had been written and given to Moses.

While attending school, Judas missed his Aunt and Uncle. He also missed Cassandra, the daughter of Uris and granddaughter of Eber Benjara. They had become very close friends and played together ever since Judas could remember. She was older by a few months, and she could do most things that a boy could do. He learned a lot from her during their playtime. She also learned that when Judas went into one of his trances, just to keep talking to him as if everything was all right. She just assumed that this meditative state was caused by the grief of never knowing his parents.

Judas had always known that his mother Sofia had died giving him birth. But the details of his conception had not been revealed to him, nor were there any plans to tell him any time soon. When they told him about his birth, Reuben and Leah also gave him the necklace that Sofia was wearing when she died giving birth to him. From the time he was twelve years old, he always wore that necklace either on the outside or inside his cassock. He was never without it.

As far as he knew, Simon Josiah had been his father, and he had died saving his fellow freedom fighters prior to his birth. Only Reuben and Leah knew the horrible story of how Judas had been conceived, and how Simon Josiah was not his real father. Judas had also not been told the real story of how Simon Josiah had died. Reuben had shared that information only with Leah a long time after Sofia's death.

Throughout his scholastic life, Judas seemed to have conflicts within himself. On the one hand, he was being taught in a synagogue where the most of the priests were Roman sympathizers and accepted Roman rule. The priests did not want nor did they support any kind of rebellious conflict. They felt that any sort of conflict would be worse on the Jewish people then outside rule. Besides, Tiberius was continuing Augustus Caesar's policies of allowing Jewish consultation rights in the governing of their conquered Palestine. This consultation was accomplished through the Sanhedrin and the surviving sons of the deceased Herod the Great.

On the other side of the ledger, Judas was now old enough to understand what was going on in the Resistance Planning Committee meetings, and had learned the love of freedom and home rule from the Zealots that visited and participated during these meetings. It was not hard to dislike the Romans, especially after hearing how barbaric they were towards the Jews without any provocation. It was even easier to loathe those of Jewish blood that collaborated with the Romans. It was one thing for the Emperor of Rome to issue a Decree ordering humane treatment for the Jews but quite another for the lower echelon leaders, Procurators, and soldiers to comply with those decrees. The truth of the matter was that the soldiers and their generals thought of the Jewish men as less then dogs, and their women as slaves and concubines. This conflicting erudition affected Judas' emotions immensely. It was therefore inevitable that he became heavily indoctrinated in the patriotic movement.

He was now a participating member of the Committee. His appointment was solidified when he was twelve years old. He was in attendance at a Committee meeting when Joel, one of the Zealot leaders was sharing their plan to bivouac about two hundred revolutionaries on Mount Gerizim near the village of Sychar. The plan was to wait there by the narrow mountain pass for a shipment of weapons that was being sent from Caesarea to Jericho, and attack the caravan as it made its way through that narrow pass. It was Judas that spoke up against that plan.

"That plan is useless."

"Be silent lad, you know nothing about these matters," claimed Reuben.

"With all due respect Sir, I do know. I hear many things that are said in the Synagogue. Just a few days ago a diplomat from Caesarea came to the Synagogue to speak with the Administrator about that shipment. As I was performing my daily cleaning chores, I overheard him say that not only were weapons being sent, but also gold and silver shekels collected as taxes to be put in the palace coffers. Because their weight would be excessive for the mountainous trip, they are being sent by ship from Caesarea to Joppa, then by land to Gophna and from there to Jericho. This way there are fewer Roman miles to travel by land, and less steep mountains to traverse." The group looked in amazement at each other as Judas continued. "The dates have changed also. This is now scheduled to happen one week later then what you have been told to allow time for the Gabbai and the Mokhes who collect the taxes to bring the tax money to Caesarea from the surrounding villages."

As it turned out, all that Judas had told them happened, just as he had said. From then on, he was not only considered a casual visitor at these meetings, but a welcomed participant. He continued to stay alert while at the Synagogue with his ears and eyes open at all times and shared whatever information he learned with the Committee. He became an excellent and reliable source of inside information for the Resistance Planning Committee and therefore to the Zealots.

With his acceptance by the group, Judas thought for a while that he had finally found what for years he felt he had to do; yet the feeling did not subside. Often, he still sensed a calling to do something, but he did not know what. This feeling of trepidation, and anxiety caused him many sleepless nights. What was it that he had to do? Why did he feel as if something in his life was incomplete? It is true, he never knew his parents, but no child could ever wish for more loving and caring parents then Reuben and Leah. They always went beyond their means to give him everything he ever desired. The love he could have expected to receive from his parents could not have been any truer or deeper then what he received from them.

At night he would pray to the God Jehovah to please release him from this feeling.

"God, I can not bear this feeling that at times overcomes me. I have always placed my trust in You, and have done Your will. I have always tried to be a good and honorable person who has studied and kept Your words and commandments that You gave to us through Your servant Moses. I do not know what I have done, or have left undone to deserve this empty insufferable feeling that is demitting me within my soul, but I pray with all my heart that You,

in all Your wisdom and Your glory, take this agonizing cup from me. But Lord,
if this is Your will, that I carry this burden, then Lord, let Your will be done."

He became an excellent student, so much so, that by the time he was ten years old,
he could speak and read three languages, Hebrew, Aramaic, and Latin. Along with
John Barzacarias, he was one of the most advanced students in the group. Both were
used extensively to read from the Old Testament in Hebrew until John left to study
with the Essenes sect at Khirbet Qumran in their monastery on the Judean desert.

The Essenes at Khirbet Qumran were mostly Rabbis that were led away from the
Temple in Jerusalem under the leadership of a Priest named Levi who felt that the
Temple had been defiled when a Chief Priest was appointed to the Sanhedrin from the
Hasmonean reign. The Khirbet Qumran people were Essenes in their philosophy, and
are credited with the writing of the Dead Sea Scrolls.

When John left, Judas hated to see him leave. By that time, they were both about
eighteen years of age. They had developed a very close relationship for as long as
they both could remember. John's father, Zacarias had died leaving John totally devastated. He never completely got over the loss of his father. While he had a good relationship with his mother Elizabeth, he spent most of his time with Zacarias, either at
home, or in the Temple. Judas was the first to know that John was leaving to join the
Khirbet Qumran sect.

"Why do you want to leave Kerioth and the Synagogue?" asked Judas.

"Because I can no longer stay here without my father," replied John.

"Who says you can't stay"

"No one, it is I that say I have to leave. I miss my father so, that I can not stand to
be in Kerioth anymore, must less in the Synagogue where he spent most of his life.
Everywhere I turn, I feel him there, or I see him. I have to go some place where I can
grieve for him and make peace with myself."

"But what about your studies here?" inquired Judas.

John replied, "I will continue studying the Torah with the sect at Khirbet Qumran.
This will not only give me the solitude that I am seeking, but will also expose me
more to the beliefs of the Essenes. I feel that I must get back to the basic Laws given
to us by Moses. I'm beginning to feel that the myriad of interpretations has skewed
and deluded God's intent in His Laws. Since I was a child, I have always felt that I
had to prepare my own way for the Lord and make straight the path into my heart for
when the Messiah comes as promised."

"I too have felt as if I am ordained or destined for something, but I don't know
what. Many nights I have laid in bed, praying that God reveal to me what it is that I
am feeling, and that I must do or accomplish, but I get no answer. I sometimes think

that maybe this strange and unbearable feeling is caused by the sadness I feel at never knowing my mother and father."

"You and I are very much alike Judas," said John with a friendly smile on his face as he put his arm around Judas' neck. "We both are probably destined for something that is completely out of our control." With that, the two embraced and were not to see each other again for almost twelve years. After completing his studies with the Khirbet Qumran, it was rumored that John became an active member of that group.

By the time he was twenty-three years old, Judas had completed his studies at the Synagogue and had been certified as a Scribe by Johanna, the Chief Instructor. He had taken Judas as his understudy for four years. It was an unwritten requirement that those aspiring to become Scribes had to serve a minimum of three years as understudies. Judas was such a good Scribe, and liked by so many people, that Johanna did not want to release him for fear that his own business would suffer. Still, he had to release Judas as his protégé.

As a Scribe Judas performed many and sundry duties that included writing official documents, deeds, marriage scrolls, copying documents, and any other clerical duties that might become necessary for his client. Because of his excellent reputation that he gained while at the synagogue as a learned and excellent biblical student, he also was call upon to interpret Jewish laws for the people. He had learned the Torah and the Laws of Moses well. He was hailed as one of the most brilliant alumni scholars to have completed his studies at this prestigious Synagogue. Most people knew Judas Iscariot as an intellectual with a keen sense of fair play.

He was now living in his own apartment in Jerusalem, and experiencing a better than average existence due to his trade. Although he was now considered somewhat well to do, he seemed to always be an advocate for the poor and for those less fortunate then most. Quite frequently the Sanhedrin sought his counsel, and they too were amazed at the wisdom and knowledge that he seemed to possess.

Even though he was in great demand by the elite and the collaborators of the Roman Empire, he never forgot that he was a Nationalist, or Zealot as they were sometimes called. He used these connections to extract information for the movement towards self-rule. He believed the same as others did, that the time had come for the fulfillment of the Promises of God as predicted by the Prophet Isaiah.

"For unto us a Child is born, unto us a Son is given; and the government will be upon His shoulders. And He will be called Counselor, Mighty God, Everlasting Father, and Prince of Peace. Of the increase of His government and peace there will be no end, He will reign on the throne of David and over His kingdom establishing and holding it with justice and righteousness from that time forward, even forever. The zeal of the Lord of hosts will perform this." (Isaiah 9:6-7)

"But you, Bethlehem, Ephrathah, through you are small among the clans of Judah, out of you will come from Me one, who will be ruler over Israel, whose origins are from the old, from ancient times. Therefore Israel will be abandoned until the time when she who is in labor gives birth and the rest of His brothers return to join the Israelites. He will stand and shepherd His flock in the strength of the Lord, in the majesty of the name of the Lord His God. And they will live securely, for then His greatness will reach to the ends of the earth and He will be their peace. (Micah 5:2-5)

Judas, along with all Nationalist, and disgruntled Pharisees, Sadduccees and Essences interpreted the coming of a Savior quite literally. They were waiting for a Messiah that would lead them into battle and overthrow the Roman pagans and Who would restore the Promised Land to world power as it had been once before in the past. He would be crowned the true *King of the Jews* and would rule the entire world from His seat of government. He would destroy all nonbelievers, and would take vengeance against those that collaborated with the enemies of the Jews.

One day, shortly after his twenty-eighth birthday, Caiaphas, who was now the Chief Priest of the Sanhedrin, called Judas to Jerusalem. Caiaphas had been appointed as the Chief Priest of the Sanhedrin some ten years before by Valerius Gratus who had been acting as Prefect of Judaea. When Judas arrived, to his surprise, they were asking about John Zacarias. They wanted to know if he had communicated with him within the past few months. He was about to tell them that he had not heard from John since he want into the desert to study with the Khirbet Qumran some ten or twelve years ago. Before he had a chance to tell them, a servant came running into the room and announced that the Procurator was in the building, and was approaching the room to speak to them.

All of a sudden through the door came this man; a Roman dressed in clothes interlaced with thread made of silver and gold. He was tall and his commanding presence was quite intimidating. He looked to be in his late fifties or early sixties in age, but the years had treated him well. He had a tremendous command presence in the way he carried himself. When he entered the door, all of the priests stood up. As he entered the room, his attention was drawn to Judas. He stared at Judas and then down to the necklace that he was wearing with a perplexed look on his face.

"Do I know you?" he asked, as he leered at Judas and at the necklace for some time.

"No Sir, I believe that I have ever had the distinct privilege and high honor of meeting you before."

"You look so familiar, and that necklace, have I seen it before? My sense tells me that we have met somewhere before, but I must be mistaken." Looking at Caiaphas he abruptly changed the subject and said, "I am troubled that there is talk about a Rebel named Barabbas and his band of Zealots raiding some of my tax collectors (Mokhes). These rebels are taking what they have collected before they can turn it in to the coffers. This is causing me problems with other tax collectors that are seeing this as an opportunity to keep their collections and then blame this rebel Barabbas. Why only yesterday, I had to execute some because their story did not seem believable to me."

"How can I serve you my Lord?"

"I need to know of anyone that you might suspect of being a member of this band of rebels." Spinning around to look at Caiaphas straight in the eye, and holding up his right index finger, Procurator Pantera averred, "If I can catch just one, I can then find out where this Barabbas is hiding. Then I can put a stop to this bandit's foolishness in Jerusalem and all of Galilee."

The Chief Priest was quick to answer, "Rest assured, my Lord, that we the leaders of our people, want nothing more then to have an amiable co-existence with our benevolent friends from Rome. Strife and battle, are not the way to accomplish this, and are not in the best interest of either of our people. We require that message be taught each Sabbath at each synagogue throughout Palestine." Extending his arms outwardly palms up, Caiaphas pleaded, "If we knew anything we would share that information with you right away."

Procurator Pantera continued, "Word also come to me that some time ago, most rebel bands became united under one leader and are being coordinated by a group of dissidents located somewhere in Judea."

"If you will permit me to speak your Highness," stepped in Judas, "I have lived in Judea all of my life, and I have not heard anything about one general leader, or any group coordinating the rebellious efforts of anyone. These are only rumors aimed at causing strain between the Jewish community and our friends the Romans. This is easy to see, if you would only stop and think. There are more non-Jews in Galilee then there are Jews. There are Greeks, Egyptians, Armenians, Arabs, and Pyreneans, to name a few who would benefit greatly by seeing us at war with each other. You have to take unfounded rumors with some skepticism."

Looking at Judas, Pantera scratches his right cheek and mutters, "Well, maybe your right, but I want to know immediately if you can confirm any rumors, or if you discover the whereabouts of any rebel, understood?"

With that he began to walk out of the room but stopped and turned to Judas again and asks,"Are you sure we have never met before? I have this feeling that I have seen you before." Putting his right index finger on Judas' collar, then by his chin, he mumbled, almost inaudibly, "That necklace, I know I have seen it some where."

"I would think that would be impossible my Lord, it has belonged to by family for well over ten generations. My mother died with it on giving me birth, and my grand aunt gave it to me when I was eight years old."

"Your great aunt you say? What is her name?"

"She is called Leah Gibeon, wife of Reuben Gibeon, the blacksmith of Kerioth. They raised me when my mother died giving me birth."

"And what about your father," Procurator Pantera asked quite coyly?

"My father was Simon Josiah Iscariot, a Scribe like me from Kerioth who served the people there and in the surrounding towns. He died attempting to save some friends."

"From the enemy, not doubt," Octavio Pantera interjected.

Judas hesitated momentarily, then said, "Yes My Lord, from the despised enemy of the people!"

Procurator Pantera looked very cautiously, then said, "Hum, well, I do not know any of your relatives. I must be mistaken then, though I rarely am."

Curtsying as a gesture of respect, Judas added, "I only wish we had met before, Your Majesty, it has been my privilege to meet you today. I can only pray that this will not be the last time."

With that, Pantera walks out of the room. When he is gone, they return to the business that they were conducting before he interrupted.

"You were asking me about John Zacarias," said Judas as a prompt to get back to their previous conversation. "Why do you ask if I have heard from him?"

"Rumors have reached us that he was a member of the Essenes and joined the group at Khirbet Qumran."

"Yes, I knew about that when he first went to join that sect twelve years ago. What is wrong with that?"

The Chief Priest responded, "It is also rumored that he has since left the group, and has started his own religious movement out in the desert and outside the villages surrounding the Jordan River. It is said that he is attracting a substantial following. People are beginning to say that he is the Prophet Elijah come back to life. He is advocating repentance and total commitment to the promised Messiah who is to deliver only those Jews that become worthy by keeping to the letter of the Laws of Moses and who are cleansed from sin through the rite of baptism." Becoming more aggravated, Caiaphas' tone of voice becomes louder, "The Baptist is professing that only by being prepared, repentant, and baptized by water can they be cleansed and ready to be favored by the Messiah."

"I am unaware of this movement. I have not heard anything at all concerning John nor the expansion of the Essenes custom of baptism."

"It is catching on so, that he is now being called John the Baptist. According to what he is saying, the Messiah tends to punish all, including Jews that do not repent and prepare for the coming of the Messiah. This is an affront to the Romans and us Pharisees and is causing turmoil between the Romans and us. You heard Procurator Pantera, he is livid about any talk of a Messiah whose main goal is the ouster of the Romans from Palestine."

"I will keep my eyes and ears open, and I will tell you if and when I hear any thing that I think you need to hear," retorted Judas.

"We knew we could count on you Judas. Thank you for your cooperation. It is well noted."

Their meeting concluded, Judas left Jerusalem to return to Kerioth.

On his way back to his adobe in Jerusalem, Judas was thinking about what he had heard about John. He kept reflecting on how the Sanhedrin priests were now refer-ring to John Zacarias as John the Baptist. He had heard that the Essenes used this rite to cleanse their body to insure that they would be worthy to meet the Messiah when he made his appearance on earth as the Holy Scriptures prophesied. This ritual's name of Baptism came from the Greek word to describe dipping someone or some-thing or submergence into some liquid, mainly water. "This must be why they are now calling him Baptist. He must be using that ritual in his new religious sect the Sanhedrin claim John is starting,"

Judas was thinking to himself as he walked down the cobblestone streets towards his abode. As he was walking and thinking he did not notice the person walking with a severe limp towards him. He appeared to have a wooden leg that caused him dis-comfort as he walked. Judas was in such deep thought that he was startled when the man called his name as he approached.

"May the Lord be with you Judas," said the man as he neared.

"O Lord God of heaven! Is it really you Asa?" Judas was elated to see his old friend whom he had not seen since he was a small child. This was the same person, but now almost thirty years older, that brought the news to Reuben that Simon Josiah had been killed.

"Where have you been Asa," inquired Judas?

"I was wounded in the battle near Cyprus about twelve years ago. I lost my leg to a sword wielding Roman soldier. That infidel had good aim! The cut was deep and it eventually became so infected with gangrene that it had to be cut off almost to the hip." He hit the peg that served as his leg, and it made a solid wooden sound.

"I am sorry to hear about your leg. Are you still with Simon Zealotes?"

"No," replied Asa, "I was no good for battle after loosing my leg, so I returned to Machaerus, where my son now lives, to spend the remainder of my days with my grandchildren. Besides, Simon the Zealot is not the leader any longer. He stepped down about a year or two ago to let the younger more zealous leaders like Barabbas have their turn. It is said that he has joined some crazy man that is saying that the Messiah is walking amongst us now. How about you Judas, how have you been? My, you have grown into a fine handsome and strong man!"

"Thank you Asa. And I have always felt close to you too since you were with my father when he was killed in action."

"Yes I was, and I will never forget that day. He was a handsome man too, but you look more like your dear departed mother, and not at all like him. She was a fine gentle person, so full of life!"

"That's what most Zealots that knew my father tell me, that I don't look much like my father. I wish I had known him at least for a little while before he was killed."

"He was a full fledged Nationalist. On the day he was killed, he knew that there was danger in delivering a negative reply to Tiberius Claudius who was in charge of the Roman Legion on that day."

"Is that how he died? I was always under the impression that he had been killed in hand to hand combat."

"No, it was worse then that. We were trapped on a mountaintop and Claudius wanted us to surrender. He even sent an ambassary to tell us that he would be lenient if we surrendered. We all decided that we could not trust him, since he had tortured and then drowned some of our men earlier the day before. Simon Josiah volunteered to take the message that we were willing to fight to the death before we would surrender."

Asa began to chock up and to behave as if he was actually reliving the experience all over again. His voice crackling, he continued, "He did not return on the same day as we expected. After it became dark, we could see a pole on fire, which looked like a Roman candle, and could hear the excruciating painful cry and screams coming from the ball of flames. When the sun came out the next day, we could tell that it had been Simon Josiah who had been crucified, and burned while still alive at the stake by the Romans."

Judas could not believe his ears. He had never been told exactly how Simon Josiah had died. He was visibly upset, and was shaking from the anger he felt towards the Romans at that moment. The most upsetting thing was the death by crucifixion and fire. The three most hideous forms of death that the Romans used were, first crucifixion, then fire, and third was feeding you to the wild beasts. These were considered the most inhuman, and were intended to bring shame and dishonor to the family of the person being executed. What was worse, these three methods did not leave a corpse to bury, and in Jewish theology a corpse needed to be buried if the soul was to find peace.

He never hated the Romans more than he did at that moment. He had never felt anger and hatred in his heart like he did at that instant. He could not hold his emotions back, and he began to cry softly as he visualized the events that had been told to him. Asa reached out and put his arm around him and made a feeble attempt to comfort him. After a while, Judas regained his composure, and kept repeating the phase over and over again, "Those savage bastards!"

When their visit was over, they embraced and wished each other well, and Judas continued to his abode. He could not help but wonder why Reuben, who had been like a father to him, had not told him the whole story of how Simon Josiah had died. It absolutely bothered him that the true story had been kept from him. Now more then ever, he wanted to become more active within the Nationalist movement. He could not help but wonder if this was what he had always felt that he was destined to do, to become a major player in the liberation movement. He set up most of the night, thinking about what he needed to do now. He was full of anger, and felt somewhat lost, not knowing what to think or do.

He remembered that when his friend John Zacarias felt that way, he decided to join the Essences sect. He also remembered that in his conversation with the High Priest, they had mentioned that John had been seen by the shores of the River Jordan near the town of Agrippina. Judas decided that he should seek his friend and share his feelings with him. If anyone could understand and identify with what he was feeling, he knew it had to be John.

Next day, early in the morning, he left Jerusalem and went to Kerioth. There he spent a full day and night with Reuben and Leah. They were now in their early seventies, and not able to get around as good as they use to do. Reuben had given up his role in the Resistance Planning Committee about eight or nine years before. It got to be too much for him, so he decided to let younger men take over that responsibility.

Judas was still visibly upset that they had never told him exactly how Simon Josiah had died. Reuben could sense something was wrong with Judas so he asked. "What seems to be bothering you son?"

"When I was in Jerusalem yesterday, I saw an old friend, whom you know. It was Asa."

Reuben looked at Leah for a split second and continued, "How is old Asa? I have not seen him in a good twenty or twenty-five years."

"He is doing as well as can be expected of a man who lost his right leg in combat. He told me it happened some time ago. He had returned to Machaerus and has lived there with his son ever since that time. He happened to be in Jerusalem just passing the time while his son was transacting some business in the city."

"I hope you told him to come by and visit with us if he could."

"No, it completely skipped my mind. I was to mad and upset at what he told me about my father Simon Josiah."

There was a long silence, then with his eyes beginning to well up with tears he continued. "Why didn't you tell me exactly how my father died? You led me to believe that he had been killed swiftly and painlessly, protecting his fellow libera-tors." He began to sob as he persisted. "He was massacred, crucified and then burned while still alive by the Roman, as ordered by the very person that is now Caesar of Rome, Tiberius himself!"

Reuben had been looking down at the floor as Judas confronted him about keep-ing the way that Simon Josiah had died from him. He slowly raised his head and uttered, "Looking back now, I know I should have been the one to tell you. But I did not want to cause you any more pain then what you have already suffered by the loss of your mother. I did not want to fill your heart with hate either. That is not good for you."

"I have always been a Nationalist. At a very young age, you allowed me to take part in the Committee meetings. I learned back then to hate the Romans."

"I disagree with you Judas. I would never allow anyone, particularly me, to teach you to hate. What you learned was to love freedom, and independence. The love of self-determination as God's chosen people in their own promised lands given to them by God is much different then hatred of another human being because of any pain he might have caused. I did not want you to have that type of feeling towards any man."

Shaking his head back and forth very slowly Judas said, "I am so confused. I don't know what it is that I must do. I feel like I am suppose to do something, but I don't know what. The frustration and anxiety this mysterious feeling has caused me since childhood, is unbearable at times."

Putting his arm around Judas' shoulders, Reuben added, "I could always sense that in you son. Ever since you were a child, playing in the shop, you would sit quietly and stare into space for long periods of time, as if in a trance. You could never describe what it was that you were feeling even then. Sometimes I think that God has touched you. When you were born, your mother, may she rest in peace, claimed to have seen what she described as angels who prophesized a destiny for you. She never really told us what that destiny was exactly. Therefore we never thought anything more about it. We later came to the conclusion that she was only hallucinating in her final moments. "

After listening almost in disbelieve, he said sobbingly, "I have to go away, I must try to find what it is that is bothering me so. I believe my mother was right because sometimes I really feel that God has destined me to do something, and it just isn't that time yet." Standing up and stretching his arms out as if in total defeat, he pleaded, "What else can it be? This feeling is about to drive me insane. I don't think I can stand it much longer. I have to find out something!"

"Where are you going? What will you do?"

Wiping tears that had streamed down his cheeks he answered, "I am going to find my friend John Zacarias. He left about eighteen years ago to study and live with the Essenes in Khirbet Qumran. He too was distraught at the death of his father, and had many unanswered questions the same as me. I am hoping that he has found some answers that he can share with me to alleviate my insufferable pain. I only pray that he or someone he knows can help me out of this dilemma."

"When are you leaving Judas?"

"I am leaving in the morning." He could see the pain in their eyes about his leaving, so he added, "I have to go. I hope you can understand."

Leah could not help but think back to the time that Sofia first told her of her ordeal. How she was brutally raped by Commander Octavio Pantera, and how she had to leave Nain and her family behind. She wanted to tell him the truth about his conception, but she could not find the courage to do so now. If he reacted this way by only finding out how Simon Josiah was crucified and then burned alive at the stake, how would he react if he were told that he was the son of a Roman Commander who now was Procurator of Judea? She could not find the heart or the courage to tell him right this instant.

They all stood up and hugged in a threesome embrace for a long time. Reuben was praying within himself that this would not be the last time he would see Judas.

The next morning, he kissed Reuben and Leah goodbye and started on his trip on a white horse that Reuben had bought for him a few years back. He was dressed in average traveling attire, and carried a saddlebag that contained additional changes of clothing. He also had a bedroll next to his saddlebag for sleeping at night. This trip was going to take at least four to five days if all went well.

The trip was long and tedious, and uneventful. He traveled past Mount of Olives, then past Jericho. He continued heading north until he came to the village of Salim. There he asked several people if they had heard of anyone performing the ritual of water baptism. He was told that there was man just north of Salim, on the banks of the River Jordan, who was baptizing Jews into some kind of new sect. Some could not understand why, since only non-Jews were baptized when they accepted Jewish theology. Some of the people that he talked to told Judas that John the Baptist was using the Essenes rite of baptism for repentance, preparation and cleansing. He was doing this to insure readiness and to guarantee acceptance of his followers by the Messiah. When he asked where the Baptist could be found he was told that he had been in Agrippina, but had since traveled south to a point about eighty furlongs (ten miles) north of Salim, by the Jordan River. It took Judas close to two full days to travel there.

When he neared the point where they said John could be found, he saw a large crowd gathered by the Jordan River. As he approached, he could hear John preaching to the multitude saying, "Repent all you sinners, both Jews and Gentiles, for the Kingdom of God is near. I am the voice in the desert that the prophet Isaiah spoke about, crying in the desert for you to prepare the way for the Lord and to make straight the path for Him into your hearts."

John's clothes were made of camel's hair, and he had a leather belt around his waist. It was rumored by the people that had seen him and had spent sometime listening to him that he survived mostly on locust and wild honey, except when some good kind hearted person shared a good meal with him.

As Judas come closer, he could hear what appeared to be an argument between some listeners and John the Baptist. He heard John's reply, "You Pharisees and Sadducees, why are you here? Who warned you to flee from the coming wreath? You claim you have repented, but your deeds do not show it! Don't think that because you are Jewish that you are saved. God could raise better Jews then you from these stones. Beware, His ax is already at the root of the trees and every tree that does not produce good fruit will be cut down and thrown into the fire."

When the well-dressed Pharisees walked away from the crowd, John looked up and saw Judas. He waved to Judas to come forward, and at the same time he walked out of the Jordan River. He reached out and fondly greeted Judas.

"Judas Iscariot, my long time friend, I am so happy to see you again. How long has it been since we saw each other last?"

"We were twelve years old, now we are thirty, that's a long time John!"

"Has it really been that long? Why it seems like only yesterday you, Cassandra and I played in the blacksmith shop, and read the Torah scriptures at the synagogue. Remember how we use to compete for the right to read during the services?"

"Yes I do John. It broke my heart when you went away. It took me several years to get over the hurt of loosing my best friend." Hugging John one more time, Judas added, "But now, I have found you and I am very happy to see you."

"I missed you too Judas. Many nights I laid in my bedroll at Khirbet Qumran and wandered if I had done the right thing. As time went by, I knew I had found what I had been searching for, my true reason for being."

"And what did you find was the reason for your existence John?"

"To bring back the true meaning of the Laws of Moses. The Pharisees and Sadducees have perverted their meaning by interpreting the Laws to benefit men like themselves. They think nothing about building a enclosure around the Covenant with ridiculous and absurd rules that quenches the thirst for God and becomes a hindrance rather then a conduit to do God's will."

Judas looked puzzled, yet he was trying to understand what John was telling him. "I think I understand what you are saying. I have felt the same way at times. It is ludicrous not to allow a shepherd to protect his sheep from a preying wolf only because it happens to attack on the Sabbath."

"Yes, I think you are grasping the point I am trying to make here. But the primary reason for my being is to be the bearer of the good news that the Messiah is coming soon, and that we must repent and make straight His path into our hearts if we are to be accepted by Him."

"Where is your campsite?" asked Judas.

"I live wherever I may be that night. Tonight, I will camp here on the bank of the River Jordan." Reaching out and grabbing Judas by his arm John the Baptist said, "Stay and partake of what nature provides for us to eat."

"Yes, I will. I will be right here and watch and listen to you until you are done for the day."

Judas stayed and listened to John preach about repentance. What he was hearing and seeing reminded him considerably of the Prophet Isaiah in the Torah. Even Elijah is said to have worn coarse garments like John the Baptist was wearing, to show that nothing material could help gain the favor of God. Their dress of animal skins displayed that all the riches and luxury in the world could not buy you acceptance into the "Kingdom of God."

At the end of the day, when the last of the curious and on-lookers had left, and John had performed his last baptism of the day, they sat together and ate some fruits and bread that an older woman had brought to John earlier that day.

"Judas, you look worried and dissimulated, what is bothering you my old friend?"

"Is it that obvious that I am troubled and depressed in spirit?" replied Judas.

"Yes," said John, "I could sense it when I saw you walking towards the lake, and once I saw your face clear, I would see it in you eyes. Tell me, what is bothering you? Maybe I can help."

"It the same old problem that we both have had since our childhood, and that we have spoken about often times when we were youngsters. This feeling of incompleteness, and uneasiness as if something is missing. It has grown more and more insupportable as I have aged instead of subsiding as we used to think when we were adolescents. I have everything that I would possibly wish or hope for or need. I have a good education, loving foster parents, an excellent vocation, some good friends, still, sometimes life is intolerable because of this supernatural feeling that something is missing, or something that I am destined to do remains undone."

"I don't have to tell you again, Judas how I used to feel. As you said, we have spoken about it on numerous occasions in the past. The wonderful thing is that I no longer have those feelings. I have found out what my destiny is, and I have never been as happy as I am today."

"How did you find it?"

John hesitated, swallowed hard, then said in an assertive tone of voice, "I have seen the face of the prophesized Messiah. He is alive and with us right now, but His time has not yet come! He will make His presence known at the right time, not before."

"How can you be sure of this John?" asked Judas somewhat suspiciously.

"I know because of what I have personally heard and seen with my own two eyes."

"Who is He? Where is He?"

"His name is Jesus and He is a Nazarene. He is there now with His mother Mary and His four half-brothers, James, Joses, Judas, and Simon. He also has two sisters, Mary the lessor, and Martha."

"How do you know Him? And how do you know He is the Messiah?"

"He is my cousin. Mary is my mother Elizabeth's sister. When His father Joseph died, He too came to Khirbet Qumran. He was only thirteen years old, and knew only about carpentry. But in less then six months, He was teaching the Priests and Rabbis the true meaning of the scripture. They could not believe their eyes or their ears when He corrected many of their false assumptions and interpretations of the Torah. They were so chagrined that they denounced Him as a false Rabbi and asked Him to leave."

"But how do you know that He is truly the Messiah and not just another imposter as all the others have been?"

"I have visited with Him and His mother Mary since that time, and have heard the story of His virgin birth, and I have seen other signs that unequivocally tell that He is the Messiah. I tell you Judas, all you have to do is look into His eyes and you will know that He is the Messiah."

"John, I have come here to try to find an answer to my inherited anxiety that is about to end my sanity, and what I am finding is cause for more distress!"

"What do you mean Judas?"

"I find a friend who comes from a well to do family wearing skin clothing and eating only when something is graciously given to him. When nothing is given, he eats locust and wild honey or Lord knows what else. He is not known as John Barzacarias any more, be is called John the Baptist because he is now using the ritual of baptism not only on Gentiles, but on Jews that have no need for baptism."

"Judas, Judas, you still do not understand."

"Wait! There is more. Now this intelligent scholarly friend tells me that he has found the Messiah, who happens to be his kin! When I ask for some evidence, this friend tells me that all I have to do is look into this so-called Messiah's eyes! I ask you John, where is His army? Where is His forces that He will need to be the savior and of the Jews?"

"That's just it! We have been waiting for the wrong kind of Messiah! He is not nor was He ever meant to be a worldly Messiah but a Messiah of the Spirit."

Shaking his head slowly as if in disbelieve Judas stated, "You and I studied the Torah, and know the prophecies of Jeremiah. He was told by God that the day was coming when God would raise up from the house of David, a righteous man, a King who would reign wisely and do what is just and right in the land. And that in his days, Judah would be saved and Israel would live in safety. I ask you John, how can He fulfill this prophecy without being a military leader with an army?"

"That is true, but we have been wrong in interpreting the Kingdom of God as if it is a new kind of political proclamation or society. His concern, and reason for coming is to save the spirit and souls of all people, and to initiate a special new relationship with God and all His people. This new relationship is His Kingdom, not any piece or parcel of land or country. He wants you and me, Jews, Gentiles, the hold human race Judas,.... that's His Kingdom! God has made it quite clear, as stated in the book of Deuteronomy, that there is nothing inherently special or righteous about Israel for which they deserve God's favor more than any other nation. God desires everyone, everywhere to know Him, love Him and to serve Him.

Judas was silent for the first time since their conversation started. For the first time, he seemed to grasp what John the Baptist was telling him. It was true that the scriptures did not describe any physical battles that the Messiah would personally lead to regain control of the lands given to them by God. Once you thought for a while about the scriptures, it made sense that God could have been speaking about bringing His people back to Him spiritually and in faith. Through time there had been too many divisions of sects interpreting the same thing but coming to very different conclusions. Even Jeremiah's prophecy that he had quoted earlier could have spiritual intent. He remembered what Jeremiah had said just prior to what he had quoted.

"Woe to the shepherds who are destroying and scattering the sheep of my pasture! Because you have scattered my flock and driven them away and have not bestowed care on them, I will bestow punishment on you for the evil you have done. I myself will gather the remnant of my flock out of all the countries where I have driven them and will bring them back to their pasture, where they will be fruitful and increase in number."

Judas could see that God could have just as easily been speaking in a spiritual rather then in a physical sense but he was not convinced by John to think otherwise. Judas still continued to disagree with John. He believed that the Messiah was referring to an earthly kingdom, and John believed it to be a heavenly kingdom. Judas was truly convinced that it meant a physical rather then a heavenly kingdom that the scriptures spoke about. The shepherds could be the religious leaders that interpreted scripture to suit their own purposes for personal gain. It would also mean the heathens who brought false idols and gods like Baal into their country and convinced some Jews to worship them. It wasn't rare at all for some barren woman to pray to Baal, the god of fertility for children even though the Laws of Moses prohibited false gods. Judas still believed that "Gathering the flock" had always meant that once the Messiah established His Kingdom here on earth, He would gather the descendants of the twelve original tribes. Once gathered, He would return the Promised Land to them and the Messiah would rule over them through twelve selected Procurators of His choice.

After a long period of silence, John got up from the blanket made of animal skin that he had been sitting on, and washed his hands and face at the river. When he finished, he looked at Judas, who still looked as if still in deep thought and he said, "I am going to lay down and rest now. I have a feeling that I am going to have a big day tomorrow. You are welcomed to share some of my skins for bedding."

"Oh, yes thank you John. I am tired too. I will make a bed and rest here with you."

Judas reached into his saddlebag and withdrew some other garments that were more suitable for sleeping. He changed clothing, made a nice bed of leaves and brush covered by the skins, and used a thin blanket to cover him from the cool night air. He looked up into the sky and marveled at the splendor of God's work. Ever since he was a child, he loved to be outside enjoying the wonders of nature. The sky was clear and it seemed to him that he could almost reach up and grab a handful of stars anytime he so desired. He often wondered why he took so much pleasure from being outdoors, especially at night. It must have come from one of his parents he thought.

Next morning, as the sun rose from the east, Judas was awakened by the sound of people beginning to gather by the Jordan to hear John speak and to be baptized.

Chapter 10
Truth Revealed

By the time that Judas arose and picked up his bedding, John was already preaching to a crowd of about twenty or thirty on-lookers. In a matter of an hour, the crowd had increased to well over fifty and still growing. Some were accepting his baptism without question, yet some were very skeptical and were asking probing questions of him before they committed to be baptized. Still others, after their discussions, chose not to accept being baptized by John in the waters of the Jordan River.

"If the Messiah you speak of is our true deliverer from the bondage of Rome, then where is His army, and what kind of Messiah is he?"

"He is the Son of God, sent here to atone for our sins. He is a loving and forgiving Messiah who wants to restore all His people to the ways that He prescribed through the original commandments given to us through Moses."

Judas listened intently as the debate went on between John the Baptist and a parade of questioners that seemed at times not to have an end. As he sat listening he looked up and to his surprise he saw Simon Judas Zealotes walking towards the river from out of the wasteland to the south. He ran to meet him as he approached.

"Simon! How good it is to see you! How have you been?" shouted Judas gleefully as he threw his arms around him in a warm embrace.

"Praise be Jehovah, if it isn't Judas Iscariot! You are a sight for sore eyes. What brings you here to the Baptist's camp?"

"I came to visit my old friend John. I have known John since our childhood days. We were inseparable until he left to join the Essenes at Khirbet Qumran. I had not seen him in over eighteen years. I heard that he was here proclaiming the coming Messiah, so I thought I would come and see what all this is about. How about you Simon, what brings you here?"

As they walked towards the Jordan River, Simon spoke, "A few years back I stepped down as the leader of the Zealots. I opined it was time for someone younger and in better physical condition to lead the movement. Since that time I have been a fisherman, a trader of wares and I have even tried raising and selling livestock. But I have to tell you Judas, when heard that someone whom people were calling the re-incarnated Elijah was telling people that the coming of the Messiah was at hand, I had to come and see if I could be of service to him."

Grabbing Simon by his sleeve and tugging hard enough to spin Simon around, Judas stopped walking momentarily and questioned, "You want to be of service to John?"

"No, not just John, I mean I want to serve the Messiah. John has said that the Messiah is not an actual earthly King or militarily inclined. John is saying that He is more concerned with the soul and spirit of His people then in actual liberation." Simon added, "But I disagree with that. All the scriptures that I have ever heard of speak of the day that the Messiah will free His people from bondage. I think He will need Leaders who can muster up men to fight the yoke of slavery that the Romans have placed around His Chosen People's neck." Simon paused a second then he said, "I am so glad to see you here Judas. We need people like you, smart, strong and educated to help govern our people when He gains our freedom."

"I agree with you Simon. The Prophet Malachi states in the Torah that surely the day of the Messiah is coming and it will burn like a furnace. He said that all the arrogant people and every evildoer will be stubble and that day that is coming will set them on fire. I believe that the evil doers are the Romans. Surely anyone can see that. He plans to destroy them all and restore Judea to its former glory."

Shaking his head in agreement, Simon added, "I don't know much about the Torah, but this much I know. Malachi also said that God spoke through him saying that not a root or a branch will be left to the evil ones. Only for those who revere his name, will the Son of righteousness rise with healing in His wings. Malachi also warned us to remember the laws of Moses, which God gave him at Horeb for all of Israel. There is no doubt; the Zealots are the ones that he speaks about as revering

God. The Messiah will surely need an Army to lead against the Romans to regain the glory that was once Judea's. We the Zealots, the ones that love our Motherland given to us by God, are the favored over the Pharisees who twist all the Laws to suit themselves.

Judas then said, "I agree with what you say, but then sometimes I don't know, I am more confused then I was when I got here."

"What is so confusing?" asked Simon.

"Everything! Don't misunderstand me Simon, I too want it to be like you have pointed out. And I too am prepared to lead the poor, the disillusioned. God knows they are the ones that have lost all they possess because of taxes levied upon them by the Procurators, Ceasars and their noblemen. They ruin good God fearing Jews so they can continue to finance their evil, vile orgies and revelry here as in Rome."

"I am glad to hear you talk like that Judas. Your real father must have been a true Zealot!"

"You knew him Simon," said Judas, somewhat puzzled. "He died the same time that Judas Zadok died. His name was Simon Josiah Iscariot."

"I knew Simon Josiah very well. As a matter of fact, he was the one that recruited me into the movement. It was because of that close bond between us that he confided in me that your mother Sofia was already with child when he met her."

Judas could not believe what he was hearing! "What did you say? Tell me again, I'm not sure I heard you right."

Looking surprised, Simon said, "Judas, I was under the impression that Reuben had already told you the truth about how your mother Sofia had been attack and raped. I always told Reuben not to wait too long before he told you the whole truth. He always assured me that he would, so I thought you already knew. I'm sorry I said anything."

"No, no, they never told me anything other then Simon Josiah was my father."

Judas was shaking so that he had to sit down on the hillside and gather himself together. Simon sat next to him and hugged his neck in an attempt to comfort him.

"Judas, you know that who your real father is does not matter. Everyone in the movement always felt that you were our son. Why we use to fight to attend the Committee meetings just so that we could see you when you were a baby and then a toddler, getting into everything. When we would return to camp, we had to tell everyone how you were doing and how much you had grown. To tell you the truth, not one child could have had as many fathers as you did during your formative years."

"I remember those times, and I enjoyed all the attention and affection that I got from everyone, especially you Simon. Next to my Uncle Reuben and Aunt Leah, you are the one that I most admired and wanted to be like. But I have to tell you, I am devastated. I have never felt as low and depressed as I do right now."

"Why Judas?"

"I came here to see if I could fill in a void I have felt all my life. Instead I find a childhood friend that I don't really understand anymore. I hear talk of a Messiah that is not what he is supposed to be. My good friend Simon, the only man to unify all freedom fighting factions and the best military techician I have ever known is no longer the leader of the liberation movement. And now I am told that the person I always thought was my father, is not my really father. Don't you think these are enough reasons for feeling like I do?"

After a short while Judas got up and began to walk away. "Where are you going Judas?"

"I am going back to Kerioth to speak to my Aunt Leah and Uncle Reuben about this matter. I need to find some answers."

With that said, Judas went and gathered his belongings, saddled his horse and began his journey back to Kerioth. Many questions needed to be answered. As Judas traveled back to Kerioth, many thoughts ran through his mind. His moods ran from anger, to disappointment, from love to hate and in many other directions.

"God must be testing me," he thought, "This must be what has been going on ever since I can remember. He has been testing me to see if I am worthy of Him. Yes, that must be it, He is testing me as He tested Job. The Scriptures in Job say that testing gets rid of impurities and other unrefined qualities in our character the same as a fiery furnace removes them from silver and gold. God is testing me, I know He is. Lord God, I may not know whom my real earthly father may be, but I know You are my heavenly Father. Is this what You want me to know? Is this what You are trying to tell me? Are You questioning my faith the same as Job? I am devoted to You Lord God. Do not doubt me O Lord, my devotion to You is genuine and staunch. Comfort me in this time of despair."

When he stopped and camped at night, he would close his eyes and recall favorite scriptures and he would recite them to himself, sometimes at a loud angry scream. This was the only thing that seemed to keep his mind off all the tribulations that he seemed to have encountered the past few days. Each night he camped, it took him until way into the night to fall asleep. His mind was overactive, thinking a thousand thoughts, and not finding any answers. Most of the time he cried himself to sleep. He hardly ate anything during his trip back to Kerioth. His mind was totally engrossed in thought and in prayer. He even overlooked his personal hygiene so that by the third day, be looked more like a mendicant beggar then a well to do Scribe.

When he arrived at Jerusalem, he decided to stop by his quarters to rest and renew himself before he went on to Kerioth. He took a warm bathe, changed clothes and when he was dressed, he sat down at a table to consider how he was going to confront Leah and Reuben. He was angry with them for concealing the truth from him, but he could not help believe that they did it out of love for him. These feelings were still one more disconcerting dichotomy that created more anxiety, which he did not need.

He was home less then three hours when he heard a knock on the door. He went to see who was there, and to his surprise it was Cassandra Benjara, the granddaughter of Eber whose son Uris, the father of Cassandra had been killed in the same battle as Simon Josiah. They had been very close friends ever since he could remember. From childhood they seemed to know that they shared a moment in time that effected their lives forever, the death of their fathers. She had never married because she felt an obligation to care for her aging grandfather Eber who had been in poor health for the past ten years or so. When Judas saw her, his heart jumped with joy.

"Cassandra! You don't know how happy I am to see you. Please come on in."

After exchanging a friendly hug she said, "Judas, where have you been? One day you are here, then the next thing I know, you are gone. I thought that you might have gone to see your Aunt and Uncle in Kerioth, but you are never gone this long. Where were you? I was worried for you."

Pacing the floor Judas declared, "Cassandra, I feel like I am going mad with all this consternation. It has become unbearable. Lately it has compounded ten fold!"

In a failed attempt to touch his shoulder, Cassandra asked, "Why Judas? What is going on?"

Still pacing, Judas said, "In the past three weeks I have found out that I am not who I have always thought I was."

"What do you mean?" she asked grabbing his hand and sitting Judas down next to her on the divan.

"A few weeks ago I met an old friend here in Jerusalem who I had not seen in almost twenty years. We began reminiscing about when I was a child, and he told me that Simon Josiah had not died as I had been told. I was always told that he had died fighting, defending himself and his men in battle, and that his death was quick and painless." Judas paused a moment, took a deep breath, then continued, "I could and did accept that. At least that way, he had the opportunity to defend himself. But my friend Asa told me that this was not the way he died at all. He was taking a message from his troops to the Romans and he was under a flag of truce. They did not like the reply he gave them so they did not release him. Instead, they crucified him to a pole and burned him while he was still alive!" He was sobbing emotionally when he reached this point of the story. "Can you imagine the pain? He was burned alive!"

"Yes, I can only imagine, but that does not change matters. That only makes him more of a hero if anything."

"You don't understand. I feel and have always felt a lot of love towards Simon Josiah, but what bothers me most is that my Aunt Leah and Uncle Reuben kept the truth from me. What else could they be keeping from me?"

Stroking his head Cassandra said in a reassuring voice, "I seriously doubt that they did it to harm you. If anything, they did it because they have always known what I know about you, that you are a very emotionally sensitive and loving person who feels other people's agony and pain. I do not think that there are other deep dark secrets that they may be keeping from you."

"That's just it. I then went to find our friend John Zacarias. I had heard that he was living by the River Jordan, baptizing both Jews and Gentiles into some new order or sect. I went there to speak to him to see if he had found relief for his feeling of emptiness and incompleteness, which is the same way I have felt ever since I can remember." At this point, Judas choked up, swallowed hard, then added, "While I was there, I found out that Simon Josiah was not really my father. An old friend that I had not seen also for about twenty years told me that my mother was already with child when Simon Josiah and she met. He married her to keep her from being castigated and banished from Kerioth."

Cassandra was silent and in awe at what she had just heard. It was hard to believe what she was hearing. "Did he tell you who your real father is?"

"No, no, he did not know. I think that only Leah and Reuben know. They must know. I was just sitting here, before you came, contemplating how I want to approach them with this question. I would really like to go home and confront them savagely, but I can't do that. They are old now and not in good health. I don't think that they could stand the shock of being put in that position."

Cassandra smiled, wiping a tear from her eye. She kissed his right cheek and hugged him with another friendly embrace. "That is just like you Judas, no matter how hurt you may be, you always think of the other person before you think of yourself. You always feel the other person's pain much more so than your own. That's what I have always liked most about you Judas, your sensitivity."

They visited for a long time, talking about what would be the best way to affront his Uncle and Aunt. They both agreed to pray for an answer and so for the next hour or so, before Cassandra went back home and Judas went to Kerioth, they prayed for divine guidance and intervention in this matter.

When he arrived in Kerioth the next day in the early afternoon, Leah and Reuben were in the back of the house tending their garden. When they saw him they were so filled with joy, that Leah dropped the hoe in the excitement and it almost hit Reuben on its way to the ground. She ran as fast as she could, which was not fast at all due to her advanced age, and fell, almost exhausted, into Judas' arms. She hugged and kissed him as if he was the prodigal son returning from his travels. Meanwhile, Reuben, who was on his knees, took a little more time getting up from the furrow that he was weeding. When he arose, he too walked just as fast as he could towards Judas.

Oh Judas, Judas, I am so glad you are home with us," said Leah rather jubilantly. "We had no idea when we would see you again. Thank God Almighty that you are safe with us now."

"Son!" said Reuben, taking Judas' hand and embracing him as tight as he could with his left arm. "It is good to have you home, safe and sound. We were very worried about you. We have heard so many stories about people being killed without provocation by the armies of Romans that are chasing Barabbas and his troops. Ever since more and more peasants and farmers have been forced off their farms after losing everything including their wives and families, the resistance has gotten more aggressive. They are now joining Barabbas rather then to live in the streets as beggars. Most are in the movement now more for revenge then for the love of freedom."

"That is the power and glory that is Rome!" said Judas in a very sarcastic fashion.

"Tell us, did you find John Barzacarias," asked Leah?

Still in complete control of his emotions, Judas answered, "Yes I did and he sends his warm love and affection to you and Reuben. Ever since his mother Elizabeth died he has immersed himself into what he says is his calling, preparing the way for the coming Messiah. "

"Well Judas, did you find out what you wanted when you met with John?" asked Reuben.

"No, I am still at a loss about my feelings of incompleteness and anxiety." Beginning to loose his grip a little he added, "But I did find out some other disturbing facts."

"Pray tell us Judas, what did you find out," implored Leah, "What is bothering you?

Fighting within him to keep his composure Judas said, "While I was there with the Baptist I met up with Simon Zealotes. He told me that he had stepped down as the leader of the Zealots a few years back to give the younger more energetic insurgents the opportunity to lead."

Reuben did not look surprised at hearing this information, instead he said, "I had heard that he had relinquished his rank soon after a battle near Sebaste. It was rumored that he had a manifestation telling him that he could win freedom for more souls if he followed 'a voice in the wilderness, crying in the dark' then with a sword. Could that be John, or the Baptist as you say he is now called?"

"I don't know." Unable to hold back any longer Judas then uttered, "He did tell me something else that really upset me terribly. He told me that Simon Josiah was not really my father; that my mother was with child when Simon Josiah met her." Looking at them straight in the eyes he added, "That's why I am here, to find out the truth from you. Please, tell me the truth. I have to know the truth!"

Reuben had placed his arm around Leah while Judas was talking. He looked at Leah, who was beginning to weep very nervously, then he looked up at Judas and said in a very atoned voice, "Son, Simon is right, Simon Josiah was not your father."

Judas was so shocked hearing it from Reuben that his strength gave way, and he fell to his knees in the garden where he stood. Somehow he had hoped that Reuben's answer would have been different; that Simon was mistaken, or that all of that was just a bad quip. As he knelt, he kept shaking his head in a slow cadence, side to side, and saying, "No, no, it can't be so, it just can't be so."

Kneeling down next to him, Reuben put his arms around Judas and said, "Judas, please listen to me, I want to tell you first that Leah and I have loved you as our own child. We would never do anything on purpose that would harm you. We both felt that Sofia's secret was safe with us, and when Simon Josiah died, we also felt that the secret had died with him also."

Judas turned towards them again, tears running down his face then asked, "I am not Simon Josiah's son? He is not my father? Then who is? I want to know. Can't you see, that I need to know?"

They helped Judas up from his knees and gave him a cloth to dry his tears. They walked to the far corner of the property, near a grove of olive and fig trees where Sofia was buried. Her grave was always kept neat and trim with lots of fresh flowers that Leah and Reuben always planted around it. While they walked, Judas was able to regain some of his composure again. There, on the benches that Reuben had build, they sat down and Reuben began to speak as he gazed, looking out into empty space.

"I remember that day as if it was only yesterday. I was working in the shop when I looked up and there, to my surprise was Sofia with an older man, Simon I believe was his name, a Merchant from Nain. I must confess to you Judas, that at first I deplored the idea of her coming to stay with us even though she had no other choice. You see, she had to leave Nain because she was exiled as a defiled woman."

"As a defiled woman? Are you saying she was promiscuous?"

"Oh Lord God, no! A more devout and holy person you could have never met." Swallowing hard Reuben added, "She was raped one day as she was watching her parent's herd at the foot of Mt. Tabor near Nain."

"Raped!" echoed Judas with a teary and louder then average tone voice.

"Yes. Raped. As she watched the herd, a Roman cavalry Captain came upon her, and as much as she fought, begged and pleaded, he had his way with her."

Leah then continued telling the story. "She wasn't even aware that she was with child until she was with us almost two months. It was I who found out about her condition by her morning sickness and her missed lunar cleansing. She was so young, so innocent, that she did not even know she was carrying you."

A little puzzled at something that had been said, Judas questioned, "You said that you did not want her to stay here?"

Reuben replied, "I was reluctant at first. Leah and I had been alone for a long time and I feared the change in our life style that I thought would be necessary by having her here with us. But Judas, I was wrong, so wrong! She was the best thing that ever happened to Leah and I. She was a gift to us by God! Within a matter of a short time, my entire attitude towards everyone and everything, especially Leah, changed completely. She became the daughter we thought we would never have. And at her death, you became the son that we had always prayed for to our God in Heaven."

Somewhat reluctantly, but needing to know the answer Judas then asked, "Did she ever mention if she knew the name of the Roman Captain who had raped her?"

Delaying a moment to look at each other, Reuben then answered, "Yes she did. The day that she arrived she told us the whole story of why she had to leave Nain. She told us that first day that the man who assaulted her was a Roman Commander named Octavio Pantera, who commanded the cavalry troops of the First Legion of Rome."

"Who? What was his name?" He could not believe his ears! He thought that he must have been hearing things. "What was his name?"

"Octavio Pantera," repeated Reuben, "The archfiend that is now the Procurator of Judea."

This was almost too much for Judas to handle. He was all but at the point of total breakdown. There was no way to describe that gut wrenching feeling, that sense of complete loss of perspective, self, and direction. He felt like a feather, floating in the air, with no control over its own destiny, totally dependent on the four winds that blow to decide his future.

Leah reached out to Judas, drew him to her bosom and hugged him as tightly as she could while he cried profusely. He could not hold back any more. It seemed that the events of the past three weeks had completely altered his life, as he had known it. He had found out about Simon Josiah's death and the transformation of his friend John to someone he hardly recognized. Judas had also found out that his mother had been savagely violated. To top it off, he found out that he is the bastard son of a Roman, not just any Roman, but the one, who is now the chief oppressor of the Jews in Judea. All the pain climaxed at that point in time. He cried long and hard with deep emotional feeling for some time.

After he had released all the pinned up rage, hurt and anger by crying and had regained his composure somewhat, Reuben spoke. "Judas, son, there is something else that we did not tell you. We never meant to keep it from you, we just did not give it much thought. Your mother Sofia told us that before she was assaulted she experienced an occurrence that seemed to her to be more real then a dream as she first thought. For many years after her death, we dismissed it as an illusion. But now, Leah and I believe it to have been an apparition of some sort.

In a dream state or trance, there appeared to her, two men with glowing faces and dressed in white shiny robes. She could vaguely remember what they had said to her. She told us that first they called her by name saying, 'Sofia, Sofia….do not be afraid.' They then revealed to her that what her future held, she would not be able to comprehend, nor would she be able to control it. She said that the figures mentioned that what was to happen to her would seem as if someone other than Jehovah had ordained it to happen. But she was to rest assured that it was God's will and that it had to happen if Scripture was to be fulfilled. They told her that as with Jacob, son of Isaac, God would not condemn her or her offspring, meaning you. That as the Lord God had found favor in Jacob, so it would be for her and her descendent to come. Sofia said that she kept asking them, 'What Scripture? What will happen? What are you talking about?'

"But the glowing figures only told her not to fear for the Lord of Abraham has chosen her and you, as her only offspring, to help fulfill the Scripture written in the Torah, and as foretold by David and the Prophet Zacarias. They concluded their visit by telling her not to fear for herself or her family or for her descendant, meaning you. As they were leaving they told her it would be hard to understand but the Lord has found favor in her and in you as her future offspring."

After giving Judas a few moments to ponder on that story, Reuben then spoke, "Don't you see Judas, the Lord God has found favor in you. It has to be a real omen, the dream has to be true. What has happened in your life does not come from evil, but from God Himself!"

"How can rape and a personal vicious assault on my mother come from God?" shouted Judas angrily.

"Judas!" lauded Reuben, "You more then anyone else should know and understand the answer to that question. You are the most versed in the Holy Scriptures. You can not have forgotten the lessons we learn from the Book of Job. God is the Supreme Being, the Ruler of all, even Satan. Yet he allows Satan certain limits of power within certain constraints through God's own indulgence. It is nothing for God to use Satan to help fulfill prophecy or for whatever reason God desires. It is God who uses Satan, not Satan who uses God. The fact remains, I now believe that you have been touched by God, chosen by Him for some event that will change the lives and history of the Jewish people."

Looking somewhat perplexed Judas then asked, "Do you really think so Reuben, Leah?"

Leah looked at Reuben and then at Judas and proclaimed, "I had not thought of Sofia's dream for some time, until now, because I had no reason. But now, looking at all that has happened, I am convinced that it was not a dream, but it was as real as that fig tree over there." Taking Judas' hands in her hands she continued, "Sometimes we feel like we have lost all control over our lives and are being manipulated by events that we do not understand. We sometimes feel that we are forced into situations that we do not want or do not understand, like having Sofia come to live with us. Sometimes those situations or events are so unpleasant that we would not choose them if we had any control. At times this may seem unfair, but we must accept them as opportunities that God is giving us to fulfill His will and not our own will. Your reward for doing so is not necessarily given to you on this earth, but in heaven. When it comes from God, what may seem to be unjust here on earth is made just and holy in heaven." Gently lifting Judas' head up with her hand so she could look into his eyes she asked, "Can't you see that Judas? Can't you see that son?"

What Reuben and Leah said seemed to comfort and ease his pain somewhat. He began to think that maybe this is why he had felt so lost, like a ship without a rudder most of his life. Maybe God was manipulating him for a purpose that was beyond his comprehension and he had yet to discover and understand that purpose. In response to Leah's query, he nodded his head and uttered, "Yes, I see what you are saying. But I am still upset about this whole thing."

"It is understandable Judas, but beware. When justifiable feelings of anger, rage or frustration are not handled the right way they can lead to unacceptable behavior like bitterness and rebellion towards God. That's what Job had to guard against, and he was rewarded for it," advised Reuben.

"I'll be alright," he responded. "I just need some time to gather my thoughts and my composure. I need to be alone for a little while here by my mother's grave."

"Fine," replied Leah, "We are going inside the house to make some herbal tea. Please come inside when you are ready." They both kissed Judas and hobbled towards the house helping each other as they walked.

Judas sat on the bench nearest to Sofia's grave. His elbows were on his knees, and he held his head with both hands on his forehead. So many new revelations impacted his life now, that he did not know what to think, much less what to do now. He looked at the well cared for grave, bordered with yellow, blues and pinks flowers. He reached for the necklace that hung around his neck. Clutching it tightly he began to speak.

"Mother, I wish that I had known you. From what I have always heard about you from everyone that knew you, you were a very loving and understanding person. You seem to have been the type of person that would have understood the pain and suffering I am going through at this moment." He sobbed a little as he talked, "Sometimes I think that you are still here with me. I can feel your presence. I always have, ever since I was a child. Sometimes I feel as if any moment you will appear before me and tell me what it is that I am suppose to do. I feel so lost and alone. Everything that I have ever believed to be true about me has been shattered. I am at a crossroads now, not knowing where to go from here or what to do. The man that fathered me is the most hated man in Judea. I feel nothing but rancor and hatred in my heart for him. I want to kill him with my own two hands, but I know what God commands about killing. I also know what he commands us to do about loving each other, but how can I love a man that hurt you so deeply? If you can hear me from beyond, please intercede on my behalf with God and help me find peace within my heart and to learn my destiny." He paused momentarily then said, "But whatever be His will may be, let it be done as He commands."

He continued in meditation and prayer, comforting his mind and soul, crying still from time to time, as he sat there for the next few hours.

Chapter 11
Judas the Disciple of John

Judas decided to spend a few days with Reuben and Leah. He past the time mostly praying and meditating in the fig and olive grove by Sofia's grave. Before leaving Judas told his grandaunt and granduncle that he fully understood the reasons they had kept those events a secret from him. He told them not to feel bad about anything, because he knew that they loved him like their own son, and would have never purposely committed or omitted anything hurtful towards him.

Leah and Reuben could not help feeling bad, but for an altogether different reason. They had no idea what Judas was going to do next, yet they both sensed that this might be the last time that they would see him, for a long time to come, if not for ever. He seemed to have regained all of his peacefulness, but the hurt could still be seen in his eyes contrary to what he said. Although she was totally broken hearted about Judas leaving, Leah gave him a protective blessing when he left.

"May you always walk in one accord with our Lord God. May He keep you save from all harm and make you an instrument of His love and divine plan. May He help you find your destiny and may it be filled with love, blessings, comfort and prosperity. May God's patience and mercy follow you for the rest of to your life. And may all these things be done to and for you according to God Jehovah's will."

He kissed and hugged them goodbye, and returned to his dwelling in Jerusalem.

The first thing he did upon his return was to go visit Cassandra, to talk with her about his findings, and what he had resolved to do. They both walked outside her home and sat on the back porch under a canopy that was made of thickly cut tree trunks for corner pillars and smaller tree limbs as cross members up top. On these cross members there were whole palm tree leaves laid in a staggered fashion and tied down as shingles to create the roof. After recounting what he had found out in Kerioth, she sat awed struck and silent for a brief moment.

"What are you going to do now?" asked Cassandra.

"I am going to join John the Baptist.

"Why? Why would you want to do that? What purpose would that serve?"

"Every day, good and honest men who have lost their lands to the Romans for taxes, and who have been ostracized by these evil monsters, come to the Baptist in search of hope. I witnessed this happening daily while I was there with him for a few weeks. They come every day to find answers to their troubles with the Romans. They are like lost sheep, looking for a good shepherd to lead them. They are zealous for someone to step up and lead them into victory over these Roman tyrants. Even though they don't know anything except farming, they are willing to become freedom fighters. They are willing to face and do anything, even death, to help establish the new order that John the Baptist advocates and to regain their right to self-rule and their right to self-determination. How can God's own chosen people accept any less? "

"And what are you going to do, lead the insurrection?" Cassandra averred somewhat sarcastically.

"No, but when the Messiah comes, and He will come, I want to be there, in the forefront to help insure the demise of Roman rule in our land." Clinching his fists he added, "I want to be the one that personally destroys Procurator Pantera, with my own bare hands!"

"I fear for you Judas. You have changed. You are a man obsessed with thoughts of vengeance. You must remember that vengeance is not ours to give, but for the Lord Yahweh to deliver."

"That's easy for you to say, you are not the one who found out that you are the bastard son of a Roman tyrant!"

"Yes, you are right. But do I need to remind you that I too suffered a great loss at the hands of the Romans when they killed by father; in the same battle that Simon Josiah was killed? I too never knew him since I was only a baby when he died." Her voice was starting to show some anger and emotion as she continued to castigate Judas for his statement. "And if that isn't enough, my mother was killed by a drunken Roman soldier who was driving a chariot as fast as he could, running over Jews, just for sport! So don't tell me that I don't know about feeling the need for revenge. Yet, I remember when you were going to school in the synagogue that it was you, Judas, who told me that we must learn to forgive and let our Lord God decide the murder's fate. What has changed you now?"

Looking down at the ground, feeling remorseful at what he had just said to her he uttered, "I don't know Cassandra, I can't answer that because, I really do not know. Hatred for the Romans is eating my insides, yet I know that to hate and to despise anyone is wrong." Lifting his head and looking at Cassandra in her eyes he said softly again, "I don't know. Maybe I'll find the answer and learn about love again with the Baptist."

"I hope and pray for your sake that you do. You have been more then a friend to me. You are like the brother that I never had, and I would not want to loose you to evil spirits because of what you are feeling inside of you right now. I want you back, as you were before, happy, cheerful and ready to help anyone that needed your help. That's the Judas that I grew up with and fondly remember. That's the Judas I deeply favor."

They sat outside in the porch for hours, just talking about the past, the present and what the future might hold for them. It was not until late that night that Eber, Cassandra's grandfather called to her, "Cassandra, the hour is late and it is time for you to come inside."

"Yes Grandpapa, I will be there in a minute." Turning to Judas she asked, "When do you plan to leave for John's camp?"

"I am leaving tomorrow morning at sunrise." Very reluctantly Judas then said, "I have been trying to avoid telling you this, but I must tell you. I do not plan to return until I find out exactly what I have been destined to do by God, and have actually achieved my fate. I may not know what it is that I am destined to do, but I feel in my heart that whatever it is, it will change the course of Jewish history and possibly the world."

"I will miss you Judas, and I will pray for you daily, and I will look in on Reuben and Leah from time to time for you. Think of them and me once in a while, and know that you will always be in our thoughts and prayers, no matter where I or where you may be."

"I will, you know that. I have so much to be grateful for, stepparents like them, a true friend like you, it's more than most men have in these times of strife and trouble. It is so hard to say goodbye so I'll just say until our paths cross again. Who knows, I might appear at your door when you least expect it!"

"I would love that very much," added Cassandra, "No matter where I might be, you are always welcomed into my house."

They caressed and he watched her as she entered the house. Once inside, she turned to look through the window and sweetly blew a kiss at Judas who was standing outside looking back at her. She then watched Judas walk slowly with his head bent and looking down at the gravel road. His hands were clasped behind him as he walked. He looked like a man who was carrying the destiny of the world on his shoulders.

The next morning Judas hitched his horse to a small two wheel wooden cart that he owned and gathered as many of his belongings as he could carry with him, and headed for the Jordan River. He did not know where the Baptist might be, but he knew that if he traveled as close to the river as possible, he would eventually run into him. He had traveled three days when he heard that John was preaching and baptizing where the Jordan and the Jabbok Rivers come together, at a place called Bethany. It appeared that the Baptist had traveled towards the south of Samaria, towards Judea. It was mid-morning when he reached the place where John the Baptist was preaching to a gathering of seekers. Simon Zealotes was helping him control the crowds that were waiting in line to be baptized by John in the river waters.

Judas noticed two other people that were helping John the Baptist besides Simon Zealotes. He wondered how long they had been followers of the Baptist. They seemed to know and outwardly approve of what the Baptist was saying and doing.

Judas worked his way passed the crowds and when he reached the front of the river, he noticed some priests from the synagogue in Jerusalem, and some Levites who assisted them at the Temple and the Tabernacle. The Levites claimed to be direct descendents of Levi, the son of Jacob. They claim to have been selected by God to assist as servants of the tabernacle.

"Who are you?" Judas heard one of the Priests asking the Baptist.

John turned to him and began to testify in the name of the coming Messiah. He confessed freely, "I am not the Christ."

They asked him, "Then who are you? Are you Elijah?"

"No," he said, "I am not him."

One of the Levites asked him, "Are you a Prophet then?"

Somewhat aggravated the Baptist avers, "No. Are you so blinded by our own self-worth and your own rituals that you do not know who I am?"

"Seemingly stumped they finally ask,"Who are you then? Give us an answer to take back to those who sent us. What do you say about yourself if you are not the Messiah, Elijah or a prophet?"

John replied in the words of Isaiah the Prophet, "I am a voice of one calling in the desert, 'Make straight the way for the Lord.'"

This did not seem to satisfy some of the Pharisees, who had also been sent by the Chief Priest Caiaphas, especially since he was baptizing Jews who did not need any baptism. Only Gentiles who were converting to the Jewish faith were given the ritual of baptism. They asked, "Why then do you baptize if you are not the Christ, nor Elijah, nor a Prophet?"

"I baptize with water," John replied, "But among you stands One you do not know. He is the One who comes after me, the thongs of whose sandals I am not worthy to untie."

Demonstrating their disgust with hand gestures at not being able to understand the Baptist's answers, the whole entourage left the riverbank making their way back to Jerusalem to report their finding to the Chief Priest. As they left, Judas could hear their grumbling between each other about the Baptist's replies to them.

When they were gone, Judas noticed a very old man and woman, who must have been husband and wife, attempting to come down towards the river to receive their baptism. He moved over and helped them reach and enter the water's edge. John the Baptist and Simon Zealotes looked at Judas and smiled. Not a word was said between them but all five of them, the Baptist, Simon, the two other followers that Judas did not know, and Judas, knew at that split second that he was there for good as a disciple of John the Baptist. He continued to help the rest of the afternoon controlling the lines of people that wanted and were waiting to be baptized.

When the sun went down behind the Mount Gerizim range, some of the people began to leave and some began to camp by the banks of the River Jordan. John the Baptist and Simon the Zealot, as they were now referred to, stopped preaching and performing the Rite of Baptism. All three walked to their campsite located about one hundred yards from the river. As they walked Judas was pulling his horse and cart behind him. He stopped on several occasions by other people's campsites and gave all his belongings away except a few articles of clothing. When it was all gone, he gave the cart and horse to an old woman that was helping her lamed husband who could barely walk. "Here my good woman, you have more need of this then I do," he said to her.

In total disbelieve at the precious gift, she replied, "Thank you Sir, May God bless you seven times seventy for your goodness." The Baptist's approval at what Judas had done could be seen by the glow of his face.

Although exhausted from the day's labor, John expressed joy at the return of Judas. "My dear friend, you have no idea how I prayed each day that you would return again. When Simon told me that you had left about a month ago, my heart was sadden for both of us."

"I had to go back to Kerioth to confront my past, John." Hesitating a little, Judas then added, "There were some answers that I needed in order to resolve some issues that were disturbing me. I found out the truth, and now I am back to help you in your ministry."

"I knew you would," replied John, "I had a vision of you and I working together, spreading the good news throughout the countryside. In this vision, I saw myself leading the advent of the Messiah, and you were the one offering up the sacrificial lamb to God to atone for our sin."

"I knew Judas would come back too," chimed in Simon the Zealot, "But I also knew that you had to affront your psychic fiends that you have complained about ever since I have known you as a child. I hope and trust that all past issues has been resolved to your satisfaction."

Looking at Simon the Zealot Judas answered, "They have. I don't think that they will be a problem in the near future. For now, all I want is to be a part of your ministry and care for our people."

"Judas," added Simon as he placed both of his hands on Judas' wide shoulders, "I have known you since you were a baby, not bigger then the palm of my hand. I have seen you grow up to be a fine, strong, learned, and compassionate man. I want you to know that I will always be there if you need someone for whatever reason. I have always cared for you and have been proud of all that you have accomplished, just as if you were my own son. I will always be there for you when you need me."

After a few more words of welcome had been exchanged, Judas noticed the two disciples that he did not recognize and asked about them. He was interested in finding out who they were, but he also posed the question in an effort to steer the conversation away from the direction it was heading. He had already experienced too many emotional events to feel comfortable with more sensitive talk, even though it felt good for his soul.

Simon answered, "The taller one is Andrew, a fisherman from Bethsaida, a little village in Galilee. He is one of several brothers who, along with their father, a man named John, own some fishing boats. He was on a business trip to Jerusalem. On his return trip he happened to run into the Baptist preaching and baptizing on the Jordan. He became so overpowered by the Baptist's message, that he has not even hinted about returning to Bethsaida. The other one is John, the son of Zebedee. Zebedee is a well to do fishing business owner also. He runs the business with the help of John and his older brother James. He too heard of the Baptist, so he came looking for him to see if what he and James had heard about him was true. He too has never made an effort to return home".

Later that evening, all five eat supper and talked together by the campfire for sometime into the night. They spoke about the old times growing up together and they spoke about the future and the coming of the Messiah. Late that night after they had made their sleeping pallets up and had lain down, Judas felt a calmness and tranquility that he had not felt since he was a child. He looked at the vast universe with it's seemingly never ending blue blanket of twinkling stars and quarter noon that looked like a man's face, smiling down on him as if to say, "Judas, you are on the right track for what you have been looking for. Your destiny has begun." Feeling more content then he had ever felt before, he closed his eyes after he ended his night prayer, and fell right to sleep.

For the next four to six weeks, they continued to preach and baptize people that came to listen to John the Baptist. It seemed that the crowds grew larger and larger each day as the word of mouth spread throughout Samaria and Judea. Most people came because they believed what was told to them by those that had come before, that John was the Prophet Elijah come back to life. John never once gave anyone reason to say that, and he always denied it glowingly when ask if he was the reincarnation of Elijah.

One day as they were performing their ministry, something caught John's attention. It was a tall, handsome figure of a man, with well-groomed long hair and beard. It was Jesus Barjosephus coming towards him. John declared loudly in a joyous loud and firm voice, "Look! There is the Lamb of God who will take away the sin of the world! He is the one I meant when I said, 'A Man who comes after me has surpassed me because He was before me. I myself did not know Him, but the reason I came baptizing with water was that He might be revealed to Israel."

Judas was awe struck. He looked at Simon who seemed to be frozen, like a statue made of stone. His mouth was agape and his eyes wide open and they seemed not to even be blinking. "Simon, Simon, that is Him, the Messiah!" Judas shouted. He did not know if it was the way the sun shone on Jesus' tunic that emitted the glow or if it was an aura of gold ray slivers that seemed to project from Him.

Jesus stood about five feet ten inches tall, slender but firmly built and appeared muscularly well developed in the upper torso. He had light olive-brown skin, and light brown shoulder length hair and a moderately long, but well-trimmed moustache and beard. He wore leather sandals and a white tunic that seemed to glisten with the sun. His eyes were light brown and penetrated deep into your soul when He looked at you. His face was more oblong then round, and had excellent definition due to his strong chin and high cheekbones.

Then John the Baptist, still looking at Jesus, gave testimony saying, "I saw the Spirit come down from heaven as a dove and remain on Him. I would not have known him, except that the one who sent me to baptize with water told me, 'The man on whom you see the Spirit come down and remain is He who will baptize with the Holy Spirit.' I have seen and I testify that this is the Son of God!"

"John," spoke Jesus in the most soothing voice Judas had ever heard, as he neared the waters.

"Yes Son of Man. What would you have me do?"

"Baptize me John."

Falling to his knees John answered, "It is I that should be baptized by You!"

Reaching out to lift him back on to his feet, Jesus replied, "Let it be so now; it is proper for us to do this to fulfill all righteousness."

So John the Baptist consented and baptized Jesus. As soon as He was baptized, Jesus went up out of the water. At that moment the heavens were opened. John, later that night, told Judas and the other disciples that he... "saw the Spirit of God descending like a dove landing on Jesus." At the same time he heard a voice from heaven saying, "This is my Son, whom I love; with Him I am well pleased."

After being baptized, Jesus went up to a nearby mountain to pray. He spent the rest of the day and that night on the mountain. The next day, around mid-morning, John the Baptist was at the same location preaching and baptizing with his disciples when he saw Jesus passing by. As Jesus passed by John the Baptist said, "Look, there goes the Lamb of God!"

When Andrew Barjona and John Zebedee heard the Baptist say this, they left the Baptist and began to follow behind Jesus. After a short while, Jesus turned around and saw them following and He asked, "What do you want?"

Andrew answered, "Rabbi, where are you staying?"

Looking at both of them He replied, "Come and you will see."

They followed him a short way up a mountain where He was camped. They both stayed with Him for the next few days, until Jesus announced to them that He was going higher up the mountain to pray. After listening to Jesus for those few days, they were totally convinced that he was indeed the Messiah, so both John Zebedee and Andrew went to their respective home, anxious to tell their brothers about who they had found.

Jesus went up the mountain and stayed for forty days. During this time, He fasted and prayed to His Lord Yahweh. While on the mountain, His faith and destiny was tempted but He defeated all the evils before Him.

Judas and Simon the Zealot remained with the Baptist helping him in his ministry and baptisms, but every free moment that had, all they could talk about was their first impressions of Jesus. Judas could not help think how strange it was that John the Baptist had referred to the Messiah as "The Lamb of God." "Lambs are used for sacrifices," he thought to himself, "Jesus should be referred to as a 'Lion or Bear' something that it strong and aggressive."

Looking at Simon, Judas said in a voice that projected total awe, "Did you see those eyes? They seemed to go deep inside me and totally reveal my most inner feelings to Him. Nothing more could have been revealed then was revealed at the moment he laid His eyes on me, not even if I had been cut wide open with a sword!"

"Yes," replied Simon, "I experienced the same feeling. I have never seen anyone exhibit the command presence that He manifests. He must surely be the King of the Jews that will command the army that will free our people from the chains of slavery, the same as Moses and David did. He must truly be the Messiah."

Then Judas averred, "I want to be in the forefront of any and all battles that will destroy Octavio Pantera. I am going to get the greatest pleasure in seeing him gravel in the dust and beg for mercy!"

Looking somewhat puzzled Simon asked, "Judas, this is the second time I have heard you mention wanting to destroy the Procurator personally. Is there something that happened to you or to your grandaunt and granduncle that I don't know about? Did he take their lands, or did he hurt them in some way?"

Giving Simon a long blank stare Judas then replied, "No Simon, this is strictly a personal matter between the General and Procurator Pantera and me. The time is coming when I will have my day and way with him." Judas was rubbing the necklace that he was wearing around his neck with his right hand as he was saying this to Simon.

Each day the Baptist would preach and perform the ritual of Baptism somewhere on the Jordan River. He continued preaching repentance for the forgiveness of sins, and referred to himself as "A voice of one calling in the desert." He advocated that all should prepare the way for the Lord and make straight paths for Him. Some of the on lookers would ask him, "What should we do?"

He would answer, "The man with two tunics should share with him who has none, and the one who has food should do the same. If you are a Tax Collector, don't collect any more than you are required to collect. If you are a laborer, don't extort money and don't steal from your employer. Be content with your pay, for there are others that would be willing to do that labor for the same pay."

Many of the curious who came to listen to the Baptist wondered in their hearts if John might possibly be the Messiah but he would always say that the Messiah would soon reveal Himself though His deeds that would soon be known throughout the land.

The Baptist heard, from hordes of people that came to him, many stories of despair, maltreatment and exploitations they had experienced at the hands of the Herod Antipas. Herod was the son who received Galilee and Perea when his father Herod the Great died. The Baptist also heard that Herod Antipas had rejected his first wife so that he could marry Heodias, who had been the wife of his half-brother Phillip. This went against the Laws of Moses, and the Baptist began to preach against this practice, and particularly against Antipas, who was Jewish and should have known better.

As time passed, rumors would reach the Baptist's camp that Herod Antipas was beginning to get agitated with John's personal attacks. However John did not have any fear for he knew that he only spoke the truth. By this time Judas had now been with John the Baptist for about six months or so. He still experienced a little anxiety once in a while, but he could not remember the last time that he had felt this good about himself.

One late afternoon as Judas was helping the Baptist with his rites, he heard some-one call his name. He looked around to see who was calling, and to his surprise, it was Barabbas, the Leader of the insurrectionist. Barabbas was of average stature with longer than normal hair that seemed to be sparse in the front part of his head. It seemed to curl at the ends, particularly at the side-burns. He had light brown eyes that seem to connote some sad eulogy about his life thus far. Even though he was only in his late thirties, he had seen and experienced more tragedy then most man twice his age. Judas walked down to the shore where Barabbas was standing and they began to talk.

"Judas, my friend, how have you been? I heard you were here with the Baptist."

"I have been here for about six months now." Looking around to see if anyone else was with Barabbas, Judas added, "How did you find out about me?"

"Some of my army officers told me that you have been sending men to them who are tired of all the oppression and exploitation by the devil Romans. They told how you had convinced them to find us and to join us, since the foretold King of the Jews is soon to lead us into victory."

"That I have, and will continue to do. Everyday I see good families torn apart by the mordant Romans treachery and devious attitudes towards them. I tell them that it is much better to choose to die on our feet, fighting to regain our freedom then to choose to live long lives, on our knees, as servants and slaves of these pagans pigs."

Amazed at what Judas had just stated, Barabbas said, "Well put my dear friend! I knew that you were not yet through working for the revolution and us. I knew that we could still count on you to work with us in our cause."

Judas felt a good feeling just hearing what Barabbas had said. He asked, "So tell me Barabbas, why are you here?"

"I want to know more about this man Jesus that people are talking about and are calling the Messiah. Have you met him?"

"No, I just saw him for a few minutes about four months ago when he came to be baptized by John."

"What was your impression of Him? Is He the Messiah, or just another false prophet?"

"I tell you Barabbas, I have never seen a man like Him in all my life! All you have to do is look at His eyes and you can see the presence of something that is almost impossible to verbalize. If I did not know better, I would swear that He could speak directly to your heart without uttering a word!" Looking straight at Barabbas eyes, Judas added, "No, there is no doubt left in me that he is the Messiah."

"Where could I find this Jesus now?"

"I don't know. He did not stay long that day that He was baptized. Two of John's helpers, Andrew Barjona and John Zebedee left with Him and have not returned to this day. I did hear that Andrew and John went home to tell their brothers about Jesus after staying with Him two or three days."

"You say they have brothers? How many?" Then raising his fists he said, "And will they fight with us?"

"I don't know if they will join the cause, but they do have brothers. Andrew said that his brother was named Simon. He described him as being a man of action, and eager to do whatever he sets his mind to do. He said that Simon tends to be very inquisitive, and feeds his curiosity by not being shy and asking questions about what he does not understand at the time. They both live in Bethsaida, on the north side of the Sea of Galilee, near Capernaum."

Judas continued, "John's older brother is named James. According to John, when James gets committed, he gets very aggressive about his commitment. He would be the type of person that would do good in our movement because he is very zealous and ambitious."

Looking around very suspiciously, and getting real close to Judas' face he asked, "What about Jesus? What have you heard about His whereabouts?"

"I heard that he was seen going into the dessert, and then was seen coming back out a few months back. But where He went from there, I have not heard."

"Keep an eye out for Him Judas; get word to me when you find out where He might be." More like an afterthought Barabbas then said, "Oh, keep up the recruiting also, we need all the men we can get that are willing to fight. You know where I can be found if you need me."

"Yes I do, and I have to confide in you that I personally want to see Procurator Pantera destroyed!"

"You may get your wish. I hear word from some of my people working as servants at his palace that Rome is very dissatisfied with his inability to stop the looting of the Tax Collectors and with their lose of revenue. They may be replacing him sooner then even he thinks."

"I just don't want him removed as Procurator," Judas said as he tightened his jaws and pounded his palm, "I want him disgraced and dead, I want to see him die!"

"You give us the Messiah that will lead, and I will gladly relinquish my troops to Him as His Army of liberators to run the Romans back across the sea to their land where they belong. I will then personally guarantee that Octavio Pantera will die! Look, I must be going now. I will keep in touch with you."

"Be careful Barabbas," Judas warned, "There are as many traitors among the Jews as there are friends. Caiaphas the High Priest is one of them. He sends people here in an effort to cast bad light on the Baptist, but John is too smart for his emissaries."

With that, Barabbas walked back through the crowd and was gone in a matter of a few minutes. Judas resumed helping the people that wanted to enter the waters to be baptized by John. After an hour or so, Simon the Zealot came near to speak to him.

"I heard some people talking and they were saying that Barabbas was here. What did he have to say?"

"Not much, he just wanted to ask me about Jesus, and if I knew where He might be right now."

"What did you tell him?" asked Simon the Zealot.

"I told him that I did not know, but as soon as I found out, I would send word so he could meet Him for himself. I think that he wants to offer his army to Jesus whenever He is ready to begin the conflict to free His people from the Romans."

"I hope you told him that you and I stand ready to fight along side of him and Jesus at a moment's notice," averred Simon.

"Yes I did. For now he wants us to continue recruiting fighters from the hordes of people that have been banished from their homelands and farms and who have come here looking for a leader. He said they make excellent fighters."

After a short pause Simon stated, "Judas, I have been thinking that it is time for us to seek Jesus and offer our services to Him. I think it is time that we find out first hand what His intentions really are. Some people are saying that He has been seen on the outskirts of the desert, preaching much the same as the Baptist."

"Yes," said Judas, "I was thinking the same thing just the other day. If we are to be of help, we have to be around when He begins the revolt. That is one fight I do not want to miss out on. Let's talk to the Baptist tonight and take our leave in the morning."

"That sounds good to me," replied Simon.

"I just hope that my friend John will understand why we have to leave his tutelage. I love him like a brother, but I must do what I have to do. For the first time in my life, I had not felt that overbearing anxiety for some time, until the last few days. I really thought that this was my destiny, to help John the Baptist prepare the way, but something inside me tells me now that I have not found it yet. I really hope the Baptist understands."

As the late afternoon gave way to the evening shades and shadows, most of the curiosity seekers and converts had gone home or to their camps near the hillside for the night. John the Baptist and several other disciples along with Judas and Simon set around the fire partaking of some tidbits of food that had been given to them by some of the newly baptized. As they sat talking about how the multitudes were growing every day, the conversation turned to John's brusque verbal criticism of Herod Antipas.

"John," said Simon, "Some friends of mine from Machaerus who work at the Palace of Herod told me that Herod Antipas is becoming very disturbed about what you are saying with reference to his sister-in-law Herodias and her daughter. It is rumored that he has made threats and denunciations towards you. I would be very careful for the next few weeks. Let the ill-tempers subside before you denounce him again, for your own safety."

"I speak only the truth, Simon" replied John, "It is not I that Antipas should fear, but the Son of God who will sit in his judgement. As for me, I do not fear any man or anything that is against God Almighty and His Laws."

Judas echoed Simon's concern by saying, "We are asking that you decrease your criticism of him for just a little while because Simon and I do not want anything bad to happen to you. We will not be here to defend you if this should occur. That's our worry."

Looking somewhat puzzled, John asked, "Where are you going to go Judas my friend?"

This was a hard thing to say for Judas. Simon and he looked at each other, then Judas said, "Simon and I wish to find Jesus of Nazareth to follow Him for a while and to listen and learn more about His teachings. We want to be part of His ministry and Kingdom. I have not been able to shake His image since I first laid eyes on him a few months ago when you baptized Him. I hope you can understand."

Somewhat melancholy John the Baptist answered, "I do Judas, but I thought you were content here with me under my pastoral care."

Standing up and re-sitting himself next to John the Baptist, Judas stated, "I have never been more at ease then I have been these past few months, John, but deep down inside me, I still feel that this is not my genuine destiny. I do feel that I am closer to it now then I have ever been, and I have you to thank for it. I had hoped and prayed that you would understand."

Placing his hand around Judas' shoulder John the Baptist replied, "How could I not understand? I too have been guided by the same feeling of divine intervention all my life, the same as you. I will pray that God will guide you and show you the way to your calling in life."

They hugged and exchanged kisses on the cheek, then Judas said, "We will be leaving in the morning. Do you have any idea where we might find Jesus?"

"He can be found in Nazareth. He has been ministering in the surrounding area for some time. Go there and you will find Him."

Before retiring for the night, Judas once again implored, "John, my most endeared friend, please heed Simon's warning. I don't know what I would do if anything were to happen to you. Please be careful."

"Do not worry about me, nothing will happen to me that it not preordained by God Himself. I am His, totally, to do with as He sees fit. My only wish is that you find whatever it is that you have been chosen to do. I will pray for you everyday. May our Lord be with you and Simon during your travels and always." They all set and talked for a little while longer, then they retired for the night.

Next morning as the sun was starting to rise from the east, Judas and Simon the Zealot left and began to make their way towards Nazareth. A week or so later, when they arrived they asked some of the Nazarenes if they knew the whereabouts of Jesus. No one would give them any information until an old man who said his name was Ornan. They asked him if he had heard about Jesus and he replied, "Oh yes, He was here in Nazareth." Winking his eye at Judas, he added, "He was raised here you know. He is the son of Joseph, the Carpenter. He taught in the synagogues around this area, and everyone praised and admired His wisdom, until about two weeks ago when He came into the synagogue here in Nazareth, and He stood up before the congregation and read from the book of Isaiah." Scratching his head and looking up as if to remember something, the old man said, "He chose to read that part that says,

"The Spirit of the Lord is on me, because he has anointed me to preach good news to the poor. God has sent me to proclaim freedom for the prisoners and recovery of sight for the blind, and to release the oppressed, and to proclaim the year of the Lord's favor.'"

"So what happened then?", inquired Judas.

"Well, when He was through with that reading, He rolled up the scroll, gave it back to the attendant and sat down. The eyes of everyone in the synagogue were fastened on Him and then he said to them, 'Today this scripture is fulfilled in your hearing.' Imagine that!"

Ornan let out a childish giggle, shook his head and continued. "For a while, all spoke well of him and were amazed at the gracious words that came from his lips. They could not believe that this was the son of Joseph the Carpenter. How could He be so wise? He is only a carpenter, and not a very good one at that!

As Ornan giggled, Judas asked him, "So, what happened? Where is Jesus now?'

"Like I said, every thing was fine, but the congregation turned on Him when He began comparing them to the faithless Jews of Elisha and Elijah's time. He also had the boldness to suggest that Gentiles could enjoy the blessings of God while some Jews would not."

"So what happened next?" queried Judas beginning to get agitated at getting the story from Ornan in bits and pieces, yet heightened in curiosity at what had transpired.

"Well, by that time all the people in the synagogue were furious when they heard this. They got up, and like a mob out for vengeance, drove him out of the town. They took him to the brow of the hill on which the town is built. They were going to throw Him over the cliff, but He just looked them all straight in the eyes and they all acted as if they were all paralyzed. Believe it or not, He just walked right through the whole large gathering, and went on His way." Ornan giggled again, this time for a longer period of time, since he thought it was quite hilarious the way Jesus dealt with the stiff-necked Pharisees.

All of a sudden his face became very serious and he said, "Yes Sir, He just looked at them with those eyes!" He paused as if he was trying to visualize something, then he said it again, "Those eyes! What a look He had. It seems as if He could melt iron by just looking at it. I have never seen anything like it, He just parted them like Moses parted the Red Sea, and walked right through the middle of them."

"So where can we find Jesus now?" asked Judas.

Still looking intently at outer space, as if reliving the account, he was brought back into the moment by Judas' question that he really did not hear because of his deep concentration. So he said, "Huh? What did you say?"

Judas repeated the question, "Where can we find Jesus now?"

"He can be found around the Sea of Galilee, preaching the good news. Where ever there is a crowd, you will find Him."

They thanked him and continued on their journey to find Jesus of Nazareth. After they had walked a few steps, Judas looked back at the old man and saw that he was walking away, his head shaking from side to side as he continued that childish giggling louder and louder as he walked.

Chapter 12
The Master's Dozen

After traveling seven days they saw a large crowd by the Sea of Galilee and they heard a voice telling the people gathered," Repent for the Kingdom of heaven is near." It was Jesus. They pushed and squirmed their way through the hordes of people, up to the front of the large crowd until they were so close, they could reach out and touch His garments. They stood there in total awe listening to Him preach. They had never heard anything like Him in their entire life! Just listening to him made the fires of hope for liberation burn unquenchably in Judas' heart as well as in the hearts of many that were there listening to Him.

"Liberation! What a sweet savory idea!" thought Judas, "And it needs to be realized whether it be through divine intervention or by all out warfare."

As he stood there listening with his mouth gaped; Jesus turned and looked straight into Judas' eyes. He could feel Jesus' eyes down deep in the most obscured recesses of his heart and mind. It seemed as if He stared at him for hours, yet it was only for a fleeting moment. Almost instantly Jesus turned and looked at one of His disciples that was helping Him control the crowd. This man was a tall formidably built man with dark brown eyes and a somewhat long black beard and mustache that hung past his strong chin. His face was weather beaten, and the lines formed by the vertical wrinkles in his cheeks added years to his looks. Without hesitation, this burly man, about forty years of age came over to Judas and said, "Welcome brother, can I be of service to you?"

"My name is Judas Iscariot, and my friend is Simon Zealotes. We have been witnesses and disciples of John the Baptist for the last six or seven months, and we now wish to become witness and disciples of Jesus the Nazarene."

"Yes, I knew who you were from the moment I saw you."

"How do you know me?" replied Judas.

"My name is Simon, or Cephas (that is Peter) as the Master has renamed me. I am Andrew Barjona's older brother. Andrew has spoken of you often to me and to the Master." Turning to Simon he added, "And you my brother, must be Simon the Zealot. We have spoken of you often too."

"Is Andrew here with Jesus also?" inquired Judas.

"Yes, and so is James and his brother John Zebedee, and others that the Master has personally selected as His pupils and witnesses." Pointing each one out as he identified them, Peter continued speaking, "There is Philip Rossi who is also from Bethsaida like my brother and me. He is the one that is in charge of our daily sustenance and provisions. Also with us is a man named Nathanael Bartholomew. He comes from Cana in the Providence of Galilee. His father is Tolmai the Rabbi in Cana."

"When did you become one of Jesus' disciples?" asked Judas.

"It has been about three months now," replied Peter. "Andrew and I were casting our nets, fishing with our father Jona here at the Sea of Galilee when Jesus came walking by and stopped and talked to us." Peter hesitated for just a second, and his face got this look of awe, as if he was reliving the moment. He added, "When we saw His eyes, and heard His voice saying, 'Come, follow me and I will make you fishers of men', there was not doubt that He was all that my brother Andrew had told me a month or so before. So we left our nets, our father, and our belongings and have followed the Master ever since."

"How about James and John Zebedee?"

"It is very much the same story. A few days after we joined the Master we walked by the Sea again and He saw James and John, fishing with their father Zebedee. He called them to follow, and they left everything, just like we did." Simon Peter paused for a moment, then he added, "There is one big difference though. We were a poor family fishing operation, but Zebedee had a fleet of boats and men working for him. He is very well to do, and James and John stood to inherit it all, but when they left, their father disinherited them. Their mother is quite the opposite, she is a true believer of Jesus, and is very happy for them."

Seeing that Simon the Zealot had sat down on the ground, Peter said, "Come with me to our camp and rest. You must be tired from your long journey."

As they walked towards the campsite Judas continued his inquiry. "How about the other two that are with you also?"

"You mean Phillip Rossi and Nathanael Bartholomew. They joined us a few weeks after James and John. We knew Nathanael through Phillip. They both studied at the same Synagogue in Cana when they were children. We have known Phillip and his family since childhood. We use to ride his fathers Arabian horses at his father's cropland."

Judas then said, "It has been a tiresome journey, but I am glad we have found the Nazarene and all of you. Let me see if I can remember the names of the followers that you just pointed out. Of course, you are Simon, that is, Peter, then there is Andrew, your brother, those two over there are James and John, the sons of Zebedee, and on the far side are Phillip and Nathanael. There are six of you all total."

"That is correct," answered Peter.

By now they had walked a few hundred yards from the crowd to a simple campsite. Out of inquisitiveness Judas asked, "Why did Jesus change your name? Does He do this to all of His disciples?"

In a proud, almost boastful voice he replied, "Oh no! He has done this only to me! When my brother Andrew brought me to Him and introduced us for the first time, Jesus looked at me and said, "So you are Simon Barjona. From now on you will be called Cephas (in Aramaic and Petros or Petra in Greek which then translates to Peter which means the Rock). You will be the rock upon which I will build MY church."

"What did He mean by that? Had Jesus known you before?" asked Simon.

"No." replied Peter, "I had never met Him before, but He acted as if He had known me all my life. As for building a church on me as the rock, only the Master knows what He meant." They walked for a little while longer, and when they reached the Apostle's campsite, Peter directed, "Stay and partake of our food and rest. The Master will want to talk to you when He finishes professing to the crowd."

"Thank you Simon."

Sticking his chest out, much like a soldier when he stands at attention, Peter replied, "Peter, call me Peter, please."

"I beg your forgiveness, Peter. Thank you for your kind offer. We will rest for a while, then we will join you and Jesus by the River."

"The Master will want to talk to you and find out how John Zacarias is doing. He will come to you when He has finished. For now, just rest."

When Peter left them to return to where Jesus was preaching, Judas and Simon laid down to rest and they fell asleep. They must have slept for about two hours. During his sleep Judas had a dream about his mother Sofia. He had not dreamed about her since he was a young boy attending school in the Synagogue in Kerioth. He saw her as plain as day. She had on a white robe that seemed to glisten as if the sunrays were reflecting off of it. It was strange, but in the dream, she seemed to be walking, but her feet never touched the ground! They were always a few hand spans off the ground. In his dream, he was also asleep, and Sofia came to him and told him, "Judas, my loving son. You have grown into a fine strong man. Do not let hatred stand in your way. Listen to the Master; forgive those that have offended you as I have forgiven them. You have been hand picked to insure that prophecy is fulfilled as it is written. Then we will all be together in the Kingdom of God, forever and ever. This has been promised to me by Yahweh, the God of Moses, and our God."

Suddenly, Judas was awakened by what felt like a ton of clay bricks in weight being place on this chest. When he was fully awake, and in control of all his faculties, he noticed that someone was standing over him and that this person's shadow had fallen upon his chest. He could not make out the face at first since the evening sun was behind the man. Almost immediately, the person that was standing over him knelt down beside him. It was then that Judas saw that it was Jesus the Nazarene.

"I did not mean to startle you Judas," said Jesus, with a voice that was as soothing as anything he had ever heard rolled up into His voice.

"You did not alarm me, I was just having a dream and it was very realistic for a dream, that's what startled me."

"You must be Judas, from Kerioth, Judas Iscariot. I am Jesus Barjosephus from Nazareth. Peter tells me that you and your friend want to be disciples and help spread the good news."

"Yes," replied Judas, "We were disciples of John, John the Baptist for about six or seven months and now Simon Zealotes and I want to be of service to you in anyway that you see fit."

"I know you were with my cousin John, now called the Baptist. I saw you there about three months ago when I was baptized by him."

"You remember me from then?" asked Judas somewhat surprised.

"Yes, I knew then that you would eventually be one of my disciples, and one of my chosen Apostles."

Judas could not hold back his feeling of joy and he knelt down and kissed His hand and said, "Ask anything of me and it will be done. Tell me how I can best serve you Master?"

Jesus replied, "You are a Scribe, or so I have been told. You are a scholarly man; therefore I want you to handle what little funds we get from the faithful. I want you to keep an accounting of these funds, making sure that we pay the taxes that the Romans may impose. This will be your role in addition to that of helper, student, and eventually, evangelist of the Good Word." Then Jesus' face took on a look of deep seriousness. His eyes seemed to once again burn deep into Judas' being. Jesus then added, "The main thing I want you to do is to follow your heart. Do what must be done when the time comes for it to be done."

Judas did not quite understand the last part concerning what he needed to do. He asked rather bashfully, "What do You mean when You say to follow my heart and do what must be done when the time comes?"

Jesus answered, "In due time it will all become quite clear Judas, in due time."

From that moment on, Judas and Simon the Zealot went with Jesus wherever He preached. They would stay in one place for a few days, or a week, depending on the reception that they would receive in the area. Often times, if accommodations were made available by residents or friends that lived nearby, or by people that came to hear Jesus talk, they might stay for longer then a week at a time. Once, while in Capernaum on a Sabbath, Jesus went into the synagogue and began to teach. As usual the people listening were amazed at his teaching because he taught them as one who had authority, not as the teachers of the law. When he was teaching, a man in the synagogue who was possessed by an evil spirit cried out, "What do you want with us, Jesus of Nazareth? Have you come to destroy us? I know who you are, you are the Holy One of God!"

Upon hearing this, Jesus whirled around to face the man. Peter and Judas had begun to move towards the man in an attempt to silence him, but Jesus motioned them to stop and very authoritatively responded, "Be quiet! Come out of him!" The evil spirit shook the man violently and came out of him with a shriek.

The people were all so amazed that they asked each other, "What is this? A new teaching, and with authority! He even gives orders to evil spirits and they obey him!"

News about Jesus spread quickly over the whole region of Galilee. Jesus' plan was to spend more time at Capernaum since they had excellent accommodations in the household of Peter and his wife, and expenses were almost nothing. After preaching at the Synagogue the fourth day, Peter's brother-in-law came and told Peter that his mother-in-law was in bed with a very high fever. Peter convinced Jesus to change His plans for the evening. Jesus usually dined with the Rabbi and his family, explaining further the teachings that He had taught that day. Instead that night they all went to Peter's house and they found his mother-in-law in bed with an extremely high fever.

Upon entering the house, Jesus went to her, took her by the hand and helped her up. Immediately the fever left her and she began to wait on them, and to feed them. All of her friends that had been tending to her rushed out into the streets and began to tell how Jesus had cured her. That night after sunset, the people brought to Jesus all the sick and demon-possessed. The whole town gathered at the door, and Jesus healed many people that had various diseases. He also drove out many demons, but He would not let the demons speak because they knew who He was, and it was not yet time to reveal Himself.

Very early the next morning, while it was still dark, Jesus got up, left the house and went off to a solitary place where he prayed by Himself. After a time Judas and the rest of the six disciples missed Him, so they went to look for Him. When they found Jesus they exclaimed, "Everyone is looking for you!"

Jesus replied, "Let us go somewhere else, to the nearby villages, so I can preach there too. That is why I have come." So for the next six or so months they traveled throughout Galilee, preaching in synagogues, healing and driving out demons. Judas could not believe what he was witnessing. Demons were ousted, the sick were being healed, and the lame made to walk, all by just the word of Jesus the Nazarene.

One day, Simon the Zealot came running towards Jesus and the rest of the group that was with Him. As he ran he kept yelling very excitedly, "Lepers! Lepers! They are coming this way. Judas rose up from where he was sitting and started towards them to stop them from reaching Jesus. Immediately Jesus took his arm and motioned Judas to sit back down. When the people infected by leprosy reached Jesus, one of them got on his knees. While removing his wrappings from one of the affected area he spoke beggingly.

"I have heard about you, and all the good things that you are doing." Holding up a rotten knob that was once a human hand he continued, "I know and believe in my heart that if you are willing, you can make me clean."

Filled with compassion Jesus reached out and touched the man. "I am willing," He said. "Be clean!"

Immediately the leprosy left his hand and face and he was cured. Jesus sent him away at once with a strong warning, "See that you do not tell this to anyone. Just go and show yourself to the priest and offer the sacrifices that Moses commanded for your cleansing, as a testimony to them."(Book of Leviticus Chapter 13 and 14)

But the man did not listen, instead he went out and began to talk freely, praising Jesus and spreading the news. Because of the hordes of people that resulted from the publicity of His miracles, Jesus could no longer enter a town openly but stayed outside in sparsely populated places. Yet the people still came to him from everywhere.

During his stay with Jesus during these few months, Judas witnessed many more miracles and heard many sermons about the coming of the New Kingdom of God.

One day, when Jesus was resting Judas came to Him and said, "Master, may I have a word with You?"

"Judas, yes, sit here next to Me. What is it? Do we need more funds?"

"No Master, we are financially sound. I just want to clear my mind about something."

"What is it Judas? Don't tell Me that you do not understand some of the parables that I have been using to bring My points across. I can understand some of the others not grasping the point, but you, an educated man should not have this problem."

"No Master, I feel that I understand them well, although sometimes it requires some deep though to decipher all of their meaning. But this is not what I want to ask about."

"What is it then?" Jesus replied. Judas always felt very uneasy each time that he questioned Jesus. It was as if Jesus already knew the question before he asked it.

Judas fidgeted a little then said, "You have been speaking about establishing Your Kingdom and being the savior of our people, and I totally believe that. My question is, when will it happen? I do not know if our people can stand anymore of this devastating oppression."

"Judas," said Jesus putting His arm on his shoulder, "My time has not yet come. Rest assured that when the time comes, you, Judas, of all my disciples will be the first to know. Then you must be ready to do what you have to do. You must do what in your heart you know is right."

Judas was alternatively happy and sad to hear what Jesus had just told him. He was sad because it was not yet time, but happy to hear that he would evidently be a major player in the liberation and in setting up Jesus' Kingdom. When the conversation ended, Judas left Jesus alone to meditate.

After returning once more to the town of Capernaum and curing countless people, Jesus met up with a Tax Collector, or as they were better known, a Mokhes named Matthew Levi Baralphaeus, (the son of Alphaeus). Alphaeus was Jesus' uncle and His stepfather Joseph's brother. This made Matthew Jesus' cousin. As a Mokhes, Matthew was one of the most hated people by the Jews. There was nothing worse than a Jew like him who was a blackmailer, a thief and traitor, who would take full advantage of his own people for his own gain. He was a Publican, that is, hired by the Romans to keep the other Jews in check. He would overtax and keep the difference for himself once he remitted the true taxes to Rome. He would set up his table of operation anywhere that he could have the best access to the most people, such as where roads crossed and at the lake harbors. He then collected personnel taxes and taxes on exports and imports.

A few days later, Jesus was walking by the lake, and as He walked He saw Matthew again, sitting at his collection table. Jesus looked at him with a look that Matthew had never experienced before. It seemed as if he was outside his body looking down at the dreadful man he had become. He had never viewed himself in that light. About that time Jesus said a simple phrase to him, "Follow me," and Matthew got up and followed him, leaving all his earthly belongings and monies behind.

It was hard for Judas to accept Matthew, even if he was Jesus' cousin on his stepfather's side. John the Baptist was also Jesus' cousin on His mother's side. Judas could not help but marvel at the difference between the two cousins. All of his live, Judas had been fighting oppression and corruption imposed on the Jews by the Roman provisional government. Enemies were many, especially Jews that collaborated with the Roman. Now here was Matthew, a prime example of what they hated the most! Trusting Matthew came very slowly for Judas, but Simon's heart had softened substantially by now from listening to the Master speak about love and forgiveness. Therefore it was easier for Simon the Zealot to accept Matthew.

Judas had more difficulty accepting the "turn the other cheek" philosophy. Too many harsh things had happened in his life, such as the rape of his mother, the executions of his stepfather to list a few, for him to feel love and compassion at this point.

It really upset Judas further when that very night Jesus went to Matthew's home and had supper with him and other tax collectors and known sinners. This act was against the Mosaic Law. Someone went and told the Pharisee teachers from the synagogue, and they had to come and see for themselves. They could not believe it when they saw it. They were shock, and asked Jesus, "Why do You eat with tax collectors and sinners? They do not even exercise ceremonial washing of their hands when they eat as required by Law. They do not hold to any of the traditions of the elders such as washing their cups pitchers and kettles before partaking food in them."

Hearing this Jesus said to them, "Isaiah was right when he prophesied about you hypocrites when he wrote, 'These people honor me with their lips, but their hearts are far from me. They worship me in vain, their teachings are but rules taught by men.' You have let go of the commandments of God and are holding on to the traditions of men. You have a fine way of setting aside the commands of God in order to observe you own traditions! Besides, it is not the healthy who need a doctor, but the sick. I have not come to call the righteous, but the sinners."

It was difficult for the Pharisees to reconcile His actions so from then on, Jesus became a "Persona non-grata" at the synagogue at Capernum. Since Jesus could not use the Synagogues anymore, He preached in open-air forums. Even so, the crowds that followed Him on a daily basis grew and grew as His deeds and miracles gained notoriety. The disciples had their hands full with crowd control. There were seven hand picked disciples now with the addition of Matthew, but there were hundreds more that came on a daily basis and assisted Jesus during His sermons and baptism. It was not Jesus who baptized by water, but it was a rite that His helpers performed before, during and after His sermons. One day Jesus went up on a mountainside to pray. He continued all night in prayer to God. He was praying for Divine Guidance in selecting the disciples that he would ordain as Apostles. The next day, He called those He wanted. The ones He chose came to Him. He appointed twelve, designating them Apostles, to be with Him and to preach and to have authority to drive out demons. These were the twelve He appointed.

1. Simon whom Jesus called Peter, and who was the brother of Andrew Barjona.
2. James, son of Zebedee who He called, Boanerges that is "Son of Thunder" and who was the brother of John.
3. John, son of Zebedee, James' brother who He also called Boanerges.
4. Andrew Barjona, the brother of Peter.
5. Phillip Rossi, who was half-Greek and a horseman by trade. He was from Bethsaida and was a childhood friend of Peter and Andrew.
6. Nathanael Bartholomew, a student of Scripture from Cana His father was Tolmai Tholomew, the Rabbi in Cana.
7. Matthew Levi son of Alphaeus, the Mokhes, (that is Tax Collector) and paternal cousin of Jesus and was also a brother to James.
8. James, the son of Alphaeus also, brother of Matthew the Tax Collector, also known as James the Lessor.
9. Thomas, the tender hearted, and the doubter.
10. Lebbaeus Thaddaeus (who today some believe his first name was Judas) and who was a half brother to Jesus.
11. Simon the Zealot
12. Judas Iscariot.

Alphaeus was Jesus' uncle and brother to Joseph, the stepfather of Jesus. Therefore Matthew and James the lessor were cousins of Jesus the Nazarene and of Lebbaeus Thaddaeus. Therefore, three of the twelve were related.

Of the hundred or so disciples that had followed and served Jesus during this time, Jesus chose these twelve as His Apostles. As disciples they were students, listening and learning the ways of the Lord, but as Apostles, they were now to be zealous advocate and teachers. He gave all twelve, including Judas, the authority to heal the sick, raise the dead, and cleanse those who have leprosy and to drive out demons.

As time passed, Jesus sent them out in pairs with the following instructions. He told them, "Do not go among the Gentiles or enter any town of the Samaritans. Go rather to the lost sheep of Israel and preach this message, 'The Kingdom of God is near.' Do not suppose that I have come to bring peace to the earth, I did not come to bring peace, but a sword. For I have come to turn a man against his father, a daughter against her mother, a daughter-in-law against her mother-in-law to the point that a man's enemies will be his own household."

Upon hearing what Jesus had just said, Judas felt exuberant for he was certain that it meant it would not be long before He would lead the battle to establish His Kingdom. Simon the Zealot was just as jubilant. He had learned from His cousins that Jesus was a direct descendant from the lineage of King David. Simon had always been a great admirer of King David. As a matter of fact, he always attempted to emulate David during his fifteen-year stint as the Commander of the freedom fighters. It was Simon Zealotes who, after the massacre at Bethel, convinced all sects of Jews to join together for a common cause and forget all of the philosophical and religious differences between them. He was successful in convincing young Essenes, Pharisees and Sadducees that self-rule in their beloved Promised Land was primary and essential before any philosophical matters. Not since King David had this unity been accomplished until Simon Zealotes had achieved it. Now he just knew that he was going to have the opportunity of commanding some of the fighting forces under the direct leadership of one of King David's descendants. What an honor and privilege, he thought!

Judas and Simon the Zealot were one of the pairings that was sent out by Jesus. They traveled to the towns and villages on or near the Sea of Galilee beginning with Korazin, Magdala, Tiberias, back to Magdala, then to Cana, down to Nazareth and then to Nain then back again to Cana and Nazareth.

When they left Nazareth, they walked about ten miles to Nain. About a mile before reaching their destination, they came upon a lovely lowland area by the side of a small mountain. It was covered with wild flowers of numerous colors, and wild green grasses. Judas could not get over how beautiful this spot seemed to be. He was so impressed and emotionally moved by its peaceful serenity that he told Simon, "Simon, I know we have less then a mile to Nain, but let us stop here to rest and meditate before we enter the village."

Simon responded, "Why Judas, are you already tired? We just rested less then an hour ago."

"I know Simon, I just want to enjoy the splendor of these hills and dale." Looking around at all of nature's beauty, Judas added, "I have never seen anything so picturesque and gorgeous anywhere else in all of my travels. I just want to enjoy it for a little while. You know Simon, my Uncle Reuben told me that my mother had been born and had lived in Nain before coming to Kerioth. I wish I knew where in Nain so I could at least visit the land she walked on." After a short silence he added, "I bet she loved these hills and scenery as much as I do. Don't you think it's possible?"

"Yes I do Judas," replied Simon. "You would have to be blind not to love this gorgeous view."

They set down on a hillside under an old cedar tree. From there they could see the vegetation, trees, and the newly grown green grass that would have provided a feast for any livestock. From his sitting position, Judas laid down on his back and noticed the fluffy cumulus clouds as they lazily and slowly moved across the sky on there way from the sea to only God knows where. He could not believe how calm and peaceful he felt at that moment. He never felt this much at peace except when he was in the presence of the Nazarene.

"Have you ever seen a place as lovely as this in you life?" he asked Simon once again.

"No," replied Simon, as he chewed on some blades of green grass and as he followed the flight of the clouds too. "I can't say that I have. Here I even forget that we are at the mercy of the Romans. I get the feeling that all is at peace."

Just then a rabbit made a scurrying sound as it ran out from behind a rock that was behind them and to their right side. Turning to see what had made that noise, they watched the rabbit run behind some bushes directly behind them about twelve feet up the hill.

"It's a rabbit!" said Simon, "and I am so tired of eating dried fish! Let's catch him and make a feast out of our next meal," he added while rubbing his hand on his stomach in a circular manner.

"Simon! You know that the rabbit is an unclean animal, and we are forbidden to eat it."

Leaning towards Judas, he said sheepishly, "Don't you remember Judas what Jesus told the crowd when the Pharisees questioned Him about eating with unclean people because we failed to wash our hands in ceremonial washing?" Trying to sound as much as he could like the Master, Simon then said, "He very staunchly told the crowd, 'Listen to Me everyone and understand this. Nothing outside a man can make him unclean by going into him. Rather it is what comes out of a man that makes him unclean.'"

"That can't be what the Master meant," responded Judas

"Yes it was. I know because after the crowd had left, He came back into the house and we asked Him what he meant. Well, He told us 'Don't you see that nothing that enters a man from the outside can make him unclean? For it does not go into his heart, but into his stomach, and then out of his body. Jesus then told us that what comes out of a man is what makes him unclean, for from within, out of men's hearts come evil thoughts, sexual immorality, theft, murder, adultery, greed, malice, deceit, lewdness, envy, slander, arrogance and folly. All these evils come from inside and make a man unclean, not the food.'"

Judas was still somewhat skeptical and Simon the Zealot noticed this so he added jokingly, "Come on Judas, you have heard the Master tell us to accept all whose faith is weak, without passing judgement on disputable matters. Well, I am weak, weak from hunger and I think that the future of that rabbit is in dispute!"

Judas laughed at his comment, and could not help but join Simon in his attempts to snare the rabbit. They went to the brush where they last saw the rabbit hid, and in his zeal to get the rabbit, Simon became all snarled up in the thorny vines. He began to holler and shout in pain, and it seemed that the more he tried to back out, the more entangled he became. For some reason all of this struck Judas as comical, and be began to laugh almost uncontrollably! He felt like a child at play at this very moment. As a matter of fact, the last time he remembered laughing this hard was when he was a child, playing a game of tag with Cassandra and John Zacarias.

Judas gave up the chase because he was laughing so hard. He laid on the hillside, face up, still laughing heartily as Simon pleaded for help to extricate himself from the tangled mass he had gotten into by himself. Judas finally arose again to help his friend. Doing so, he noticed that the rabbit had gone into what appeared to be a cave behind all this thorny rubble.

"Look Simon," said Judas curiously, "There is a cave behind these bushes. I wander what's inside. Come on and help me push this rubble and thorny bushes aside so we can go inside and take a look."

Reluctantly and still in some small pain from the thorns, Simon agreed to help as some form of payback for Judas' help. Using their shawls to protect themselves from the thorns, they pushed until the thorny weeds broke at the base and rolled away from the entrance of a cave. As Judas went in, he could see his long shadow in front of him caused by the early evening sun behind him. As he entered, it took a while for his eyes to become acclimated to the darkness but after a short while, he could see almost to the back of the cave. He saw some small boulders close to the entrance and a larger one close to the back of the cave. He got an eerie feeling as he stood near the center of the cave. He walked slowly to the back of the cave and looked down behind the large boulder and he saw the eyes of an extremely frightened little creature, squatting to keep from being seen. Judas could see that it was shaking from fright. It was the little rabbit. At that moment, a feeling of sadness and compassion came over Judas. He thought to himself, "How can anyone hurt any thing that is that scarred? You would have to be devoid of a compassionate heart to cause it any harm."

About that time Simon called out, "Do you see our next dinner in the cave, Judas?"

Looking down at the terrified little animal Judas, for some unexplainable reason, almost tearfully replied, "No. No, I do not see anything."

With that he turned and walked outside of the cave where Simon was sitting, still picking some thorns from his legs and arms. Judas set down next to him and said, "Simon, do you ever wonder about how many people have used this cave as their refuge or home, or just a resting place in the past?"

Simon shook his head to indicate a no answer as he continued to pick little bits of thorns out of his leg.

In a melancholy fashion, Judas then said, "I do. I can't help but wonder what has happened in caves like this one at one time or another. Scrapping the ground with his hand as he talked, he uncovered something that appeared to be a round metal object. "Look Simon, look at what I just found!" To his surprise it was silver. Upon closer examination, Judas found it to be a shekel coin referred to by the Romans as a Piece of Silver. "I wonder where it came from, and to whom it belonged?"

After sitting by the cave long enough for Simon to clean as many of the thorns out of his flesh as he could, they continued on their trip to Nain. They walked along a gravel road until they saw a farmhouse that had long been deserted. There was a walkway to the house, and a large fig tree where the walkway met the gravel road.

"What a quaint home," remarked Judas, "I wonder who owns this place."

"I doubt if anyone has lived there in sometime," replied Simon, "It looks as if it has been deserted for quite something."

Judas walked under the fig tree and set down on what must have been a makeshift bench at one time. It had almost rotted apart. Looking at the tree he noticed what appeared to be some carvings. He pointed it out to Simon saying, "Look Simon, this must have been a favorite place for someone to play. They have carved their names on the tree. Let me see if I can make out the writing. It reads, Seth and a little lower down it reads Zev. I wonder who they might have been? I wonder where they might have gone?"

"I don't know," said Simon, "But if things went here as in most places, they might have lost the place to the Romans for taxes. This could have been one more Jewish family that lost its home because of the Romans."

"You might be right," added Judas, "But it's a shame that the people who once lived here, and who I am sure were once happy, had to experience the heartbreak of loosing their family due to ignorance, philosophical and religious differences."

After resting briefly, and looking inside the house through the cracks on the shudders, they continued on their journey.

Everywhere they traveled, they did what the Master had told them to do. They searched for some worthy person there and stayed at his house. Each time they entered the home, they blessed it. When they were not welcomed or when they were taunted by the citizens as it happened in Tiberias, they shook the dust of their feet upon leaving and told the townspeople what the Master had told them to say. They said to them, "It will be more bearable for Sodom and Gomorrah on the Day of Judgment than for you the people of this town for you have rejected the one that sent us."

Everywhere they went, they talked about how the scripture and prophecy found in the Book of Isaiah had been fulfilled, and that the Messiah, in the form of Jesus of Nazareth would soon "..Bring justice to the nations." Since both Judas and Simon truly believed that Jesus was soon to establish his earthly Kingdom, they very enthusiastically spread the word of the coming salvation and recruited heavily for Barabbas' army.

Recruiting was one of the many positive things that came out of this evangelical trip. They both tried to heal the sick, and even to restore sight to a blind man, but neither of them could do it at first. This was very disappointing to both of them. Eventually, after extensive praying and fasting, they could perform miracles as the Master had instructed them to do. They continued to preach the coming of the New Kingdom and about the miracles performed by Jesus the Nazarene, which they had witnessed. "We have seen it with our own eyes," they told the crowds, "The Master, Jesus of Nazareth, raising the dead, healing the sick, and even commanding the winds and waters, and they obey Him.

"How can this be?" questioned the unbelievers. "Tell us more about these things."

Simon Zealotes then said, "Well, one day the Master told us, 'Let's go over to the other side of the lake.' So we got into a boat and set out. As we were sailing, the Master fell asleep since He was exhausted from ministering to the hordes of people for days. As we were sailing, a squall came down on the lake, so that the boat was being swamped. Believe me when I tell you, we were in great danger and we all feared for our lives! I then turned and asked Peter, another one of His servants, to please wake Jesus up because we were sure we were going to drown. Well, Jesus got up and rebuked the wind and the raging waters. He ordered them by shouting to them, 'Quiet! Be still!' I tell you the truth, immediately the wind died down and it became completely calm, as if nothing had ever happened."

Murmuring could be heard in the crowd as they discussed among themselves the validity of what they were hearing. Simon then continued, "I know how you feel, because you see, I felt that way too until I saw for myself. One day a man with an evil spirit came from the tombs in the region of the Gerasenes. No one could bind and hold him any more, not even with a chain. He had often been chained hand and foot, but he tore the chains apart and broke the irons on his feet. No one was strong enough to subdue him. Night and day among the tombs and in the hills he would cry out and cut himself with stones. When he saw the Master from a distance, he ran and fell on his knees in front of Him. He shouted at the top of his voice 'What do you want with me, Jesus, Son of the Most High God? Swear to me that you won't torture me!' Jesus had said to him, 'Come out of this man, you evil spirit!'"

"What happened next?" asked several people in the crowd. "Yes tell us the rest of the story," you could hear more people say.

Simon continued saying, Then Jesus asked the voice, 'What is your name?' and the spirit answered, 'My name is Legion, for we are many.' The evil spirits begged Jesus again and again not to send them out of the area. But a large herd of pigs was feeding on the nearby hillside, and they asked Jesus to allow them to go into them. Jesus gave them permission, and the evil spirits came out and went into the pigs. The herd of pigs, about two thousand of them in number rushed down the steep bank into the lake and were drowned. I tell you, Jesus is the Messiah for even the devils ask Him for permission and do His bidding."

Judas spoke to the crowd then. "Even one of the synagogue rulers from Capernaum named Jairus knows and can testify to the powers of Jesus of Nazareth. He saw Jesus one day and fell to Jesus' feet. He pleaded earnestly, 'My little girl is dying. Please come and put your hands on her so that she will be healed and live.' So Jesus went with him. A large crowd followed and pressed around Him. A woman following Jesus also had been subject to bleeding for twelve years. She had suffered a great deal under the care of many doctors and had spent all she had; yet instead of getting better she grew worse. When she heard Jesus approaching the spot near where she stood, she came up behind him in the crowd and touched his cloak. She thought that if she just touch it, she would be healed. Well, as soon as she touched the Masters cloak, she immediately stopped bleeding. She felt that her body had forever been freed from her suffering. When the Master found out what she had done, He told her, 'Daughter, your faith has healed you. Go in peace and be free from your suffering.'

"What happened to the man's daughter?" someone asked.

"Well, while this was happening with the woman, a man came from the house of Jairus and told him that his daughter had just died."

Gasps could be heard from the crowd. Someone yelled out, "What did the Nazarene do about that?"

Judas continued, "They told Jairus not to bother the Master anymore since she was now dead. Ignoring what they had said, the Master told Jairus, 'Do not be afraid, just believe!' The Master asked Simon who is standing next to me now, and I to hold back the crowd. He took Peter, James and John with Him. He told the crowd standing outside the house, crying and making a big commotion, 'The child is not dead, she is only asleep.' But they all laughed at Him. After that Jesus ordered everyone out of the house and he entered only with the father, the mother and the Apostles that he had taken with Him, and went to the room where the child had been laid. He took her by the hand and said to her ' Talitha koum!' (Which means little girl, I say to you, get up!) Immediately the girl stood up and walked around. At this they were completely astonished. He told them to give her something to eat."

Simon added excitedly, "I tell you, anyone who has power even over death, is truly the Messiah. Some of you have seen even us heal the sick, and cast out demons from some people, but our powers, although they come from God through Jesus, it is not comparable to His powers. The time for Him to set up His Kingdom is at hand and He will win our salvation when He does establish his reign." This was what Simon and Judas preached throughout their travels.

Once, in Cana, while they were talking about the great miracles that the Nazarene was performing daily, one of the onlookers began to jeer them saying, "You must be insane! The Messiah is a Nazarene? Nazareth is full of Gentiles. They are the most pathetic, uneducated, and disgusting bunch! What good can come out of Nazareth? I'll tell you the answer to that question myself, nothing!"

Shortly another man came forward and said, "I know you, you were with the Baptist about a year or so ago, you were his disciples. How did you escape the wrath of Herod Antipas?"

"What do you mean?" asked Judas.

"A few months ago, Herod Antipas took the Baptist to Machaerus and has imprisoned him for professing against him. All of his disciples left him and scattered all over Palestine."

"When did this happen?" asked Simon the Zealot.

"It happened about two or three months ago. Some say that the only reason Antipas has not executed him yet is because he fears that the Baptist is the Prophet Elijah returned from the grave."

"Do you know for sure that the Baptist is still alive? Judas asked with great concern.

"Yes he is," the man replied. "I think that Antipas is saving him for his own evil purpose. Otherwise the Baptist would be dead by now."

Turning to Simon Zealotes Judas said, "Simon, we have to go to Machaerus to check on John." Simon agreed, so the very same day they both left Cana and began their journey to Machaerus. It took almost two weeks to get there. They first traveled to Magdala where they talked a sailboat owner into taking them south on the Sea of Galilee, down through the River Jordan, south to another large lake that some peopled called the Salted Sea. There they disembarked and walked eastward for about 13 miles to Machaerus. They only stopped periodically to sleep and eat. They did not preach or recruit on their way since they wanted to reach Machaerus as soon as possible. They both knew that going there was in direct disobedience of Jesus' instructions to remain in Galilee, yet they felt sure that Jesus would want them to see what was happening to John the Baptist.

Chapter 13
Loss of Judas' Loved Ones

When Judas and Simon the Zealot arrived, they went directly to the Palace of Herod Antipas and requested an audience with Herod. At first the chancellor in charge of granting audiences flatly refused. They left the Palace to regroup. Their plan was to return again the following day. As they were leaving Judas spoke, "I really do not blame the chancellor for not giving us an appointment."

"Why," asked Simon, somewhat confused at what Judas had said.

"Because Simon, look at us. We look worse then two destitute beggars from the street. We have not trimmed our beard, moustache and hair since Jesus sent us out like 'lambs among wolfs'. Secondly, we have not bathed since we left to come here over two weeks ago. Look at our clothes! If I had been the chancellor in charge, I too would not have allowed an audience with the like of us either. I would have been afraid that we were some kind of street outcasts, looking to do harm to Herod. We need to find a place we can trim and clean ourselves up and then try again."

"Where can we go?" asked Simon.

After some quiet thought Judas said, "I know a man who lives here by the name of Asa. He lives with his son and his grandchildren. Maybe they will be kind enough to provide us with a bath and some clothes."

"How will we find them?" asked Simon.

"Let's ask at the synagogue, I am sure they would know.

They went there and as expected they knew the family and gave them the directions. When they arrived, a man looking somewhat older then Judas was sheering a lamb.

"May the Lord be with you friend!" said Judas. The man quickly whirled around as if he had been startled. He lifted the sheering scissors blades that he had been using on the lamb up in a defensive posture. "Please, do not fear. We mean you and your family no harm. I am Judas Iscariot, and this is Simon Zealotes. May I ask your name?"

The man looked surprised at first. He looked at both strangely, then a smile came over his face as if he had just seen an old friend. "Simon Zealotes you say; and Judas Iscariot?" He dropped the scissors blades and walked swiftly towards them. Taking their hands in his, and squeezing them tightly he said, "Welcome, welcome to my home. I am Mark, Barasa. My father Asa spoke of you so often that I feel I know you." Looking at Simon he continued, "He told me countless of times that if it had not been for you, he and hundreds of others would have died near Bethel. I am so honored to finally meet you! Welcome to my humble home, my house is yours during your stay."

"And what news do you have of Asa?" asked Judas.

The question brought on a sad look to Mark's face. He replied, "He passed away in his sleep about ten months ago. I buried him by his garden that he tended until his last days." Trying to contain his sadness he asked, "Would you like to have some cool water, some food, a bath, a change of clothes, a room for your stay? I am at your service; just ask, and your needs will be taken care of immediately. Judas and Simon looked at each other and could not help but marvel at his offer. It was exactly what they needed, and they did not even have to ask for any of it.

After some minutes of initial conversation, both Judas and Simon spent the next few hours cleaning up. They bathed, trimmed their beards and hair, and put on some fresh clothing that Mark Barasa had laid out for them. Afterwards, as they were sitting around a wooden block in the kitchen that served as a table, drinking leaf tea, Judas said, "We are here in Machaerus because he heard that Herod had taken John the Baptist prisoner. We want to get an audience with Herod to plea for his release. What you offered and gave to us was exactly what we needed. It seems that you must have been reading our minds when you offered your kind hospitality."

Looking at both of them, Mark grinned and said, "It is not all that eerie. My father always told me that whenever freedom fighters came into a village, it was because they needed food, supplies, and shelter for a few days, a warm bath, a change of clothes and a warm place to sleep. I loved my father very much and I do honor to him by what I do for you. I would be happy to do this for any member of the rebellion, but it is a special privilege for me to be helping the renowned Simon Zealotes, the Zealot!" Judas looked at Simon and could not help but smile at the way that he acted. It was clear that Simon did not know how to accept a well-deserved compliment. You could tell that he was blushing and somewhat uneasy at what was being said about him. Yet, it was the truth.

The next morning they got up and dressed in the fine clothes that Mark had provided for them. As they walked out of the house, they thanked him once again. Judas and Simon had turned away and had taken just a few steps when Judas stopped suddenly. He turned around and gave Barasa's home the blessing that Jesus had instructed them to give all the homes that welcomed them.

They hurried back to Herod's Palace, and this time Judas introduced himself as a Scribe of Jerusalem, and personal friend of Procurator Octavio Pantera. They got the audience with Herod without having to wait longer then ten minutes. They waited for Herod in the castle's Great Hall, a large room about one hundred feet wide and two hundred feet long. At the far end there were some steps leading to a stage with a beautiful ivory throne with gold inlays throughout it. Long large felt drapes hung behind the throne down to the floor from the top of the ceiling that must have been twenty or thirty feet tall. There were four posts made of ivory containing beautiful hieroglyphics on each corner of the stage. These posts supported a canopy made of red satin material with a fringe of dangling golden colored cloth balls. They were nervously admiring the room, when they heard conversation coming closer and closer from a side entrance directly behind the stage. Soon Herod Antipas and his aide came up the steps to the stage and Herod sat on the throne. He threw his blue and gold colored cape over his right shoulder, and he placed his scepter in front of him as he held it with his right hand. It was made of silver with exquisite carvings of lions, camels and bears, and a man on horseback giving chase.

"Who are you?" he asked, "And what business do you have with me?"

Walking to the foot of the stairs Judas replied, "I am Judas Iscariot, the Scribe from Jerusalem. I bring you greetings from Procurator Pantera and his staff. We have been told that you have imprisoned the one they call the Baptist." Using the most authoritative tone of voice he could muster he added, "Is this correct?"

"Yes, yes I have. He was preaching insurrection against me, so I took it upon myself to put an end to such nonsense. I should have done it a long time ago when the word came down from General Pantera to have him arrested on sight, but I did not see any harm to what he was doing until now."

This caught Judas by surprise. He did not know that Pantera had actually put out the word to have the Baptist arrested. This spoiled his plan to ask for his release in the name of Octavio Pantera. He had to think fast.

"I am here because I need to see and speak with the Baptist. There are certain questions that I must ask him so I can relay his answers to Procurator Pantera. We need to see him by ourselves only, with no one else around."

"That will not be a problem." Turning to the aide Antipas instructed him to take Judas and Simon to the dungeon to see John the Baptist, and to do whatever else they needed him to do. "Will you have need of a torture specialist? We have an excellent one. He can make anyone talk. There is not a tongue in all of Palestine that he can not loosen! I love to see him at work!"

"No, there will be no need for his services, I assure you," said Simon, clinching his large hands into tight fists. "The Baptist will talk to us." They then walked with the aide and soon they were in the dungeon.

When they saw John in his cell, he was kneeling in prayer, looking up at a small window cut into the solid rock wall. The window was about fifteen feet high. The light beam that came through the window shone on John's face and chest. He appeared to be in a deep meditative prayerful state. The entire dungeon prison smelled strongly of human excrement and urine. The straw that each cell had for bedding and for cleaning purposes appeared not to have been changed in a long long while. Judas had to call out John's name two or three times before he could get his attention. When he turned to see who was calling, he looked shocked at seeing Judas.

"Blessed be God!" he said. "Judas my friend, I was just praying that Yahweh had given peace to your heart. How are you?"

"No John, the question is how are you?"

"I am as good as can be expected for the time I have spent in this sasspool. About three months ago or so Antipas sent some troops to arrest me. He claims that I am preaching sedition, and causing his subjects to exhibit disrespect towards his reign. I told him that I was only warning him that what he is doing with his brother's wife is going to cost him more then his reign. It is going to cost him eternal damnation."

"John, we warned you before we left not to speak ill of Herod Antipas. When I saw Barabbas by the Jordan River he told me that you were continuing to chastise Antipas. Even if it is the truth, it is really upsetting Antipas." Judas then quickly asked, "How are we to gain your freedom?"

"My concern is not for my freedom, Judas, my concern is Jesus. I am hearing that He is curing the sick, restoring sight and hearing to the blind and deaf, even raising the dead, regardless of their sect or political affiliation. I often wonder when He intends to establish His Kingdom."

"I don't have an answer for you," replied Judas, "Simon and I have been wondering the same thing. All He will tell me is that when the time comes, I will know what I must do. When I ask Him what it is that I must do, He answers only that I will know when the time is right."

"Judas, I want you to do something for me, please."

"Yes John, just ask and it shall be done!"

"Go to Jesus and ask Him if He is the one to come or should we expect someone else? I need to know that my efforts have not been in vain. Please, leave now and find Jesus. Do not worry about me, I will be fine. Go now and ask Jesus what I want to know."

After visiting with John for a little while longer, and convincing Herod's aide that John's cell needed new clean straw, Judas and Simon left Machaerus. They traveled back eastwardly crossed the Dead Sea and some time later arrived in Jerusalem. There they heard that Jesus had been seen nearby, so they traveled to the northeast and found Jesus preaching and bringing a widow's son back to life in Nain.

When they reached the place where Jesus was, they could not help but notice that all of the other Apostles had returned from their evangelistic journey. In conversations with them, Judas and Simon the Zealot discovered that they all had experience much the same treatment. Some people were believers, some were hecklers, and some were friendly and some not so friendly. All of the Apostles had tried to cure or restore sight, hearing, and life, but only those that prayed and fasted fervently were unable to do so. This, in a way, made Simon and Judas more comfortable in knowing that they were not the only ones that had trouble in performing miracles as the Master.

When the right opportunity came later that day, Judas approached Jesus and told Him about his trip to Machaerus. "Master, It was not my intent to disobey your orders to us, but while near here I got the news that John the Baptist had been thrown into prison by Herod Antipas. I knew that you would want to know about his well-being, so Simon and I went to Machaerus to see him."

"And did you see and speak to him?" asked Jesus.

"Yes Master, with the help of an old friend's son, who offered us shelter, food and clothing, we made an appointment with Herod, and obtained permission to speak to the Baptist."

"How is John? Is he in glad spirit?" inquired Jesus.

"Physically, he is well. Even though he is in a filthy environment, he is holding up well."

"And how is John spiritually, Judas?" Jesus asked again.

"Spiritually? I am not too sure. He seemed to be questioning whether his work up to now is valid, futile or in vain."

"What do you mean Judas?" asked Jesus with some perplexity.

Taking a deep breath so as to gain the courage to say what needed to be said, Judas answered, "Well Lord, he asked me to ask You if You are the one that is to come, or are should we expect someone else?"

Jesus looked down at His feet, and began drawing small circles in the sand with His right foot's toe. As He did so, He replied, "Go back and report to John what you hear and what you see. The blind receive sight, the lame walk, those who have leprosy are cured, the deaf hear, the dead are raised, and the good news is preached to the poor." Almost as an afterthought Jesus added, "Tell John also that blessed is the man who does not fall away on account of Me."

Judas then said, "Master, John wanted to know when You plan to establish Your Kingdom?" Judas waited with great anticipation for Jesus' answer since he too wanted to know Jesus' reply.

Jesus looked up and seemed to stare right into Judas' eyes for a fleeting moment, yet it seemed like an eternity to Judas. "Of all my Apostles and Disciples, you Judas, will know the day and hour before any one else."

The next day, as Judas was preparing to return to Machaerus the crowd had already gathered and Jesus had begun to preach to them. As Judas was leaving, he could hear Jesus saying to the crowd, "What did you go out into the desert to see? A reed swayed by the wind? If not, what did you go out to see? A man dressed in fine clothes? No, those who wear fine clothes are in kings' palaces. Then what did you go out to see? A prophet? Yes, I tell you and much more than just a prophet. He is the one about whom it is written: 'I will send my messenger ahead of you who will prepare your way before you.' I tell you truthfully, among those born of women there has not risen anyone greater than John the Baptist. Yet the one who is the least in the Kingdom of Heaven is greater than John the Baptist. For from the days of John the Baptist until now, the Kingdom of Heaven has been forcefully advancing and forceful men have lay hold of it. For all the Prophets and the Law have prophesied it until John. And if you are willing to accept it, he is the Elijah who was to come. He who has ears let him hear."

Jesus continued, "To what can I compare this generation? They are like children sitting in the marketplaces and calling out to the others saying 'We played the flute for you, and you did not dance. We sang a dirge and you did not mourn.' For John came neither eating nor drinking and they say, 'He has a demon inside him.'

I, the Son of Man, come eating and drinking and they say, 'Here is a glutton and a drunkard, a friend of tax collectors and sinners.' But wisdom is proved right by her actions."

By the time that Judas returned back to Machaerus, he learned that John the Baptist had been beheaded. Judas was told that it had happened on Herod's birthday. During a feast that was held in the Great Room in his palace, Herod had enticed Herodias' daughter to dance for him by offering her anything she wanted, even half of his kingdom. When she had finished dancing, she asked for the Baptist's head on a silver platter. Since Herod had promised under oath to give her what she wanted, he had the Baptist beheaded and his head brought on a silver platter and laid at Herodias' feet.

Judas was crushed by this news. He did not know what to do. He was so angry that he thought about killing Herod himself. It was a good thing that Simon was not with him on this return trip because he surely would have been the incendiary to light the fire of revenge in Judas' heart. He prayed for divine guidance and for the strength to restrain his desire for revenge. One of the commandments given to the chosen people through Moses kept going through his mind. *Do not seek revenge or bear a grudge against one of your people, but love your neighbor as yourself, for I am the Lord.* What ever Herod Antipas was, he was still Jewish, one of God's Chosen People.

Judas stayed in Machaerus for a few days with Mark Barasa's family. He felt too emotionally crushed to travel right away, but after a few days his heart began telling him that it would be best for him and for all concerned if he left and did not look back at what had happened for the moment. In his sorrow, he decided to stop by Kerioth to see his granduncle and grandaunt before returning to Jesus and the other Apostles to tell them the news of what had happened to John the Baptist. He stopped first in Jerusalem to see his old friend Cassandra Benjara. He had not seen Reuben and Leah or Cassandra for almost two years or so, since he left to follow the Baptist.

When he arrived at her grandfather's home, he knocked on the door but did not get an answer. He walked around to the back of the house were the porch was located, and there, working in the garden, he saw a man that he did not recognize at first. After a closer look, he knew it was Amos, Cassandra's Uncle.

"The Lord be with you Amos," said Judas, trying not to startle him.

Amos jumped a little, since he did not expect anyone, especially around the back of the house where he was working in the garden. After a long stare to focus his eyesight, he replied, "Ah Judas Iscariot, it is you! How are you, how are you, how are you?"

"I am fine and in the grace of our God Yahweh. And you Amos, I see you are still doing gardening for Cassandra and her grandfather."

After a very short but noticeable pause Amos said, "Come, let's sit under the porch. It will give us some refuge from this hot sun. Would you like some herb tea?"

"Please Amos, don't go to any trouble making any tea. I am alright."

"It's no bother, it is already made and in this earthen jar to keep it cool. Here, here is a nice clean glass for you." As he poured, he questioned Judas saying, "What brings you back around to Jerusalem? Last I heard you had left about a year or two ago to join up with Zacarias' son, what is he called? Ah yes, the Baptist."

I did serve as his disciple for about six months. Then I left to serve Jesus of Nazareth, who some believe, as I do, that He is the Messiah, and the Savior spoken about in the ninth chapter of the Book of Isaiah."

"Yes, I have heard of this Nazarene. I hear tell he heals people, and there are even claims that he has brought some people back from the dead. This is hard to believe Judas."

"Amos, believe it! I have witnessed it with my own eyes! He is the Son given to us by God and upon whose shoulders our eventual liberated government will rest. He is the Wonderful Counselor, and the Messiah. Some even call Him the Prince of Peace, since He constantly speaks of peaceful coexistence with all people. When He sets up His Kingdom, there will be no end to it and to the peace it will bring to His chosen people. He is from the House of David therefore He will reign from David's throne over His Kingdom, establishing and upholding it with justice and righteousness from that time on and forever. I tell you Amos, the zeal of the Lord Almighty will accomplish this."

"Well, I hope He is prepared to fight the Roman villains that killed my sister with their chariots, and my brother-in-law in Bethel. If I wasn't so old, I would join in and fight right along side of Him."

After sitting for a while, drinking tea and enjoying the conversation with Amos, Judas asked, "Where is Cassandra? Is she here or at the marketplace?"

"A puzzled look came over Amos. "Judas, I am sorry, I thought you had heard by now."

"Heard what?" replied Judas, with a stumped look about him.

"That Cassandra does not live here in Jerusalem anymore. When her grandfather died, she married a traveling Merchant from Cyprus in Greece that she met about seven months or so ago. She sent word to you with some of the Zealots, but I guess none of them got to see you before now."

Visibly moved, Judas asked, "Is she living in Cyprus?"

"Yes she is. She prayed for you every day that she was here." Putting his hand on Judas' forearm, Amos continued, "She felt your pain Judas, but she believed that she would never see you again when you left."

Somewhat melancholy Judas uttered, "Well, I am very happy for her. She deserves all the happiness that she can find. Next to John Zacarias, she has been my best friend. I have missed her dearly, and I will always have her deeply in my heart and in my prayers."

After a few moments of silence Amos looked at Judas and sadly spoke, "You probably don't know about your grandaunt and granduncle either do you?"

"What? What has happened to Leah and Reuben?" asked Judas anxiously.

"Last spring our God called Reuben back to heaven. It wasn't but a few months later that Leah followed him in death."

"Oh God, no! No, not them." He was visibly emotionally upset. Amos could see tears beginning to run down Judas' cheeks. "Did they suffer in their final hours?"

"No," replied Amos, "Both of their deaths were very peaceful. It is told that just before Leah succumbed, she kept insisting that all of her family were in the room with her, including her father, mother, her sister Sarah, your Uncle Reuben and your mother Sofia. She died with a happy smile on her face. They were both buried next to your mother Sofia's grave."

Amos tried to comfort Judas who cried copiously for the next half-hour or so.

"They left you their home and blacksmith shop. They wanted you to have it."

Judas asked Amos for some paper and a writing instrument. As a Scribe, he knew how to write a legal land deed. He therefore deeded his granduncle and grandaunt's property to Barabbas; authorizing him to sell under the condition that whoever bought the property would have to promise to take care of the three graves by the grove of trees near the back of the property. After he finished writing he asked Amos, "Amos my dear friend, would you do something for me?"

"Yes, of course I will. Just tell me what you want done."

"I want you to give this deed to Barabbas the next time you see him. I understand that he comes to Jerusalem quite often. Will you do that for me?"

"Yes, yes I will. I even know some of the people that are Zealots in his service. If he does not come in the next week or so, I will personally take this deed to him myself."

"Tell him it is for the cause of freedom. Next to giving it to me, I am sure Reuben and Leah would have wanted it to be used for the cause of freedom."

There was nothing to hold Judas in Jerusalem or Kerioth anymore, so he said goodbye to Amos and returned to Jesus and the rest of the Apostles.

When he met up with them, they were on their way to Nain to preach the good news. When he told Jesus of the Baptist fate, they both cried on each other's shoulder and comforted each other. Jesus said tearfully, "For this John was conceived, to prepare the way for the Son of Man. He is now in My Father's Kingdom. He has fulfilled his destiny." Looking at Judas with a look that Judas had never experienced before He told Judas, "You and I have yet to fulfill our destiny Judas. I tell you truly, even though my destiny is to be a sacrificial lamb, still I do not envy your destiny."

"What is my destiny Master? If you know, please tell me. Are you saying that you are ready to establish your Kingdom? Are you telling me that I will die in this struggle? If you are, I am prepared to lay down my life for the liberation of our people. Tell me Lord, what is my destiny?"

Touching Judas on the shoulder, Jesus said, "In due time, Judas, all will be made clear, and prophesy will be fulfilled. You will know what to do when the time comes."

Simon was happy to see Judas again. He had been worried that danger might have befallen Judas. When he saw him, Simon ran to embrace him and to tell him how he had prayed for his safe return. He also told Judas about a miracle that he had witnessed which he never would have believed Jesus would have performed because of the people involved.

"Just prior to leaving for Nain," recalled Simon, "Jesus and I and the rest of the Apostles had been in Capernaum. There a centurion's servant, whom the centurion loved and valued highly, was sick and about to die."

"A Roman centurion's servant?" repeated Judas, "Was he Jewish?.

"No!" replied Simon. "The centurion heard of Jesus and sent some elders of the Jews to Him asking Jesus to come and heal his servant. When they came to Jesus they pleaded earnestly with Him saying, 'This man deserves to have you do this because he loves our nation and has built our synagogue.'"

"So what happened next? Don't tell me that Jesus heal the centurion's servant?"

"Well, Jesus went with them. When He was not far from the house, the centurion himself came to Jesus and said, 'Lord, don't trouble yourself for I do not deserve to have you come under my roof. That is why I did not even consider myself worthy to come to you. Just say the word, and my servant will be healed. For I myself am a man with authority like You, with soldiers under my command. I tell one to go and he goes, and another one to come, and he comes. I say to my servants, to do this, and they do it. I know you command sickness, the weather elements, and even death! Just say the word, and I know with out doubt that he shall be healed.'"

"So what did Jesus do next?

"When Jesus heard this, He was amazed at the centurion's words and at the centurion's faith. He turned to the crowd following Him and he told them, 'I tell you, I have not found such great faith even in Israel. Go home now, for your faith has heeled your servant.' Then the centurion returned home and found the servant well!"

"I don't understand it," averred Judas, "what is the Master doing healing the enemies servants?"

"I don't know," replied Simon, "I sometimes wonder if and when the Master proposes to liberate His people. He is a hard Man to try to figure out."

As Simon was talking, a commotion got the attention of Judas. It looked and sounded like a funeral procession because of all the crying and wailing that could be heard. As the procession approached, Judas could see that it had also caught Jesus' attention. It had to pass right by where Jesus was preaching since He was preaching on the road that led to the cemetery. When the procession came to where Judas and Simon were standing, Judas asked one of the mourners who was the dead person in the open coffin.

"He was Caleb, the young son of Mariana, a widow from Nain. He was her only son, and her sole supporter."

The funeral procession went by Judas and when it reached the place where Jesus was standing, Jesus waited for the coffin to approach. When it came to Him, Jesus placed His hand on the coffin, and those carrying it stopped. Jesus looked at the grieving mother and friends, and then back down into the coffin. He then raised His eyes and made visual contact with Judas. He could feel Jesus' stare, burning down deep into the recesses of his soul. Jesus seemed to feel the same pity for the entourage of mourners that Judas felt. Although there were hundreds of on lookers, the silence became overpowering.

Judas saw Jesus look down at the corpse once again and then say with much authority, "Young man, I say to you, get up!"

The dead man sat up and began to talk and Jesus gave him back to his mother. The huge crowd that was listening to Jesus plus the crowd that was following the funeral procession were all filled with awe and began to praise God.

"A great prophet has appeared among us," some could be heard saying. Others were saying, "God has come to help his people. It is true that He has total command. He even rules over death, and it listens. He is truly the Messiah that will free us from the Romans as He frees this young man from the clutches of death!"

Even though this was not the first time that they had seen Jesus perform the miracle of raising the dead, Judas and Simon both stood there in complete wonderment.

The Pharisee Priests that were with the funeral procession began to question, doubt and looked at Jesus with much suspicion.

Jesus sensed this and He began to preach saying "I am the good shepherd; I know My sheep and My sheep know Me, just as My Father knows Me and I know the Father. I will lay down My life for the sheep. I have other sheep that are not of this sheep pen. I must bring them also. They too will listen to My voice, and there shall be one flock and one shepherd. The reason My Father loves Me is that I lay down My life—only to take it up again." Turning to look at Judas He continued saying, "No one takes it from Me, but I lay it down of My own accord. I have authority to lay it down and authority to take it up again. This command I have received from My Father."

At these words the Pharisee's were again divided. Many of them said, "He is demon-possessed and raving mad. Why listen to Him?"

But others said, "These are not the sayings of a man possessed by a demon. Can a demon open the eyes of the blind, or give life again to the dead?" To Judas, it was becoming more obvious with each passing day that the ruling Jews of the Sanhedrin were beginning to fear and object to Jesus and His teachings. Yet, he could not comprehend why, since every thing that Jesus did was for the good of the Jews.

It just so happened that at that very moment, in Jerusalem, the Sanhedrin Priests led by Caiaphas were meeting, discussing some complaints from concerned Pharisees that had seen Jesus and had heard Him speak. "What are we accomplishing?" asked Caiaphas. "Here is a man performing many miraculous signs. If we let him go on like this, everyone will believe in him. Then the Romans will come and take away both our authority and our nation."

"You know nothing at all," averred Caiaphas, "You do not realize that it is better for you that one man die for the people than that the whole nation perish." From that day on, they looked hard for ways to find Jesus guilty of any religious infraction that would be punishable by death, yet the harder they tried, the less they could find. If they were going to kill Jesus, they would have to find some false reason, because Jesus was careful not to break any of the major messianic laws.

Late one evening when they were through with supper, Judas approached Jesus who had been praying on a small hilltop just outside of their campsite. He waited until it became evident that He was through with His meditation, then Judas went over and spoke. "Master, may I have a word with you?"

"Judas, I was just praying for the both of us." He paused for a fleeting moment, then he continued, "It is a arduous path that lays ahead of us, that you and I must fulfill."

"Master, that is exactly what I want to speak to You about."

"I am listening Judas."

"For the past two years or so, I have been hearing You speak about the salvation of the Jews and the coming of Your Kingdom. Some of your Apostles and disciples have been waiting patiently for that day to come. I have even talked to Barabbas, who leads the army of insurrectionist. He is prepared, at a moment's notice, to hand over command of the army to You at Your request. All is ready for You, as the Messiah, and as it has been prophesied, to lead us into Your Kingdom."

"Judas, I have not come to lead an army! I have watched others that the Father has sent; who have lead armies and have liberated the Holy Land on many occasions for His people. Joshua, Ehud, Gideon, and David are some of those that led armies, but their gains through wars and talk of wars did not last. I have come to be the light of the world, so that whoever follows me will never walk in darkness nor will he ever be oppressed. I have come to free the souls of man from their own condemnation and sinful ways. For what benefit is it for a man to gain his freedom or gain the world, and loose his soul in the process? There is too much evil already in this world for the Son of Man to add to it. It is only for this that I have been sent by My Father, to be the sacrificial lamb through whose blood, death and resurrection, all sin and evil will be defeated, and the Kingdom of God will be achieved."

Confused and puzzled Judas asked, "Master, how could You have watched Joshua, Gideon and David? You are younger then I, and a descendent, many generations removed, from the House of David!"

"I will tell you Judas, the same as I told the unbelieving Pharisees at the temple, before any of them, even before Adam and Eve where conceived, I am."

Judas did not really understand what Jesus had told him. He only knew that he did not get the response that he was looking for. Now he was even more confused as to whether there was going to be a war to end all wars. Was Jesus, as the Messiah, going to lead the armies to regain the Kingdom of God that rightfully belonged to the Chosen People?

Perplexed Judas asked, "Master, I am confused. Last year, when you sent us out for the first time, in pairs to preach the coming of your Kingdom, didn't you tell us to go to the lost sheep of Israel and preach the message that 'The Kingdom of heaven is near?' Didn't You also say for us not to suppose that You came to bring peace to the earth? Your words at that time were, 'I did not come to bring peace, but a sword. For I have come to turn a man against his father, a daughter against her mother, a daughter-in-law against her mother-in-law to the point that a man's enemies will be his own household."

"Judas, do not seek a shepherd that will lead his sheep to slaughter, for you will not find him here. I have come to be the spiritual salvation of man, not its earthly liberator."

As Judas turned to walk away Jesus called to him. As he turned to face Him Jesus said, "The hour grows near, Judas. Will you be prepared to do that for which you have been born to do?"

Even more perplexed Judas answers, "I, hmm I don't know Master. When the time comes, I will be there to do what You decree."

Jesus added, "Just remember Judas, I will always love you and I will be with you when you do what you have to do."

For the next month or so, Judas continued to serve the Master faithfully. The crowds continued to grow with each passing day and with each miracle that Jesus performed. Once while at Capernaum, a collector of the two-drachma tax came to Peter, Judas, and Simon who were making pre-arrangement accommodations for Jesus' visit to that town once again. Jewish leaders collected taxes to pay for the upkeep of the temple and its services. Drachmas were Greek silver coins, (worth about seventy-five cents) about a day's wages. When the tax collector reached them he asked, "Doesn't your teacher pay the temple taxes?"

Judas replied, "Yes He does, He has always paid the temple tax. I know for I am the one that keeps His funds and pays the taxes. I would pay it now, but I do not have that much with me at the present time. When we return, we will pay you the tax."

They returned to where Jesus was staying at the moment and they told him what had happened. Judas explained that most of the funds had been spent several days back for lodging and food.

Jesus then told them, "Go to the lake and throw out your line. Take the first fish you catch; open its mouth and you will find a four-drachma coin. Take it and give it to them for my tax. The remainder Judas can hold for future use."

They did as the Master had instructed. Within a few minutes they caught a large fish weighing about two pounds or so. They opened it up and inside its stomach was a four-drachma coin as Jesus had predicted. They went from there directly to the tax collector and paid the tax.

Chapter 14
Judas' Dilemma

Shortly after the fish event, Jesus and His Apostles and Disciples traveled to Bethany where Jesus was preaching about redemption and repentance. Barabbas came into the huge crowd that was following Jesus. Since many enemies of the revolution knew him by this time, he came in disguise. Judas was distributing some breadbaskets to the faithful onlookers when Barabbas approached him.

When they saw each other, they hugged and Barabbas spoke. "Judas, my friend, I heard that your Messiah was close by so I came to see you and thank you for your generosity and support."

Still in an embrace Judas replied, "Barabbas! It is good to see you. I was becoming worried about you. I had not heard a word from you in such a long time."

"I have been busy fighting on various fronts and dodging the whole Roman army. They are really making an all out effort to squash our rebellion. I have never seen so many Legions of Roman Soldiers in Judea. I fear that in the next two or three week, more Legions will be brought in from Rome, just to try and capture me."

"Why do you think the Romans are doing that?" asked Judas.

"My revolutionist are really hurting the Romans in the pocket. Most of the tax collectors are not collecting any taxes for fear that they may be robbed and killed. Those that do collect any sort of revenue, we try to relieve them of their take. Tiberius is so enraged that a few months ago he relieved General Pantera as the Procurator and replaced him with a man named Pontius Pilate. He left Pantera here in our midst, in charge of all the occupational forces with the direct order to get rid of me and my insurgents or face death himself."

"Be careful Barabbas, he is a treacherous man. He has many spies that would sell you out at a moments notice for less then a shekel."

"I know," answered Barabbas, looking suspiciously around, "That is why I am here. My sources tell me that certain powerful Pharisees and partisans of Herod, together with some of the Priests and Scribes of the Synagogue are plotting against Jesus. They want to see Him dead."

"Why?" gulped Judas, "Why would they want to do Him harm? He, and all of us are Jews, just like they are. It doesn't make any sense."

"They feel threatened by Him. Every day His following gets bigger and bigger. They are jealous because of the miracles He performs. They can not do any of that, so they are attempting to convince everyone that He is demon possessed."

"But why? What could be their charge?" questioned Judas.

Still very uneasy and fidgety Barabbas replies, "He is expelling demons, He is claiming to be able to forgive sins, and He is healing and doing a lot of 'thou shall nots' on the Sabbath. He is also making His own interpretations of the Laws of Moses. They are accusing Him of blasphemy and false prophesy which, as you are well aware, are mortal violations, punishable by death. I tell you Judas, if He is going to lead my army as the Savior of the Chosen People, He better do it soon, because things are getting hotter, tighter and tougher. Nicodemus and the few friend of Jesus can't stop them much longer, and if any more soldiers are brought over from Rome, we may not be able to handle them."

Sounding out his frustration, Judas said, "I have spoken to Jesus on several occasions about when He intends to start setting up His Kingdom, but He appears reluctant to do it."

"Is He or isn't He the Messiah?" questioned Barabbas in a restricted louder voice.

"I know He is the Messiah spoken of in the Scripture. All the signs and miracles I have seen first hand have proven it to me beyond any doubt, time and time again."

Somewhat disgruntled Barabbas states, "I don't know how much time we have left before Pantera makes it so tough that my soldiers will begin leaving me. As much as they love freedom, they are no fools, they know when the odds are against us. They seem to love life better, and I don't blame them. I know that we do not have that much time left. The feast of the Passover will soon be upon us, so I anticipate a break in the pressure being asserted. But after that, I cannot assure that I will even be around if we do not counter attack soon after."

Pausing for just a little while to allow Judas to think, Barabbas then added, "By the way, I was able to purchase much needed supplies with the money I received from selling the blacksmith shop." Putting his hand on Judas' shoulder and giving it a gentle shake, Barabbas added, "I know it was a difficult thing for you to do, but I assure you, your terms of keeping the graves properly kept were explicit and accepted without condition." As an after thought Barabbas added, "I wish I had another twenty or thirty pieces of silver, then I could really outfit my troops to the point that I would not need the Messiah to lead the insurrection. I would lead it myself and run the Romans all the way back to Rome!"

"I still feel deep in my heart that is what Reuben would have wanted, to be of service to the revolution, even in death! Where can I get a hold of you if I need to talk to you?" asked Judas.

"I am staying at my cousin Vesper's home in Jerusalem. You know Vesper don't you?"

Judas nodded his head as a sign that he knew Vesper.

Barabbas continued, "I can be reached there if you need me."

"You are staying in Jerusalem?" replied Judas in total surprise. "That is the hub of the enemy's web!"

"Can you think of a safer place then right under the enemy's nose?" He gave a chuckle, and just before saying goodbye he added, Remember Judas, we have two to three weeks at most to strike." He hugged Judas and made his way through the crowd and left.

Judas then meandered through the crowd hoping to find Simon the Zealot. The crowd was so large that it took almost an hour to work his way around it and to find him. He was sitting by an old man and woman who had their grandchild with them. Simon was holding the baby on his knee, bouncing him as if he was riding a horse while the older couple ate their bread and pieces of fish. By the time Judas found him, the woman was just finishing her meal.

"Simon!" shouted Judas from a distance. He finally got his attention and after giving the child back to the woman, he came to meet Judas.

"Judas. Have you tasted the fish? It is delicious! I wonder where in the world did Brother Phillip get all this fish and bread? About two hours ago when I was standing by him, he was concerned that all he could get were measly four or five fishes and one or two loaves of bread. How and where did he get all this food?"

"I don't know Simon, this isn't the first time Jesus has fed four or five thousand people with hardly any food available. Anyway, I have not seen any of the other Apostles in the last hour to ask them how Jesus did it. I have been with Barabbas."

"Barabbas!" said Simon loudly.

"Shhh," averred Judas putting his finger up to his lips. "Yes, Barabbas. He was here to see me and he asked for a specific day when the Master plans to lead the revolution."

"So, what did you tell him Judas?"

"I told him that I did not know." Beginning to pace a little, Judas continued, "Simon, everyday I get more and more confused. Some days I think that He is talking about being the savior of the world, then the next day He is talking about being the sacrificial lamb that will take away the sins of the world. I swear, it is getting harder and harder to tell what Jesus plans to do."

"So what did Barabbas say when you told him you did not know?"

"He told me that much pressure is being put on him by the Roman army. Pantera has been relieved as Procurator by someone called Pontius Pilate, and now Pantera is in charge of the entire Roman occupational army with only one purpose in life, that is to capture Barabbas. Barabbas does not think that he can hold his troops together much longer then the Feast of the Passover because they are afraid for their own lives and for the lives of their loved ones that they left behind. They know that it is not above Pantera to begin executing innocent people to get to Barabbas."

"There doesn't appear to be much time left then does it?" replied Simon.

"No there isn't, only two or three weeks at most. I can't seem to get the urgency of this matter across to the Master no matter how much and how hard I try."

"If the Master is wavering like you say, you'll just have to confront Him again and force His hand," stated Simon.

"How?" asked Judas in a very perplexed tone.

"I don't know, but there has to be a solution to this dilemma, there always is a solution if you think hard enough." Rubbing his beard and chin Simon continued, asking, "What else did Barabbas say?"

"Not much more. He thanked me for Reuben's property, which he sold for fifteen pieces of silver. He said that he used that money to buy much need weapons and supplies. He also said that if he just had another twenty to thirty more pieces of silver, he could outfit all of his troops to the point that he himself could lead the troops and beat the Romans all the way back to Rome without the Messiah."

A look of complete surprise came over Simon, then he said in a jubilant voice, "Judas, that's it! That's the answer!"

With a more confused look than ever Judas asked, "What's the answer?"

"If we can't convince Jesus to lead the revolution, then maybe you can raise the money for Barabbas to get the supplies and weapons that he needs to lead the militia into battle himself."

Shaking his head a little, indicating the impossibility of achieving what Simon was asking, Judas then added, "Thirty pieces of silver is a lot of money to raise in a week or two Simon. We haven't much time. Even if I borrowed whatever we raise in the ministry for the next week or two, it would never be enough. Besides, that would not be fair for Jesus and the other ten Apostles."

"I agree. What we are now getting from the ministry would never amount to what you need," concluded Simon, "But you have to do something to help Jesus establish His Kingdom.

After pondering the question and dilemma at hand for a little while, Simons eyes lid up and he said, "Maybe that's what you are destined to do! Ever since you were a child, no bigger then the top of my sandal, you have been anguished by some feeling; some vision that you were destined for something. Even your dear mother, may she rest in peace, is said to have had apparitions telling her that her offspring was destined to fulfill prophesy." Getting more exited as he talk, Simon added, "And on several occasions you have told me that Jesus Himself has referred to a task or job that you must be prepared to perform. Don't you see Judas? I would bet that this is your destiny, to insure that Jesus has His Kingdom here on earth, even if He does not lead the liberation army!"

"I don't know Simon, it all sounds so incredible," murmured Judas.

"No. No it doesn't. Just listen to me. Who are, supposedly, the leaders of the Jewish people?" asked Simon.

Not really knowing why Simon posed that question, Judas said, "There is only one group that I can think of since we do not have our own King and our own form of government now. That would be the High Priest Caiaphas and the other eighty or so priests of the Sanhedrin."

"Right! Now, don't you think that Jesus would need to have some form of support from them, or at very least not any opposition from them if He is to become the King of all Judea?"

After some brief thought Judas answered, "Well, yes, it would make it easier if He had their support, but it would not be absolutely necessary. Besides, He could use His awesome powers and snap His fingers and change their attitudes towards Him in a flash!"

"Your right Judas, He could, but He won't. How many times have you heard the Master say that He is there to lead His sheep, but it is up to them if they want to follow or not. For that matter Judas, following your logic, He could turn all Romans into Jews and force them to love our religion, our culture, and be done with it. Yet you and I know that's not the Master's way."

More bewildered then ever, Judas snapped, "What are you getting to Simon?"

"The more I think about it, the more I am convinced that it is your destiny to help begin the armed conflict by getting Barabbas' forces all the equipment and supplies they need. Judas, your destiny is to be the conduit between the fighting forces and the Master. This is your destiny, I am sure of it! It is you who must insure a glorious victory for our people, and then the Master will rise to the throne of David. Once the Sanhedrin sees that we are victorious, they will embrace Jesus with open arms; and I am now convinced that is exactly why Jesus is waiting, for them to accept Him as the Lord and Christ (meaning Savior) and as King of all Jews."

"Most Jews that have heard Jesus and have witnessed His miracles already are hailing Him the Christ," averred Judas.

"Yes," said Simon, more determined to convince, "But not the Sanhedrin, which is the most important body of the Jewish world. As a matter of fact, didn't you say that according to Barabbas, they are ready to have Jesus killed for blasphemy and false prophecy because of their petty jealousy? So what if He eats with whores, tax collectors and thieves? So what if He heals the deaf, raises the death and tells people that He forgives their sins on the Sabbath? Once they see that the freedom fighters are running the Romans out of Palestine, they will be the first to proclaim Jesus as their King."

By this time, Judas was in deep thought. Maybe Simon was right. What else could his destiny be? He finally talked again saying, "Simon, if I have to do this, I will need your help. You and I need to begin thinking about how I am going to raise that much money. Let's pray for an answer for the next few days, then lets talk about it again to see what ideas we come up with by then."

"Okay Judas, I will pray and fast, hard, and I will think about it every free minute that I have. I am sure that in a few days we will come up with something, just as sure as the Passover is coming, we'll think of something." As Simon started to walk away, he stopped and whirled around and jokingly shouted to Judas, "Hey, I just had an idea!"

"What?" asked Judas, very surprised and unaware that Simon was just joking with him.

"It's almost the perfect time for you to pester the Master again about leading the Army towards victory!"

"Why?" asked Judas.

"Because," answered Simon very coyly and with a laugh in his voice, "If He gets angry enough to turn you over to the Romans for being such a pest, just remember this. The Passover is coming, and as has happened in the past, you might be the lucky one that the Procurator Pontius Pilate forgives and release from custody as is customary for him to do on the Feast of the Passover. You won't suffer long." He let out a laugh as he walked away leaving Judas confused, standing underneath the tree where they had been speaking. After a few seconds, Judas understood that Simon was only joking with him as he usually did. He went back to serving the bread and fishes that Simon left behind, to the hordes of people that were there to listen to Jesus.

When the evening had come, the Apostles where gathered together laying on the ground, on their night bedding, resting. They were relaxing after a hard day of monitoring and servicing the largest crowd that had come to hear Jesus speak. They were discussing the fact that some people believed without a doubt the multiplication of loaves and fishes that happened that day, while others still did not believe although they were there and saw what had happened first hand.

"I could not see how we were going to feed all those people," stated Philip. "I knew that Judas did not have enough money in the coffers to buy the amount of food we needed to feed all of them."

"The last time this happened, there were only about four thousand or so that we had to feed," stated Peter, "But this time, there had to be well over five thousand or more, don't you think so Andrew?"

"Yes, there had to be, but tell me Philip, what happened out there? I saw you talking with the Master just before we began passing out the baskets of bread and fish."

Standing up in front of the other Apostles and disciples Phillip said, "Well, Jesus came to me and asked me, 'Where shall we buy bread for these people to eat?' I still wonder why he asked me that question. I can only think that He was testing my faith or me. I quickly replied that it would take at least eight months wages or more to buy that much bread and food, and as I told you before, I knew that Judas could not possibly have that much in the treasury."

"It would have taken eight months wages just for each one to have a bite or two, and not much more then that!" added Nathanael.

"I was the one that pointed out to the Master that there was a boy, who had about five loaves of bread and two fishes or so," boasted Peter, also standing up and looking around as if seeking peer approval.

"Yes you did," snapped Philip, "But you also were the first who said that you did-n't see how that measly amount would feed them all!"

There was some laughter from all the other Apostles since they knew Peter well. He was always trying to be the 'take charge' sort of man ever since the Master renamed him "The Rock". In reality he was the type that talked better then he acted. He was a brash young man, though older then the rest of the Apostles, and was very boastful and brazen, and acted too hastily at, times. When they laughed, he looked at all of them with a very commanding look. His dark thick eyebrows gathered tightly towards his upper brow when he said, "Go on with your story, Philip, but we don't need any more of those idle remarks." Peter then, very humbly, sat back down again.

Philip continued as Peter requested. "Well, it was about that time that the Master asked Peter and I to begin telling the people to sit down on the side of the hill. There was plenty of grass, so it was not an uncomfortable place to sit at all. Jesus then asked Peter to get the loaves and fishes from the boy and to bring them to him. When he did, Jesus looked up towards heaven, broke the bread and fishes into what I though were halves, then He blessed it and prayed to God. It sounded like a thanksgiving prayer. Then the strangest thing happened."

By that time, the rest of the Apostles were real curious about what happened next. Thomas seemed to be the most curious of the twelve, so he asked, "What? What happened then? Don't leave us in all this suspense!"

"To tell you the truth, I did not see anything else happen, that's what is so strange. Jesus just told us to begin distributing the food. He had several empty baskets brought to Him and He just kept taking fish and bread from the boy's basket that He had blessed, and putting them in the other baskets. He then told us to let the people have as much as they wanted. I tell you the truth, I have never seen anything like this, and this is the second time He has fed very large crowds from almost nothing."

It suddenly became very quite, as if they were all in awe. But just then Peter jumped up again to take center stage and said, "But that's not all! What is really amazing, is that when we picked up all the leftovers, as the Master commanded saying, 'Gather all the leftovers, do not let any go to waste,' there were twelve baskets completely full of bread and fish. Isn't that right Philip?"

"That's right Peter, I guess I know what we will be eating for the next few days!" This statement made in jest by Philip seem to break the intense deep concentration and tension that all the Apostles were feeling while listening to the events of the day. No matter how many miracles that they had observed first hand in the last three years, the Apostles never lost the feeling of wonder and awe they experienced every time they witnessed things like this. They enjoyed recounting what had happened, especially emphasizing what part, however insignificant, they played in each one of those miracles.

Shortly thereafter as the apostles rested, Jesus walked into the camp with a urn of water and a wash basin. He took off His outer clothing and wrapped a towel around His waist. Having loved His own that were in the world, he now was going to show the Apostles the full extent of His love. After Jesus poured water into the basin He began to wash His Apostles feet, drying them with the towel that was wrapped around Him. When He came to Peter, he said, "Lord, are you going to wash my feet?"

Jesus replied, "You do not realize now what I am doing, but later you will understand the significance of this deed."

Pulling his feet away, Peter said, "No, you shall never wash my feet! You are the Master!"

Jesus looked at Peter with a look that conveyed strong authority, but much benevolence and said, "Unless I wash you, you have no part with me." Every thing became so silent, that you would hear the waves of the river near by as they slammed on to the shore.

After looking around at the others and back at Jesus, Peter replied, "Then Lord, not just my feet but my hands and my head as well!"

Jesus washed each of the Apostles feet including Simon the Zealot and Judas. When he had finished washing all of the Apostles' feet, he then washed the feet of six disciples that were there with them. Almost all of the disciples had abandoned Jesus when He told them that they would have to eat His body and drink His blood while they were in Capernuam. They did not understand that Jesus was speaking figuratively as He sometimes did, and did not mean it literally. When most of his other disciples heard this, they thought that Jesus was trying to start some new sect that included some form of cannibalism. From that time on, hundreds of disciples abandoned Him, except a mere few and His Apostles.

When finished, He put on His clothes and returned to his place and said, "Do you understand what I have done for you?" He looked around and saw nothing but puzzled looks on their faces, so He began to explain as He normally had to do every time He did something or spoke in parables. "You call Me Teacher and Lord and rightly so, for that is what I am. Now that I, your Lord and Teacher, have washed your feet, you also should wash one another's feet. I have set you an example that you should do as I have done for you. I tell you, no servant is greater than his master is, nor is a messenger greater than the one who sent him. Now that you know these things, you will be blessed if you do them.

The Apostles wondered what the Master meant by this, so Peter, who seemed to always take the lead in asking the questions, why, what, and how of things, asked Jesus, "Lord, are we to wash everyone's feet that we meet? Is this a ritual that you want us to perform like a baptism?"

"No Peter, don't you understand why I did it? I did it to show you a lesson, that all of those who want to be first will be last, and those that want to be exulted must first be humbled and be a servant to those that follow him."

Then Jesus left them and went on His way to pray and meditate. All was quit as each tried to grasp the significance of what had just happened.

Several days had gone by since the last meeting with Barabbas. Judas had not yet come up with any clear-cut solution to his dilemma. He had attempted to ask Jesus once again about when He would begin establishing His Kingdom, but as usual, he did not get an answer that he could clearly understand.

Jesus answered him saying, "No one knows about that day or hour, not even the angels in heaven, nor the Son, but only the Father."

That same day, after the discussion with Jesus, Judas spoke with Simon the Zealot and asked him if he had come up with any ideas. "No I have not," was Simon's reply. "I have fasted and prayed and thought hard about it but I have not come up with any solutions. It's funny, every time I have had a problem like this to solve in the past, I generally have the answer staring me in the face within a day or two." Scratching his head, he continued, "But this time, it seems the more I think about it, the harder it becomes to solve. How about you Judas, do you have any ideas?"

"I only have one, and it came to me a few nights ago as I laid watching the lightening that appeared to be flashing over Jerusalem. It is a little risky I know, but it is the only thing that I can think of that would get me the money that Barabbas needs, and still not cause any harm to anyone."

"Pray tell me, what is it?" questioned Simon with mounting curiosity.

"It's an idea that came to me from something you said as a witty remark. When I told you that I did not know whether to ask Jesus again about leading the rebellion you told me something in jest. Do you remember what you said?"

Stumped and not able to remember, Simon answered, "No, I can't say that I do."

You told me that it was the best time to approach Jesus again because if the Master turned me over to the Romans for being a pest, I would not be in their custody for long." By this time Simon started to remember what he had said in jest and was shaking his head denoting agreement. Judas went on revealing his plan. "You said, that the Passover is coming, and as has happened in the past, the Roman Procurator would forgive my debts or offenses, and release me from custody as is customary for him to do on the Feast of the Passover."

"Yes, now I remember saying that! So what's the plan you thought up from that?"

"Okay, listen carefully Simon. What if I go to see Caiaphas and the other heads of the Sanhedrin. They know me, and I would not have any problem getting an audience with them. I have served them before as a Scribe, and I feel certain that they still hold me in high esteem."

"So you go to Caiaphas, then what?" asked Simon whose curiosity was peaking.

"What if I go to them and promise to hand over the Master for thirty or more pieces of silver? You know how bad they have wanted to put a stop to Jesus' ministry since they all feel that it under minds their authority"

"What?" said Simon almost in a shout. "Have you lost your mind?"

"No Simon," Judas said, shaking his open palms slightly in a left to right motion. "Just listen to me. I would agree to this if, and only if they let the Roman Procurator Pontius Pilate incarcerate Him. Then, in two or three days I can go and petition Pontius Pilate to release Jesus as the custom dictates. That way we have the money that Barabbas needs, Jesus is protected from the Sanhedrin, and His release assured in just a few days. It's a perfect plan!"

"Judas, that is a very risky plan in deed," cautioned Simon, "How can you trust Caiaphas and the rest of the Sanhedrin to do what they will promise you? No one knows better then you how sneaky those Pharisees can be."

"I know them" countered Judas, "And they know me. I will make them swear an oath before I deliver the Master to them. Be they what they may be, they will have no choice but to abide by an oath sworn in the name of our God Yahweh. Besides, they would not dare alienate that many people that have been following Jesus and have seen His miracles and have placed their faith in Him, by doing otherwise."

"How do you know for sure that the Procurator Pilate would release Him? How do you insure that?"

"Rome does not have a problem with Jesus. Their problem is with the freedom fighters. There are many suspicions between the Romans and the Sanhedrin. I was there when Procurator Pantera personally came to interrogate Caiaphas, asking him to tell where John the Baptist was preaching. They have always suspected, though wrongfully, that the Sanhedrin is behind the rebellion."

"So what does that matter?" asked Simon.

"It matters in that I can almost guarantee that Pontius Pilate will not find any fault with Jesus. How can anyone that talks about 'Peace, loving your enemy' and 'turning the other cheek', be a threat to the Romans? Can't you see Simon? The Romans have always perceived that the real threat is the Sanhedrin and therefore will do just the opposite of what they would have the Romans do?"

Simon was rubbing his beard and chin as he usually did when he was faced with a difficult decision. He was looking down at the ground trying to visualize how this whole scenario would unfold once it was put into motion. "I don't know Judas, it sounds innocent and simple enough, but there are too many unknowns for my taste."

Judas kept insisting, "It is a simple plan, and workable just as I have described. I tell you Simon, I don't know what else to do that would be as simple and that would get us all what we need."

"That's just the problem that I am having with it. It is too simple and practical," averred Simon as he walked around very nervously. "I would advise you to put this plan in reserve, to be used only if you have not come up with any other alternative in the next few days. I would also advise you to think about all the thing that could go wrong, and cover those possibilities."

"I will," answered Judas. "I only wish I could get a sign from God or the Master if this is what I am destined to do and if what I am planing is the right thing to do."

Putting his arm around Judas Simon said, "Pray for an answer Judas, prayer is what you need, and that is what you and I will do. So they knelt down and began to chant passages from the Torah for some time.

That night Jesus and His Apostles were invited by a man named Simon, a Leper that Jesus cured, to come and eat supper at his home. While they were there a woman came to Jesus with an alabaster jar of very expensive perfume made out of pure nard, which she poured on Jesus' head as He was reclining at the table. Simon the Zealot and Judas who were present began talking amongst themselves.

"Why this waste of perfume? It could be sold for at least two or three pieces of silver or more. That would be a good start towards what you need!" declared Simon.

"Yes! By the God of Jacob, I can't believe it!" Judas was shocked. "It could have brought at least one full year's wages, and it could have been a beginning of an answer to our problem. I am sure the Master knew that she was coming and was going to do that. Why did He not stop her?"

Jesus could hear the protesting since most of the Apostles were talking to each other, wondering why it could not have been sold and the money given to the poor. Jesus then said, "Leave her alone. Why are you bothering her? She has done a beautiful thing to Me. The poor you will always have with you, and you can help them anytime you want. But you will not always have Me. She did what she could. She poured perfume on My body beforehand to prepare Me for My burial. I tell you, where ever the gospel is preached throughout the world, what she has done will also be told, in memory of her."

When Judas saw and heard this, he was furious so he excused himself and walked outside of the house. Simon followed shortly. He found Judas in a state of anger.

"What is the matter Judas?" asked Simon.

Judas was pacing up and down, angered at what he had seen. He told Simon, "I can not believe that the Master would allow such waste. I am positive that He knows how much we need the money to overthrow the Romans!" After a pause, and totally upset, Judas states, "Simon, I have to go, I have something to do. Please tell the Master, if He asks for me, that I will be back later."

"Where are you going Judas?"

"I feel sure that the only way to raise the money is to do what you and I discussed a day or so back. If I do not return back here, I will see you back at the campsite."

Judas walked swiftly down the covered walkway, made a turn at the street, and began to walk the four miles to Jerusalem in a very annoyed mood. When he had walked about a mile or so, his temper had subsided. He prayed the prayer that King David composed in his desolation and despair, the one written in the Torah that Judas had memorized as a youngster. Some of the verses that he recited were:

"My God my God, why have you forsaken me? Why are you so far from saving me, so far from the words of my groaning? O my God, I cry out by day, but you do not answer, by night, I am not silent, but still, I receive no answer."

Judas placed special emphasis on the verse that says,

"You brought me out of the womb, you made me trust in you even at my mother's breast. From birth I was cast upon you; from my mother's womb you have been my God. Do not be far from me, for trouble is near and there is no one to help."

As Judas prayed, he had his hands intertwined around the necklace that his granduncle and grandaunt had given him, the one that had belonged to his mother. Ever since he was old enough to understand, they told him that the necklace had belonged to his mother and that she was wearing it when she died, giving birth to him. They also told him that it had been in the maternal side of his mother's family for about ten or so generations. He always wore it under his outer garments because it made him feel close to his mother, even though he never knew her. Sometimes when he was really down in spirits, he would hold the brooch in his hands and speak to it as if he was speaking to his mother. Tonight he was talking to her in silence saying,

"Mother dearest, how you must have loved me to give up your life for me. I have been told that on the night of my birth you had a choice of whether to miscarry me and save your life, or to give me life, knowing full well that in doing so, you would loose yours. Had you lived, you could not have shown me any greater love then what you showed by dying for me. No greater love can a person have then this. I have always felt your presence, as I do at this moment. Please watch over me in these times of trial and tribulation. I long for the day that we can all be together again in the house of our God Jehovah."

Praying all the way under a star-filled sky that shined brightly with the glow of a full moon seemed to make the two-hour jaunt shorter than it really was. The walk was somewhat hilly but it was all so beautiful under the full moon and the night sky, particularly the Mount of Olives as he neared his destination. When he arrived in Jerusalem he went to the house of his old friend Cassandra's Benjara's Uncle Amos. It was about nine o'clock at night and Amos had just retired for the night.

When Judas arrived, he knocked on the door by the kitchen entrance. Amos suspected beggars at this time of night so Judas could hear Amos saying, "Go away! I have nothing for you at all tonight. Come back tomorrow, I'll have something for you to eat then."

"Amos, please, open your door to me, it is I, Judas Iscariot. Please Amos, I must speak to you."

After a few more supplications Judas saw a lantern light appear in the kitchen where he had been knocking. As the door opened a little, Amos' head and part of his shoulders peered from around the door. When he saw it was Judas, he said, "Judas! For God's sake, what are you doing here at this hour?"

"Amos, my dear friend, I have come to ask a huge favor of you."

"What is it Judas, what can I do for you?"

"I would like the use of your facilities here at your home so I can make myself presentable."

With a confused look Amos asked, "Presentable? For what?"

"I must go to the upper city, to see the Chief Priest Caiaphas tonight."

"Tonight? Judas, everyone has retired for the night by now. No one will see you tonight."

"I have to at least try. It is a matter of great urgency that I see him and I do not have the time to discuss it now, nor am I at liberty to talk about it. Please Amos, I am not trying to be capricious, just please understand."

Moving away from behind the door and opening it wide enough for Judas to enter, Amos said in a somewhat bewildered tone, "Sure Judas, I understand. My house has always been your house. Come, do what ever you have to do."

"I need to bath, shave, and I need to get a change of clothes from you. I must look very presentable to Caiaphas. Can you help me with that?"

After some hesitation and flinching around as if thinking what clothes were good enough to give Judas, Amos replied, "Sure, sure I can help you with all of that."

Judas took a bath in a large tub that already had water in it, left over from the last time Amos bath himself. Then he used Amos' paraphernalia to shave and trim his moustache and beard. All the while, Amos was looking at the transformation in appearance that Judas was going through. He even asked Judas if he could trim his hair since it appeared to be too long and unmanageable, and Judas agreed. When he had finished, he led Judas into Cassandra's bedroom where he had laid out his best outfit for Judas to wear. Walking in to the room, Judas could not help but think of Cassandra. The whole room still held a lingering sweet smell of her, even after all this time.

Two hours after having arrived at Amos' home, he was all cleaned up and ready. He looked at himself in the reflecting tin on the wall in Cassandra's room. He could not help but wonder how many times she had gazed at herself in this tin. For the first time it came to his mind, "How beautiful, sweet and kind she was." She was so much in his mind while in her room, that he imagined that he actually saw her reflection in the tin, next to his image.

When he walked out of Cassandra's room into the kitchen, Amos gave a look of approval and said, "Now Judas, you look like your old self, you look very presentable and prosperous even!"

Judas thanked Amos for all of his help, blessed the house and said shalom. He walked to Caiaphas home that was located in the section of Jerusalem called the Upper City. His house was only a few hundred yards from the theatre pavilion. By the time he got there it was almost midnight. Judas knew from past experience that there was always a servant left on duty. His responsibility was to stay awake and serve as gatekeeper and guard near the entryway. It was not uncommon for people, especially from the Procurator's Palace or members of the Sanhedrin, to come seeking the Chief Priest at all hours of the night.

Chapter 15
Initiation of the Ill-fated Plan

When he arrived at the gate, Judas rang a bell that was attached to the gate. He did not have to ring it more then twice before the gatekeeper and a guard came to meet him.

"Identify yourself and what business you have at this hour at the house of the Almighty Chief Priest Caiaphas?" demanded the guard.

"I am Judas Iscariot, the Chief Scribe form the Synagogue of Kerioth. I came to seek the Honorable Caiaphas on a matter of great urgency for him and for the Sanhedrin."

"Who sent you?" inquired the guard.

"I come under standing orders from General Octavio Pantera to report what I know to the Chief Priest." Sensing some hesitation on the part of the guard Judas added, "The General will be very disappointed to learn that I was not admitted and given an audience with Caiaphas immediately."

"Show me your credentials or your commission," demanded the guard.

"The only commission here is the commission of error you are about to embark on. I will not stand here and argue with a mere guard. May the wrath of General Pantera come down on you personally when I tell him you denied him entrance, for to deny me, his envoy entrance, is to deny him personally." Judas began to walk away knowing that the guard would have no choice but to acquiesce.

"Stop!" yelled the guard as Judas walked. "Enter and follow me." He led Judas into an anteroom that had beautiful polished marble floors that were so sparkling and shiny that you could have eaten off the floor. The anteroom was decorated with beautiful paintings and rich hanging rugs and had a very high ceiling. The ceiling's roof was made of some form of translucent material that let in the light to feed the live trees and plants that were planted in an atrium located in the middle of the room. He waited there as the guard had instructed, for about thirty minutes. Eventually he heard the shuffling of feet coming closer to him. It wasn't long before he could see Caiaphas approaching. He was wrapped in a night coat with some form of nightcap still on his head. Under different circumstances, the sight of Caiaphas dressed like that would have been quite funny to Judas.

As Caiaphas neared, he recognized Judas and said, "Judas, what a surprise! I did not know that you were still in Kerioth. Someone told me that you had gone in search of the Baptist, God rest his soul."

"Greetings to you Caiaphas! Yes I did go in search of the Baptist, just to find out first hand if what they were saying about him was true or not."

"And what did you find out?" inquired Caiaphas interestingly.

"I found a man that was not seeking insurrection as reported, but a man that was asking people to repent of their sins and prepare for the coming of the Messiah as predicted in the Holy Book."

"Oh!" voiced Caiaphas, "that's interesting. What else have you learned?"

"I have learned that you are disturbed by the man called Jesus the Nazarene," mouthed Judas very coyly and tentatively.

"Where did you hear this, may I ask?"

Risking exposing his plot Judas very carefully stated, "Anyone who does what Jesus does, who claims to be the Messiah, eats and consorts with thieves and whores and who claims to have the power to forgive sin, I know would be of interest to you. If not, then I know He would be of interest to General Pantera!"

"So, what is your purpose here today?" asked Caiaphas prudishly.

Judas wavered a little bid, then grasped the medallion hanging on his chest with his left hand. He then uttered, "I am here to do both of us some good. First of all, General Pantera wants to capture the rebel leader Barabbas, and you want that man Jesus so that you can stop this division that is happening within your faithful followers. If I were willing to turn Jesus over to you, it appears to me that you can accomplish both feats. And by the way, I am sure General Pantera would be most grateful to you but Procurator Pontius Pilate would be the most obligated to you, if you know what I mean."

"How do you figure that?" queried Caiaphas with some interest.

"Well, to begin, I would never turn Jesus over to General Pantera. I have never liked him much ever since he came here and disgustingly accused you of harboring the rebels in front of me. However, I would gladly turn Jesus over to Pontius Pilate since he is the Procurator, and in a much better position to reward whom ever stops these rebels. Besides, I wouldn't want an underling to get the credit and thereby alienate Pilate. Pilate can do more for the Jews now then Pantera can. Anyway, I can assure you that Pontius Pilate will then want to turn Jesus over to Pantera, who can then find out from him were Barabbas might be hiding."

"How would Jesus know where Barabbas is hiding"

"I don't know, but naven't you yourself thought of Jesus as an instigator? If He is as you say, then He has to know where Barabbas is hiding!"

Looking very interested in what Judas was saying, Caiaphas asked, "And what is your need that would be filled if this happens?"

"Oh Honorable Caiaphas, I am almost ashamed to ask it, but I have no choice. For the last three years, I have dedicated my life to finding the truth about John the Baptist and about the Nazarene. I have not worked nor made a shekel during this time. I have lived from hand to mouth, eating only what the good people have given me. I am so financially devastated; that I even lost the farm and blacksmith shop that I inherited from my stepparents."

Stepping up closer to Caiaphas and reaching out and touching his hand Judas continued, "I beg you, please do not anger with me, but I would want forty pieces of silver for turning Jesus into your hands so I can re-establish myself and my business as a Scribe."

"Forty pieces of silver, huh? For that amount I would need the approval of the Ruling Group. I don't know if I could persuade them that Jesus is worth that amount."

Skittishly Judas pushed the question, "What amount can you give without the Ruling Group's approval then?"

"I can spend thirty pieces of silver without any question," replied Caiaphas.

"Then that will have to be enough," agreed Judas, trying to sound as real as he could. He persisted to push his luck saying, "But for that amount, I would ask you for two concession."

"What would that be?" Caiaphas was starting to look perplexed.

"With your indulgence Sire, one is that I get paid now, tonight so I can began to make the necessary arrangements to turn Him in, and the other condition is for your benefit."

Caiaphas was beginning to anger, so he demanded, "Don't dally with me Judas, tell me what it is!"

"The other condition is that you turn Jesus over to Pilate as we discussed earlier, so that he can have the glory of this prestigious arrest." Looking at the questioning stare on Caiaphas' face, Judas added, "You want to make Procurator Pontius Pilate happy and keep him happy so that you can continue doing the things you do for the glory of God and His Jewish people don't you?" Judas almost choked when he said that, but he quickly cleared his throat and said, "Excuse me Sire it must be the cold night air that is causing this cough!"

Quite convinced Caiaphas said, "You make sense Judas, of course you always have. I will be very glad to see you back in the service of the Sanhedrin when you restart your career."

"And what of my two conditions?" asked Judas wanting some reassurance.

"I agree to both of them. Let me go to the coffers to retrieve the money."

While he was gone, Judas took the sleeve from his coat and wiped the sweat from his brow. He took a deep breath and told himself, "This was not as hard as I thought it would be." He was convinced that what he had negotiated would be in the best interest of Jesus. It wasn't long before Caiaphas came with a sack which after counting it, Judas verified it contained thirty pieces of silver, more then enough for Barabbas to began the armed conflict himself.

"Before I go, I must have your solemn promise that you will let Procurator Pontius Pilate have Jesus."

"I swear Judas, in the Holy name of Yahweh. It makes sense, what you have said. I promise that I will do as you ask."

"Okay then, be prepared. I don't know, when I will come back, but it will be within the next three days. Have a patrol of soldiers ready for when I return, then you will have Jesus."

Judas left Caiaphas' house and began his five-mile walk back to Bethany. All the way back he kept running the plan through his mind to see what he might have overlooked, but nothing was apparently wrong with the plan that he could see. Before reaching the campsite he saw a beggar by the side of the road. There were always beggars by the road early in the morning hoping to get some food or sustenance for the travelers. He seemed to be about his size, so he gave him the new clean clothes in exchange for his old ones. He did not want to look conspicuous or raise any questions about where he had been.

Upon his return, Judas joined the other apostles and waited. He was not completely sure whether he could perform his end of the bargain so as he waited for the right time or sign he constantly prayed and meditated.

The Feast of Unleavened Bread, also called the Passover, was nearing. Therefore Jesus sent Judas and Philip into Jerusalem saying, "Go and make preparations for us to eat the Passover meal." He always chose to send them ahead to make all necessary arrangements because Philip was in charge of the food, and Judas was in charge of the money that belonged to the group. Before leaving, they both needed to know where in the city Jesus wanted them to go to make these preparations, so they asked, "Where do you want us to prepare for it?"

Jesus replied, "As you enter the city of Jerusalem, a man carrying a jar of water will meet you. Follow him to the house that he enters, and say to the owner of the house, 'The Teacher asks, where is your guest room where He may eat the Passover with His Apostles?' He will show you a large upper room, all furnished. Make preparations there." They left and found things just as Jesus had told them, so they made all the preparations and arrangements for the Passover meal. A day or so after they had completed their task, Jesus and the other Apostles arrived.

When the hour came to eat their meal, Jesus and His Apostles reclined at the table. Then He said to them, "I have eagerly desired to eat this Passover with you before I suffer. For I tell you, I will not eat it again until it finds fulfillment in the Kingdom of God."

Judas' attention was drawn to what Jesus had just said. Could this be Jesus' sign to him that He approves that which he had done? He felt good about what he had heard, so he listened more intently. After taking the cup of wine that was in front of him, Jesus gave thanks to God and said, "Take this and divide it among you. For I tell you I will not drink again of the fruit of the vine until the Kingdom of God comes."

Once again Judas took notice of what Jesus had said. Could Jesus be really hinting His approval and consent of Judas' deed? Was Simon right? Could this have been Judas' destiny? By now, Judas was feeling jubilant!

Then Jesus took some bread, gave thanks to God again, broke it and gave it to all twelve of them saying, "This is My body given for you, do this in remembrance of Me."

In the same way, after the supper had ended, He took the cup of wine, blessed it and gave it to all twelve of the Apostles saying, "This is the cup of the new and everlasting covenant that springs from My blood which will be poured out for you. The Son of Man will go as it has been decreed, but woe to that man who betrays Him."

Judas could not understand what Jesus meant by this. He felt that this was another stamp of approval since He said that He "was going to go as decreed." Everyone knew that He, as the Messiah had been "decreed" to be the Redeemer and Savior of His people. But what did Jesus mean by "woe to the man who betrays Him?" Judas was thinking to himself, "Is He predicting that Caiaphas will betray his promise to give Jesus up to the Romans? What did the Master mean?" Judas finally came to the conclusion that Jesus must be referring to the members of the Sanhedrin, who by not believing in Him, betrayed him.

Then Jesus continued, "For who is greater; the one sitting at the table or the one who serves? I tell you, it is the one who serves."

Immediately Judas felt exuberance again at hearing this for he considered himself the one "doing a service" for Jesus, by helping to begin the armed conflict that would gain Him the Throne of His Kingdom. Judas thought that Jesus must have been referring to him as the server and the rest of the Apostles were the ones He meant as the "ones sitting at the table."

Jesus proceed saying, "You are those who have stood by me in my trials, and I confer on all twelve of you a Kingdom, just as my Father conferred one on Me, so that you may sit on thrones, judging the twelve tribes of Israel."

Judas' heart was now so full of excitement because he knew now, beyond any shadow of doubt, that he was doing the right thing. He surmised that in order to establish His Kingdom for the Chosen People, Jesus would have to bring all the Jews back to the Promised Land, back to the clans and tribes from which they began. Now, Jesus was promising them that they would each rule a tribe as Jesus' chosen Royal family, on thrones! What a thrilling revelation!

Then Jesus asked the Apostles, "When I sent you without purse, bag or sandals, did you lack anything?

They all answered, "Nothing Lord, we lacked nothing."

Then Jesus added, "But now if you have a purse, take it and also a bag; and if you do not have a sword, sell your cloak and buy one. It is written: 'and he was numbered with the transgressors', and I tell you that this must be fulfilled in Me." Jesus then turned His eyes towards Judas and said, "Yes, what is written about Me is reaching its fulfillment."

Judas' heart almost leaped out of his body when he heard that! If ever he needed certainty and confirmation from Jesus that what He was doing was the right thing, this was it! "The swords are for us to fight and regain our Promised Lands back, and to defend it from any other foe that might arise in the future. The purse and cloak has to be so that we may look and be Regal. After all, we will be the Messiah's Royal Family!"

Jesus persisted saying, "Whoever accepts anyone I send accepts Me; and whoever accepts Me accepts the one who sent Me." After Jesus had said this, His spirit was troubled and so He testified, "I tell you the truth, one of you is going to betray Me."

His disciples and Apostles stared at one another, at a loss to know which of them He meant. John was seating next to Him and Peter motioned to John and asked him to ask Jesus which one He meant. John leaned towards Jesus and asked, "Lord, who is it?"

Jesus answered, "It is the one to whom I will give this piece of bread when I have dipped it in the dish." Then, dipping the piece of bread, He gave it to Judas and said, "This that you do, go and do it quickly."

As soon as Judas took the bread, he knew that this was the sign from Jesus to begin the battle for freedom. Suddenly it all became crystal clear! Jesus knew, beyond a shadow of a doubt, what Judas was doing and Jesus did not attempt to stop him! On the contrary, He encouraged Judas by saying, "Do it quickly!" Judas thought that Jesus might have felt betrayed by Judas since Judas' plan was to have Barabbas lead the army rather then Jesus. However, Judas also sensed that Jesus accepted this arrangement since he would ultimately be proclaimed the King of Judea once liberation was accomplished. He was filled with enthusiasm since he knew, unequivocally, that this was truly his destiny that had haunted and tormented him since his childhood, and that he had searched for all of his life. This was his part in the fulfillment of scripture that had been foretold by his mother's visitations in her dreams. At last, Oh God of Abraham, at long last, Jesus had revealed his destiny to him!

None of the other Apostles heard what Jesus said to Judas at the moment that He leaned over towards him. Since Judas was in charge of the money, some thought that Jesus was telling him to go buy some addition items that He might need for the Feast of the Passover. Others thought that Jesus had ordered Judas to give something to the poor, as He often requested. All the Apostles knew was that as soon as Judas had taken the wine and the bread, he quickly went out into the night.

Judas, running most of the quarter mile to Chief Priest's home, breathlessly announced to Caiaphas upon his arrival that the time to arrest Jesus was at hand. Caiaphas summoned the troops that he had in reserve as planned a day or two before, and told the Officer-in-charge to obey Judas' directions. Before leading the few armed troops back to the house where they had eaten, Judas made it explicitly clear to all of the soldiers that they were not to harm Jesus in any way. When they arrived at the house were they were partaking of their supper, the owner's wife told Judas that Jesus and the Apostles had left sometime earlier. They had gone to pray at His usual favorite place when in Jerusalem, which was about a mile away at Mount Olives. They went to that place and found Him in a deep meditative state. Judas approached Jesus and stated, "Master, I know you are well aware of what and why I am doing what I do now." As Jesus turned around, Judas noticed what looked like sweat beads on Jesus' brow and the side of His face. Upon closer observation Judas saw that the sweat drops were actually beads of blood. Concerned that Jesus was hurt, Judas cried out, "Master! You are bleeding! Are you hurt? Has someone harmed you?"

"No Judas, my friend, do what you must do." Judas kissed Him on the cheek, then the soldiers stepped forward, seized Jesus and arrested Him. Jesus was taken to the home of Caiaphas where he and the teachers of the law and the elders had assembled. Judas stayed close, just to insure that He was taken to Caiaphas with out any harm coming to Jesus. Peter followed, but at a distance. He entered and sat down close to the guards in the courtyard to see what the outcome of these events would be.

Caiaphas and the other priests of the Sanhedrin were looking for false evidence against Jesus so that they could put him to death. As much as they tried, they did not find any, though many false witnesses came forward. Finally two witnesses came forward and declared, "This fellow said 'I am able to destroy the temple of God and rebuild it in three days.' "

Throughout their questioning, Jesus remained silent. Then Caiaphas stood up and said to Jesus, "Are you not going to answer? What is this testimony that these men are bringing against You?" But Jesus continued to remain silent. Then Caiaphas, pointing his finger at Jesus, averred with a strong authoritative voice, "I charge You under oath by the living God, tell us if You are the Christ, the Son of God."

Finally Jesus broke His silence and answered, "Yes. It is as you say. But I say to all of you, in the future you will see the Son of Man sitting at the right hand of the Mighty One and coming on the clouds of heaven."

Caiaphas, upon hearing this, very dramatically tore his clothes as an outward sign of abhorrence and said, "He has spoken blasphemy! Why do we need any more witnesses? Look at Him," he said facing the rest of the Sanhedrin members, while pointing his right index finger at Jesus, "Now you have heard the blasphemy, what do you think?"

The consensus of opinion was that Jesus was worthy of death. Some of them then began spitting in Jesus' face and struck Him with their fists. Others slapped Him and said, "Prophesy to us, Christ, who hit you?" On seeing this, Peter started to run across the courtyard and was about to bullishly enter the house in defense of Jesus when he saw Judas step back into the room where this abuse of Jesus was happening. Judas had left the room momentarily to ask Nicodemus to make sure that Jesus was taken to Pilate as Caiaphas had promised.

"Stop! For God sake stop!" shouted Judas as he ran towards Jesus. "I did not deliver this man so that you could hurl insults and pain on Him! This man has admitted to nothing that would warrant this loathsome behavior on your part." Turning around and starring directly at Caiaphas he boldly stated, "Where is your manliness? Where is you honor? Are you a man of your word? Do you break oaths as you would grass twigs under your feet?"

The room became silent. Caiaphas knew that as much as he wanted to continue seeing Jesus castigated, he had no choice but to abide by the promise he had given to Judas. Therefore reluctantly he uttered, "Judas is right, we might be punishing an innocent man. Early tomorrow morning, we will take the Nazarene to Pontius Pilate. I am sure that he will do the right thing." As an after thought he added, "This should make Pilate extremely happy. Early this evening, just before the Nazarene was given up to us, I received the news that Barabbas, the insurrectionist leader had been captured here in Jerusalem. Two trouble makers in the same twenty-four hour period should make Pilate very happy and grateful indeed."

Judas could not believe his ears! He asked Caiaphas if he was sure that Barabbas had been captured, and he replied, "Yes, an envoy from Pontius Pilate came earlier this evening to relay this message to me. I say good riddance, maybe now we can live in peace with our Roman benefactors."

Once Judas made sure that Jesus would not be chastised anymore, and that He was safe, he decided to go seek Barabbas' second in command. As he went outside of the gate at Caiaphas home, he caught sight of Peter being questioned by some of the people that had gathered outside Caiaphas' home. Judas could not tell what was happening, but he could hear Peter saying, "No! No, you are mistaken, I don't know the man."

Once outside of the fence, Judas became extremely dizzy, and almost fell on his face. It was the anxiety of the situation and the lack of sleep that caused this dizzy spell. He set down just outside the gate to rest a while. He reclined his back on the fence and after a little while, he fell asleep until he was awakened by the sound of soldiers marching out of Caiaphas' house a short distance away. He was startled when he woke up. He could not believe that he had fallen asleep. It was after five in the morning, so he quickly went directly to the house of Barabbas' cousin Vesper. By this time, it was about six-thirty in the morning. When he arrived, it appeared as if no one was home. He persisted in knocking and eventually he thought that he had seen a glimmer of light from behind someone peering through the drapes at the window.

When Judas noticed that, he began calling out Vesper's name saying, "Vesper, it is I, Judas Iscariot. I must talk to you. It is important that I speak to you." He could not get an answer. Then for some reason he remembered the story of how his stepfather Simon Josiah had died and he said, "Remember Bethel!" He waited for a few more seconds, but still got no response. He was about to leave when he heard the squeaking of a door slowly being cracked open behind him. Judas turned around and said, "Vesper? Is that you?"

"Yes. What do you want here? We know nothing."

Judas could see a pair of frightened eyes peeking from behind the door. In order to set the person behind the door at ease, Judas said, "Please, do not be afraid. I mean you no harm. I am a friend of Barabbas. I am the one that gave him my land and blacksmith shop to help finance the revolution."

"Then you must be Judas Iscariot," replied the person behind the door.

"Yes I am. If you are Vesper, I need to speak to you about an urgent matter that involves Barabbas and the movement."

After a short pause, the door opened up and the rest of the man appeared from behind the door saying, "I am Vesper. I am sorry for not opening the door right away, but with what has happened yesterday afternoon, one can't be too careful."

"That is one of the things that I want to talk to you about," said Judas as he was entering the house. He set down on a chair that was next to a flat board that was used as a makeshift table. After he set down he asked how Barabbas had been captured.

With a look of frustration Vesper said, "I kept telling Barabbas not to be going to the marketplace in broad daylight, but he insisted in going to see a lady friend of his each day. I knew that she was not any good, and I knew that once the reward on his head became enticing enough, she would betray him for the money. Can you imagine what a woman like that is going to do with the three pieces of silver that she got? For three pieces of silver, she may have single-handedly stopped the freedom movement!"

"Who is the second in command after Barabbas, do you know?"

"Levi. Levi Bancasee. He has been here several times with Barabbas.

"Where can I find Levi?" asked Judas, "I must speak to him about Barabbas and some other pressing matters as soon as I can."

"He was here earlier and told me that he would be hiding in the mausoleum caves outside the city. You can find him there now." Underground tunnels that had once been used as water cisterns for Jerusalem in olden times were now caves used as mausoleums and hiding places for those that did not want to be found.

Judas thanked and told him that it was wise for him to keep a vigilant attitude. "You never know who is your friend and who is your enemy with the situation as volatile as it is now." As he was leaving, Judas momentarily forgot to bless the house as Jesus had instructed the Apostles to do whenever one was opened to any of the Apostles. So Judas quickly turned around and gave the house the standard blessing, then he hastily made his way towards the large caves that served as mausoleums outside of the city.

By eight o'clock that morning, he was approaching the entrance of the large caves when a man who evidently was keeping watch startled him saying, "Halt! Stand and be identified."

Judas looked at the man and said, "I am Judas Iscariot, the son of Simon Josiah Iscariot. I have come to see Levi Bancasee on a matter of great urgency."

"What makes you think he is here?" rebutted the man who was apparently a sentry posted for the protection of the leaders. While asking the question, he took a good look at Judas for identification purposes.

"I have been told by a mutual friend that this is where I would find him." By this time, the sentry recognized Judas and told him to follow him through the opening of the tunnel formed by the cave entrance. Judas followed through the cave, as they made some left and right turns through a number of shafts in the cave. After a few minutes, Judas was totally confused as to what direction they were heading. For a time it was very dark where they walked, with only the one torch that the guard carried for illumination. The smell in the cave was stagnant, and it felt cool and clammy inside. The walls and the ceiling of the tunnel were almost grayish black from the black soot that must have come from the burning oil in the torches used in the past. It was difficult to breathe since fresh air was in short supply. As they neared the room where the leaders were, Judas could now see more candle and torchlight flickering and he could hear someone talking.

When they entered the room, the six men that were sitting in a circle around a campfire stood up in a defensive posture and the leader asked, "Who are you and what business do you have here?"

"I am Judas Iscariot," he said looking at the men, all the time hoping that his word would be enough identification for them to recognize who he was.

"Oh yes," said the redheaded and bearded taller man. "I was with Barabbas when he talked to you last, at Bethany. I saw you there when he went to thank you for deeding your property over to him." Turning around for the benefit of the other five men with him he said to them, "This is the son of our Patriarch and Martyred Simon Josiah Iscariot." The other man then outwardly expressed a more receptive attitude towards Judas, except one whose name was Barcaba, who seemed to still hold on to his suspicions. He seemed to be the same age as Judas, and about the same height and weight. Barcaba's suspicions stemmed for the fact that he had seen Judas working and associating with the High priests at the synagogue and with members of the Sanhedrin when Judas was a Scribe about three or four years or so back. In his opinion, anyone that worked with or for the Sanhedrin, was someone to be watched.

The redheaded man then said, "My name is Levi Bancasee, what can I do for you?"

"I have a great interest in finding out how you plan to get Barabbas out of prison. Can you tell me what your plans are to get his release?"

"We had planned to have some of our friends who work as prison guards help us out by leaving their post unguarded and the door to his cell unsecured, but they are afraid to cooperate with us. They say that General Pantera has posted additional guards of his own, and they fear for their lives if they are caught helping Barabbas escape."

"So, what is your plan now?" restated Judas.

Levi Bancasee began to walk around very tentatively as if he was visualizing what he was saying as he talked. "Well, in a few days, in accordance with the public's wishes, the Procurator will be releasing a prisoner that the public wishes to have released. We plan to be at the pavilion, in mass, and request that Pontius Pilate release Barabbas."

"No! No, you can't do that!" shouted Judas frantically as he looked at each one of the men there with him. He was almost panic-stricken. "You have to find another way to get him released."

"Why? What business is it of yours how we get Barabbas released, as long as we get him liberated?" shouted Barcaba jumping to the forefront in a threatening stance. Suspicion was beginning to show on Levi's face.

Judas noticed these suspicions setting in so he added, "It's a long story for me to explain why it matters, so lets just say that I have good reasons for asking that you find another way." To ease the aura of suspicion that had grown so thick that you could have sliced it with a knife, looking around at all of them, Judas added, "I have been an insurrectionist all of my life. My father Simon Josiah gave his life for the cause, my Uncle Reuben Gibeon was the chief member of the Committee of Kerioth, and as you know, I have given all I possess to the cause for liberty. You cannot be suspicious of me. My reason, if you must know, is a simple one. I have turned over Jesus of Nazareth, the Messiah, over to Caiaphas for thirty pieces of silver. I intend to give this money to Barabbas so he can finish arming and outfitting his army. Barabbas told me the last time I saw him, that if he had another twenty or thirty pieces of silver for armament, he could insure a victory over the Romans. To keep any harm from coming to the Master, I made Caiaphas promise to hand Jesus over to Pontius Pilate before I turned Jesus over to him. I did this because I know, without a doubt, Pilate will not be able to find fault with Him, and will have no other choice but to release Him on this feast day."

"So how does this concern us?" asked Levi somewhat rudely.

Exhibiting growing frustration Judas added poignantly, "I just told you how it concerns you. Are you that dense that you do not understand?" I did this deed in order to get additional money that Barabbas told me he needed to efficiently supply the army to begin the armed conflict. Barabbas told me that once he defeated the Romans, he and I would proclaim Jesus as the one and only King of the Jews. The plan for Jesus' release is to petition Pilate to release Him during Pilate's yearly pardon program. Now, can't you see why you must find another way to obtain Barabbas' release? Pilate will only release one prisoner, and it must be Jesus."

Feeling like he must say something to excerpt his leadership Levi stated. "There is no doubt that you and your family have been true loyalist in the liberation movement, but I have to tell you this Judas. We know that Barabbas is a leader, a fighter, and a liberator. We do not know this Jesus or whether He is or isn't the Messiah. I cannot risk the wrath of the entire Roman Army that at present is right here in Jerusalem, by initiating any futile attempt to get Barabbas out by force. I know, and you know, this would be a battle that we could never win. The best way is to get Barabbas pardoned by Pilate, take the thirty pieces of silver you have and finish gearing up the troops with the arms that we need, then strike a blow for freedom on another day when they least expect it. When we liberate Jerusalem, we can then free this Jesus of yours."

"No, I can not allow this to happen. That will be too late. I know that if Barabbas was here, he would be in total agreement with me." Judas began to pace very nervously.

He continued saying, "With great meticulous care, I have initiated this plan. It is the only way to set the entire Jewish nation free with the rightful King on the throne. If you have ever read the scripture, you'd know that it has been foretold that a Messiah and Christ would be sent by God to win back our Promised Lands and gather His people back where they belong. The Prophet Isaiah prophesied it saying, 'For unto us a Child is born, unto us a Son is given; and the government will be upon His shoulder. And His name will be called Wonderful, Counselor, Mighty God, Everlasting Father, and Prince of Peace.' I tell you that I and thousands of other Jews have witnessed miracles beyond your belief that clearly tell us that Jesus is the Prince of Peace and the true King of the Jews."

Irked at what he perceived as arrogance on the part of Judas, Levi then asserted. "Well, if He is as you say, the Messiah, let Him call an Army of angels to come and get him out of prison. Because I and at least half of our army will be at the palace pavilion in just a little while, asking for Barabbas' release."

Totally sickened by their non-caring attitude Judas then asked to be escorted out of the cave. At first Levi and the other five where reluctant to let Judas go for fear that he might reveal their hiding place. They just looked at each other, none wanting to respond to Judas' request to be escorted out. It was not until Judas told them that he wanted to go see Barabbas and give up the pieces of silver that they decided to let him go, but not before a strong warning.

"If our hiding place is found out, we will have no other choice but to think that it was you Judas, who turned us in."

Before leaving, Judas asserted, "Levi, you are interfering with divine destiny and you had better rethink your plans." As the escort and Judas left the room, the echo of laughter and words such as, "The Messiah, indeed!" then louder laughter reverberated through the tunnel where they were walking.

After exiting the cave, Judas then went to Caiaphas to attempt to get authority from him to visit the prison to speak to Jesus, at least that's what he planned to say. He really did not have any intentions of speaking to Jesus at that time, he just wanted authority to enter the prison and talk to Barabbas in hope that he could convince him to tell Levi and his troops not to ask for his release.

It was nine-thirty in the morning, and at this very moment, at the Palace of the Procurator, Jesus stood before Procurator Pilate, and some of the Chief Priests and Elders of the Sanhedrin.

The Procurator was asking Jesus, "Are you the King of the Jews?"

"Yes, it is as you say," Jesus replied.

Jesus was accused once again by the priests and the elders of being a demon possessed insurgent, but He gave no answer. Then Pilate asked Him, "Don't you hear the testimony they are bringing against you?" But Jesus did not reply to a single charge to the amazement of Pilate.

Pilate then took Jesus, who was bound hand and foot with chains, out to a balcony that overlooked a large pavilion. It was full of people by this time, standing, looking up at both of them. Pilate addressed the crowd saying, "As you know, it is my custom to release one prisoner chosen by the crowd. I have two that have come into my custody within the last twenty-four hours. There is Barabbas, and there is this man, Jesus of Nazareth. Which one do you wish for me to release?" Even Pilate felt that the crowd would want Jesus released, since he felt strongly that it was out of envy that the Sanhedrin had handed Jesus over to him.

But the Priests and elders along with hundreds of Barabbas' soldiers shouted, "Give us Barabbas, give us Barabbas." The shouts for Jesus could hardly be heard because those that asked for him were stabbed or beating by the members of the Resistance standing behind them.

Upon hearing the call to release Barabbas, Pilate then asked, "And what about Jesus, the King of the Jews, this self-proclaimed Christ? What am I to do with Him?"

The Priests and elders of the synagogue led the others in shouts of, "Crucify Him, Crucify Him!"

Totally in disbelief at what he was hearing, Pontius Pilate then said, "Why? What crime has He committed? Here is a man that has preached nothing but things like, 'Love your neighbor' so why should I have Him crucified?"

The crowd was becoming more of a mob and very unruly. They kept chanting louder and louder, "Crucify Him, Crucify Him."

Pilate then had an alternative idea. He was thinking, "I will have Jesus flogged and castigated, then I will come back later in the afternoon and ask them the same question again. Maybe if they see how I have punished and inflicted harsh pain on Him, they will change their mind and ask me to release Jesus. If they continue to ask for His life, I will release Him back to the Sanhedrin. By that time, after seeing His pain and suffering, they might also change their mind and release Him themselves." Therefore, he held up releasing Barabbas. He had all day to do that if it came to that.

Meanwhile, at that same moment in time, Judas was waiting to see Caiaphas. When Judas was announced, Caiaphas came into the anteroom almost immediately and said, "Ah, Judas my young friend, you have returned, and so early, I might add. It is barely nine-thirty in the morning! I know why you are here, so I will put your mind at ease. I have turned Jesus over to Pontius Pilate already early this morning. But to tell you the truth, he doesn't have any idea what to do with Him."

Judas, trying to look composed said, "I am sure that in a few days, Pilate will know what to do. But I have come on another matter sire. I have come to ask something of you."

"Oh? Well tell me Judas, what is it?"

"I wish to gain entrance into the prison to speak with the Nazarene."

"Why on earth would you want to do that?"

Judas had to come up with something that sounded somewhat reasonable. So he said, "I have heard that Jesus amassed a great deal of money, and if I can get Him to tell me where He has it hidden, well I just might be in a position to return your thirty pieces of silver!"

"Really!" replied Caiaphas, "And what makes you think that He will tell you?

"Well, I did spend a very short time with Him, in my efforts to find out about Him, you understand. While I was with Him, I gained His confidence, and I am hoping that He will still feels the same."

"So what do you want from me, pray tell?"

"I respectfully request that you write a note on my behalf, for all concerned to allow me to visit the prison cell and to speak to the revolutionary."

"Well, I guess that would not present a problem, just as long as you do plan to return my money to me, plus possibly a little extra? Perhaps?"

"Yes sire, indeed!"

Caiaphas began to write on a very small scroll and as he wrote Judas said, "Be sure you write that I be allowed to speak to the revolutionary, that way they will know who you mean." Judas knew that by calling Him that, he could say that the note meant that he was to see Barabbas.

After a few moments, Caiaphas started to hand the paper to Judas. As he did, he kept pulling it away from Judas in a very boyish manner, as if playing "grab the note if you can" and with a smirk on his face stated in a childish high pitched musical voice, "Happy hunting!"

By the time Judas left Caiaphas' home and arrived at the prison gates it was already about eleven o'clock in the morning. This had been a longest day of Judas' life. As he approached the gate, a Roman soldier came to the gate and asked, "Halt in the name of Tiberius! Who is there? Identify yourself!"

It was quite obvious that he was one of the regular armed soldiers that Pantera had placed there as extra guards to protect the prison from an all out attack to free Barabbas. Trying to sound as composed and as authoritative as he could, he said, "It is I, the Emissary of His Honor and Chief Priest Caiaphas. I have been sent to seek information from the revolutionary Barabbas. Here is my authorization."

The Roman soldier did not know any better. He was new so he admitted Judas into the prison after reading the note from Caiaphas that read, "This will identify Judas Iscariot. He seeks to question the rebel that was caught yesterday and turned over to his Majesty Pontius Pilate. Extend him the same courtesy that the Procurator would extend to me." It was signed and contained the appropriate seal.

Walking through the door of the prison, the Roman soldier asked, "Which one of the two that were captured yesterday do you want to see?"

"I want to see Barabbas, and I want to be along with him. I intend to question him for Caiaphas, and I do not want anything to interfere with the interrogation."

They walked through some mucky and foul smelling rooms, then down some spiraling stone steps where rats were still looking for their morning prey, then through a hallway that was lid only by large torches that hung on the wall. They finally reached the area that contained some cells, and there, sitting on a cot made of filthy hay was Barabbas.

When He saw Judas, he jumped to his feet, but before he had a chance to say anything, Judas shouted, "That's right you miserable wretch, stand up when I stand before you! You better show respect to the envoy of Caiaphas you heathen! Stand there until you are told otherwise!"

Barabbas could not understand what was happening, but he went along with what Judas said. The guard opened up the cell and Judas entered. "I will be just outside," instructed the guard, "When you are finished, just yell to me, and I will come and let you out." Looking at Barabbas then at Judas, he added. "Are you sure you will be alright by yourself with him in here?"

"Yes, this heathen would not dare attack me if he knows what is good for him. Go. Leave us alone."

They waited until they heard the door slam, and were sure that they were along, then Judas said, "Barabbas! What happened to you?" They embraced as they greeted each other.

"This will teach me to trust winches!" said Barabbas, "I should have known better. Like our first father, Adam, I too had my 'Eve' that betrayed me, turned me in for three pieces of silver, can you believe that?"

"Barabbas, I have something of great importance to speak to you about and there isn't much time to talk about it." Just before Judas got into the subject, sharp popping sounds, as if leather was being hit on a tanning post got his attention. "What is that I hear?" asked Judas.

"It's the Roman soldiers. They are lashing some poor soul they brought in earlier this morning. They have been mocking him, slapping him, and now they have been lashing the poor soul for the last hour, non-stop. They even put strands of thorny vines around His head to begin with that made His head bleed profusely. Poor soul, He cried out in excruciating pain for a while, but now, I guess the pain has gotten so bad, He can hardly yell anymore. I have not heard Him screaming in the last ten minutes or so. He has only been able to give out a loud mown once in a while. That's the only way I know He is still alive. I tell you Judas, thank God it is Him that is getting that brutal barbaric beating and not us, we would have died of pain a long time ago."

Shocked at what he was hearing, Judas cried out in a sorrowful tone, "Oh God, please don't let it be Jesus, please God don't let it be!"

"Jesus?" replied Barabbas looking at Judas in a confused manner, "What is Jesus doing here in prison?"

"It was I," cried Judas, "I am to blame." Judas was leaning his head on Barabbas' shoulder, with his arms around him, sobbing uncontrollably.

Pushing Judas away and grabbing his upper arms to get his attention he averred, "Judas. Judas, get a grip on yourself and tell me what has happened?"

Judas began wiping the tears from his eyes. He sniffled a little, and attempted to regain his composure. Then Judas said, "The last time we saw each other, you mentioned that if you had another twenty or thirty pieces of silver more, you could outfit your army to the point that you could start the insurrection without Jesus."

"I did?" said Barabbas trying to think back to that day.

"Yes you did. I kept asking Jesus almost daily, when He was going to start the rebellion, but I never got any answer. The only affirmation I perceived by His actions and words, was that when the Roman's were defeated, he would then establish His Kingdom."

Still puzzled and somewhat perplexed, Barabbas asked, "So, what has all of this to do with Jesus being here?"

"The only way for me to raise that kind of money was to give up Jesus to the Sanhedrin for thirty pieces of silver. In doing so, I first obtained an oath from Caiaphas that he would turn Jesus over to Pontius Pilate. I knew that if Jesus was Pilate's prisoner, we could then urge Pilate to release Jesus on the day of the Passover Feast. That way He would be free, and you would have the money you needed to start the conflict. Once the war started, Jesus could then lead us and establish His Kingdom here in Judea. Every Jew would be triumphant."

"Judas! Didn't you consider the risk in doing this?"

"Yes, but how was I to know that you would be caught and imprisoned at the same time? Pausing a moment, and grabbing Barabbas by his shirt collar, Judas added, "We have to get Jesus released, Barabbas, we just have to get Him released."

"It's impossible now," said Barabbas, "I was just told that the crowd has already chosen to have me released. I did not know Jesus was their other choice. I thought He was just another prisoner." Hesitating a little, he looked Judas straight in the eyes then added, "What's worse, the crowd has asked Pilate to have Him crucified!"

"Oh no! God please, do not let the Master die because of my stupidity! Barabbas, we have to do something!"

Barabbas placed his hands on Judas' forearms and while holding them, he said somberly, "Judas, there is nothing I can do."

"You can send word to Levi Bancasee to attack the prison and rescue both you and Jesus," pleaded Judas.

"Levi knows better, he's no fool. He knows that Pantera has posted more then double the guard around Jerusalem and many more here at the prison. He may be a little egotist, but he is no fool. He knows that the losses would be great if he tried anything like that."

The mention of Octavio Pantera triggered an idea in Judas' head. An eerie look came across Judas' face as he stared out into space. "What are you thinking about Judas?" asked Barabbas somewhat puzzled by Judas' facial expression at that moment.

"I think I know how to get Jesus released. I will appeal to General Pantera."

"What makes you think that he will even see you much less listen to you?"

"Barabbas, there are some things that nobody knows about me, except me. I have something in common with Octavio Pantera that will gain me an audience with him. I don't know if it will do any good, but I have to try." Looking strangely at Barabbas, Judas then said, "Goodbye my dear friend. I hope to see you and be with you soon, in battle for the greater glory of Israel!"

"Be careful Judas, You can trust a snake easier then you can trust Pantera."

While Barabbas was giving this warning, Judas was hollering for the guard to come and open the gate so he could leave. When the guard came, Judas left with him. Judas could still hear the sharp popping of the lashes being inflicted all over Jesus' bloody body. Judas though, "How much pain can Jesus stand! One-tenth the amount that He had already suffered and endured would have killed the average man." As he walked out he tried to hide his emotions from the guard.

When Judas and the guard came out of the prison, Judas did not notice that Barcaba, the most suspicious one from the mausoleum was walking towards the prison. When he saw Judas, be jumped behind a wall so that Judas would not see him. Once outside of the prison, Judas asked the guard that was escorting him, "Where can I find General Octavio Pantera?"

"He is a guest at Herod Antipas Palace here in Jerusalem," replied the guard. After leaving the prison, Judas hurried to the Palace in hopes of an opportunity to see General Pantera to beg for Jesus' release. Unknown to Judas, Barcaba began to follow him to see where he went. He had motioned three other men that were near the prison, also standing watch to follow Judas along with him.

On his way to the Palace, Judas kept thinking, "This is a dream! It has to be a bad dream, and I am going to wake up and all will be fine. This cannot be really happening! No one, not even the other Apostles and disciples love Jesus as much as I do, so how could this be happening? This is not my destiny? This can not be! How can God destine anyone to do such a contemptible thing, when God does not produce evil? My destiny as foretold to my mother is that I am to help fulfill prophecy. That can only mean that I am destined to help the Master accomplish what He came to this world to do. How does getting Him crucified help fulfill prophesy?"

Chapter 16
The Divine Revelation

It was past noon and by this time Judas was beginning to get some pains in his stomach. He was beginning to get hungry. All of a sudden he remembered that he had not eaten since early last evening. He was thinking how nice it would be to have some bread to eat when his thoughts went back to something that the Master had said to a large crowd back some time ago.

Jesus had told the crowd, "I am the bread of life. He who comes to Me will never go hungry, and he who believes in Me will never be thirsty. But as I told you, you have seen Me and still you do not believe. All that the Father gives Me will come to Me, and whoever comes to Me I will never drive away. For I have come down from heaven not to do My will but to do the will of Him who sent Me. And this is the will of Him who sent Me, that I shall never lose none of all that He has given Me, but raise them up at the last day."

Judas forgot his hunger thinking about what the Master had said. What could He have meant by that? Even at the Last Supper that they had together Jesus had said that the wine they drank was His blood and that it would be shed so that all sins could be forgiven. This brought back memories of his childhood days and of the livestock sacrifices that were mandated by the scriptures to atone for inequities towards God Jehovah. In biblical times God had even tested Abraham by requesting that he kill his only son as a sacrifice for the evils and faults of the people. Judas even remembered that Jesus had referred to Himself as the "Sacrificial Lamb that would take away the sins of the world." What could all of that mean?

Then Judas began remembering John the Baptist and a conversation they had when they first met in the desert. Judas recalled he was questioning John the Baptist about how Jesus was going to establish his Kingdom if He did not have an army to lead nor any military experience.

He remembered the Baptist saying with complete assurance, "That's just it! We have been waiting for the wrong kind of Messiah! He is not, nor was He ever meant to be a worldly Messiah but a Messiah of the *Spirit*."

Judas remembered saying in rebuttal, "You and I studied the Torah, and know well the prophecies of Jeremiah. He was told by God that the day was coming when God would raise up from the house of David, a righteous man, a King who would reign wisely and do what is just and right in the land. And that in His days, Judah would be saved and Israel would live in safety." Judas also remembered asking John, "How can He fulfill this prophecy without being a military leader and without an army?"

Judas instantly remembered, clear as a bell, that the Baptist had answered saying, "Jeremiah's prophecy is true, but we have been wrong in interpreting the Kingdom of God as if it is a new kind of political proclamation or society. **His concern, and only reason for coming is to save the spirit and souls of all people, and to initiate a special new relationship between God and all His people. This new relationship is His Kingdom, not any piece or parcel of land or country. He loves and wants a spiritual relationship with you and me, Jews, Gentiles, the hold human race, …. that's His Kingdom!** God has made it quite clear, in the book of Deuteronomy, that there is nothing at all inherently special or righteous about Israel for which they deserve God's favor more than any other nation or people. God desires everyone, everywhere to know him, love him and to serve Him."

All of a sudden these conversations that he was remembering made Judas stop in his tracks. The strength seemed to leave his legs. He could not support himself and started to fall down, but he broke his fall by leaning on a tree that was just to the right of where he was walking. He gave a big gasp, and uttered, "Oh God of Israel! What have I done? I did not understand what John the Baptist was saying until now. Just now, it has become unequivocal clear to me what John was saying to me. He was right! Jesus never intended to establish an earthy kingdom! It was a spiritual kingdom that he always referred to when the Master spoke of His Kingdom! That's why He never told me when He would lead an army, because it was never meant to be that way. Oh God! What have I done? I have to get the Master released. This has all been a big mistake!"

Judas gathered his strength and hurried his walk towards the Palace. When he arrived, a guard that stood by the front entrance to the Palace stopped him saying "Halt! Stop and identify yourself!"

It was almost impossible for Judas to gather enough strength to put on an authoritative facade, but he found it long enough to say, "I am Judas Iscariot, Special Envoy of His Honor, Caiaphas, the High Priest. I have been sent to speak with his Grace, General Octavio Pantera concerning the prisoner that is in Pontius Pilate's custody. It is imperative that I see him at once."

Judas waved the order that he had acquired to visit the prison, which looked very official with Caiaphas' official seal, in front of the guard. That helped convince the guard to let Judas into the waiting area while the guard ordered another soldier of lessor rank that was standing inside the corridor to go inform General Pantera of the visitor.

As he waited, Judas kept thinking about what John the Baptist had told him, and how it now made things that Jesus had preached much clearer now when viewed from that standpoint. The thought kept going through his mind, "It was not an earthly kingdom that Jesus wanted to establish, but a heavenly, spiritual kingdom. How could I have been so blind and half-witted not to understand what Jesus was saying?" It was a good thing that he heard footsteps because he was about to have an anxiety breakdown. He knew he could not control his emotions much longer.

It wasn't long before General Pantera came into the waiting room with an entourage of four guards following behind him. He wore a toga of fine white linen with sparkling gold thread intertwined through out the fabric, with decorative borders depicting the Roman Gods of Apollo and Jupiter, and other Roman deities. He wore brown leather sandals that looked as if they had just been polished and buffed. Even at his age, he still seemed to walk with a swagger of one much younger than sixty-something years of age.

Walking up to Judas and throwing the long length of his toga over his right arm, he said in an authoritative voice, "I am General Octavio Pantera, what business does Caiaphas have with me?"

"Sire, I am Judas Iscariot, you and I have met before."

Looking baffled General Pantera declared, "We have? Where? I don't remember."

"If I may refresh your memory Sire, it was about three years ago in the Temple office of the Sanhedrin. I was meeting with Caiaphas and some of his chief priests when you came in and asked about the man called John the Baptist."

"Oh," he said, not really remembering quite fully the details of the meeting, but he did remember Judas. He remembered him not because Judas made an impression on him, but Pantera once again noticed the necklace that Judas was wearing, with the large gem in the middle. He remembered seeing it on Judas that time, and thinking that he had seen it before someplace else. Eventually Judas recounting their previous encounter at the Synagogue restored his recollection of having met Judas before.

"What can I do for you Judas?" How can I be of service to Caiaphas?" asked Pantera.

All of a sudden something hit Judas like a bolt of lightning. He could not go on with this façade any longer. He could not stretch the truth, nor attempt to lie anymore. At that very same moment, his feelings of anxiety were gone, and the hatred that he had in his heart for the Romans in general and in Octavio Pantera in particular seemed to also vanish. It seemed as if a great weigh had been lifted off his shoulders, and for the first time he was seeing things through different eyes. All the fear that he had at that moment, which was enormous, and all the fear that he had ever felt were all gone at that same moment, along with all of his anxieties, fears, hatred, and troubles that he had never felt. Judas could not believe this feeling of euphoria and well being that he was experiencing! He did not know where it was coming from, but at that instant he was wishing that it would never stop.

He finally looked at Pantera and said, "I do not come here as an Envoy of Caiaphas. That was an untruth that I told your guards so that I could gain access to speak with you. I come here to speak to you for my self. I am an Apostle of Jesus Christ, the Messiah who is currently being held in prison."

"What does this have to do with me?" asked Pantera as caution was beginning to show in his face.

"Before I come to that, let me say that it is because of me that my friend and Master, Jesus, is in prison under the jurisdiction of Pontius Pilate and you. I handed Him over to Caiaphas for thirty pieces of silver." Pantera was about to say something but Judas interrupted him saying, "Please, let me finish. I did not understand what Jesus' teachings meant until now, when I was walking from the prison to this Palace." Judas took a deep breath, walked around nervously a little, and lifted his index finger and pointed it at General Pantera to lend emphasizes to what he was going to say next.

"You know, I was the most brilliant of all students in the Sanhedrin at Kerioth when I was young, including John Barzacarias whom you knew better as the Baptist. I must have read and recited, and memorized every passage in the Torah that dealt with the promise of the coming Messiah." He paused like he was in deep thought. Judas smiled and shook his head slowly from side to side, then he added, "But we were all wrong. The Pharisees, leaders of the Jews and I myself, interpreted His mission here on earth the wrong way. Yes, He is the Messiah, the Savior, the King of the Jews, but in a spiritual sense."

After a short pause to take a deep breath, Judas continued, "You see, that's where we erred. He does not want to establish an earthly kingdom. He does not want to establish a new government, or to be the ruler or King of any part or parcel of land. All Jesus wants is to save people's souls, Jews, Gentiles, Romans, and yes, even whores, drunkards and heathens! I realize now, that's why He spent most of His time with sinners, thieves, whores, and people that were demon possessed."

Judas looked squinted eyed as if trying to recall word for word what he had once heard. He looked at the General and shaking his finger for impact said, "Do you know what Jesus once said? He once told the Pharisees, in my presence, but I did not understand until now, He told them that it was not the healthy that needed the doctor, but the sick, and that He associated and preached to them because He had come to call the sinners, not the righteous. I did not understand that until now."

Looking directly at Pantera and stretching his hands out in front of him Judas said, "Jesus is not a threat to you and the Roman Empire! On the contrary, He teaches love, patience, and kindness. He tells people to love their neighbor as well as their enemies." Putting his hand up to his own face, Judas continued. "He teaches that when someone slaps you in the face, that instead of retaliating, you should turn the other cheek. I have heard Him say that when someone takes your money, you should give him your cloak also, for he must have greater need for it than you."

Judas was amazed at himself with what he was saying. He had no idea where all of this was coming from but he could not stop talking. It was as if a fountain was within him, and it was overflowing with what he was saying. "Even in the prayer that the Master Himself taught us all to pray, He makes our forgiveness by God conditional on how we forgive those who offend us." Judas recites that portion of the prayer saying, "And forgive us our trespasses, as we forgive those who trespass against us. I ask you General Pantera, how can anyone with this philosophy, with this believes, and with this much love in His heart be a threat to the Roman Empire?"

General Pantera had his head down, looking at the floor by this time. Judas did not notice, but General Pantera was really paying attention to him and to what he was saying about Jesus. Judas' declarations were really getting to him. The General raised his head up and looked Judas in the eyes and uttered, "I never knew that anyone could ever exist that would teach His people to love unconditionally like that, especially their enemies. You are right, I agree with you, a man like that is not a threat to anyone. But I must ask you Judas, you who was with him for three years, do people really take to heart what Jesus teaches?"

Judas looked straight into the General's eyes for a few seconds then he looked up to the ceiling, shaking his head slowly with a sly grin on his face. After a second or two his eyes made contact with the General again and he said, "Believe it or not, I am an excellent example of what you are asking." Judas seemed almost surprised at what he was thinking and about to say.

"How are you a prime example?" asked General Pantera, still expressing great interest at what Judas was saying.

Judas turned away from the General and walked two steps back to a large pillar that was behind him. He rested his back on the pillar, rubbed the back of his neck with his hand, then pointing his hand at the General he slowly said, "All my life; up until a few minutes ago, my most fervent wish was to kill you, or see you dead!" Judas pushed himself away from the pillar with his buttocks and raised his hands and head up towards heaven and laughed softly in disbelieve at what he had just said.

Upon hearing this, the guards made a move as if to attack Judas in order to protect the General Pantera, but the General waved his hand and told them to get back. "Leave us!" he commanded of his troops, and they obeyed. Looking confused at Judas he asked, "Why would you want to kill me? If you were a follower of this Jesus, how could you harbor such thoughts? Is He not what you say He is?"

"Yes, yes, yes, He is, and much much more. I did not understand Him and what He was trying to teach the world and me until just a few minutes ago. He is the Christ, the God of love. He even told us that He was giving us a new commandment. That we are to love one another, regardless of whom he and she might be. We are to love one another as much as He has loved us. Jesus told us that by this unwavering love for everyone, regardless if they are Jews, Gentiles, sinners, heathen, and regardless of his or her position and status in life, by this love the whole world would know us, and therefore would know Him."

"I know now and understand why you changed your mind about killing me," stated General Pantera, "But why did you want to see me dead in the first place?"

Shaking his head a little, Judas gave out an hopeless giggle and then answered, "For many reason. The least of which is that you represent the worst of what men can become in their quest for power over people. The worst reason is the inhumanity towards man that you as the leader of the Roman Legions represent."

Judas could not evade the subject any longer, so after a second of hesitation in an attempt to hold back tears, Judas added, "But most of all, I wanted to see you dead for what you personally did to my mother."

General Pantera was astonished, he did not know what to say, so after a few seconds he said in a repentant tone of voice, "If I incarcerated your mother, if I took her property or even caused her death in battle, those are the wages of war!"

Judas rebutted with a crackling voice as a few tears were starting to run down his cheeks, "It was not the wages of war that I speak of, it was the wages of sin, lust, and wantonness that made you do what you did to my beloved mother Sofia."

Totally aghast, General Pantera asked, "Tell me, who is your mother? I don't even know who she is. Where is she now?"

Pounding his chest with his right thumb while holding on to the necklace around his neck with the same hand, Judas averred, "My mother died giving birth to me…your son." For the next few moments, the silence was overpowering.

"My son?" repeated the General, "No, it can't be. I have never had any Jewish lady friends or lovers, much less any significant long-term relation with them. I have never even engaged with a Jewish concubine woman. You must be totally mistaken."

Judas began to recount the story word for word, as he had heard Leah tell it to him. "It was thirty-four years ago. My mother's name was Sofia. She was born and at the time lived in a small village called Nain. She was only fourteen years old when it happened. She was tending her father's flock by the side of Mount Tabor when you surprised her and raped her."

General Pantera's mouth was gaped in total shock. His face was flushed at first, then it turned pale, as the color of parchment paper. In a dazed state, he looked at Judas and after a short period of silence, he said, "That necklace! I know now where I have seen it before! I remember now. I had been in Palestine for about six months and I was homesick. I saw a young girl watching her flock so I approached her. I was a brand new captain then, and very young and foolish. My desires and lustful feelings overcame me and I took her against her will. You have to believe me, that is the only thing that I have ever done that I wish I could change. From that very moment, I have felt ashamed of what I did. For a long time, I searched for her, to ask her personally for forgiveness, but I never found her."

General Pantera paused for a moment, walked around rubbing one hand and then the other. Then looking remorsefully at Judas he added, "After the act, I felt really sorry, so as I left the cave, I threw a sack of money containing my re-enlistment bounty and seven months pay to her. I don't know why I did that, I just wanted her to have the money. But as I rode away, she flung the money back at me. I know she did because I heard it making dinging sounds as the pieces of silver hit the rocks."

Gazing at Judas' chest Pantera added, "That necklace! From the first time I saw you wearing it, I knew I had seen it before. She…," he hesitated momentarily, "She was wearing it that day in the cave!" Putting his hands to his mouth he added, "Oh God, what did I do? I am so sorry, so sorry."

Judas thought back to the time that he and Simon the Zealot had stopped just outside of Nain, on a hillside, and he had found that one piece of silver. Could it have been one of those flung away by his dearly beloved mother? Then he remembered the cave they discovered where the rabbit had hidden behind that boulder inside the cave. He remembered the pitiful scared look on the rabbit. It was so terrified that it made Judas take pity on it and made him lie to Simon telling him that the rabbit was not in the cave. Most of all, he remembered those frightened eyes looking up at him. He envisioned his mother being just as scared.

Judas continued, "My mother had to leave her family and go live with her Uncle and Aunt Reuben and Leah in Kerioth. She never saw her parents again. I never knew her, because she died, giving me birth. This necklace is all I have left of her and my heritage."

Judas could not stop talking. "All my life, I have wanted to see you destroyed, for what you represent. Then a few years back when I learned that you had raped and ravaged my mother, and that you were my father, I wanted the pleasure of killing you myself." Judas snickered, looked down at the floor and shook his head. "Now, I don't know why, but I have no hatred towards you at all, none whatsoever. It's not even difficult for me to say that I forgive you for what you have done." Looking up to heaven Judas asked, "God, what is happening to me? I don't feel any hatred. I don't feel any anxiety or frustration. What is happening to me?"

General Pantera made a move towards Judas as if to hug him. As he did, he proclaimed, "My son!"

Judas evaded his embrace saying, "Yes, I am your son by birth, but I do not have any feelings, neither bad nor good towards you at this moment. If you feel that you must atone to me for what happened, thirty-four years ago, then have Jesus released into my custody. Don't you see that He has never been a threat to you or to anyone, and never will be."

"Yes, yes I will. I'll do it right now." General Pantera went to a table that was near by and drew some paper and a writing implement and began to write. He was verbalizing what he was writing. He was saying, "This will introduce Judas Iscariot Pantera, my son. He is to be given immediate custody of Jesus the Nazarene. They are to be given an escort back to Herod's Palace accompanied by as many Physicians necessary to bring Jesus back to complete health." The order was signed, General Octavio Pantera. As he handed the release to Judas he added, "I truly hope that this will make some small atonement for the pain and suffering I caused you and your mother. Go now, and do what you must. I will be here waiting for both of you"

Taking the release in his left hand, Judas place his right hand on General Pantera's left forearm and squeezed as a sign of appreciation. They looked at each other and each had the beginning of what could have been a smile on their faces. When Judas turned to walk out of the Palace, General Pantera said, "Judas. Come back soon. I want to meet and hear more about this man named Jesus."

Judas looked at him and gave a smile and nodded his head in the affirmative, then left the Palace.

The prison was about a mile from Herod Antipas Palace. On his way there, Judas decided to take a minute and stop to see Caiaphas one last time. He wanted to return the thirty pieces of silver that he had received from him for turning Jesus over to him. Barcaba and the three other men stayed out of sight as they followed him there.

When he arrived at Caiaphas' home, all four of them hid behind some bushes but with clear view of the anteroom. They could not get close enough to hear, but they could see them as they spoke. Judas did not wait to be announced, but entered the anteroom on his own and yelled out Caiaphas' name as loud as he could several times. It wasn't long before Caiaphas showed himself.

"Judas, what brings you back again? Don't tell me you want another favor from me! Looking lustfully at Judas he added, "This one will cost you more than you may be willing to share with me!"

"No Caiaphas, I do not need anything from you, not any more. As a matter of fact, I have come to return something to you." Having said that, he flung the thirty pieces of silver at Caiaphas and some of the coins came out of their sack and made a dinging noise on the floor as they slid and rolled past Caiaphas.

"What is this Judas?" he said bewildered at this defiant act.

"I do not need your money Caiaphas. I have since found something worth more than money, I have found my salvation in my Lord and Master, Jesus Christ."

"Judas, you're not the same man that came to me earlier, begging for a favor. You have changed."

"Yes I have," replied Judas, in a strong affirmative tone. Turning and pointing his finger at Caiaphas Judas strongly added, "And you would change too if you only believed what is right under your nose. But because of your greed, and you fear of loosing what little power you have over our people, you condemn instead of loving and accepting and understanding Jesus the Christ." Judas looked at Caiaphas and could not help but laugh at the pathetic old man that considered himself the religious leader of the Chosen People. "I feel sorry for you Caiaphas. Your are a good example of the person Jesus spoke about when the Master said 'it will be easier for a camel to pass through the eye of a needle than for you to pass through the doors of heaven.'" Judas turned around and walked out of the anteroom and he could hear Caiaphas shouting as he walked.

"Judas, Judas Iscariot, you will regret this day for as long as you live. I will see to it that you are remembered by all as the traitor that gave up a friend for thirty pieces of silver. You'll see, mark my words. History will never record that you repented. I will insure that you are remembered only as the one that betrayed the Nazarene. I'll see to that, I promise you, I'll see to that! Judas, do you hear me Judas?"

Judas could not remember the last time he felt as good as he did that very moment. The only time he could remember feeling this good was when he was a child and played children games with his friend Cassandra Benjara. Even though he had not slept nor eaten in almost twenty-four hours, his step was lively and he felt good. To his recollection, his spirits had never been so high and in such state of elation in recent times.

He was about halfway to the prison building when three men that he did not know accosted him and held him tightly until a fourth one came from around a corner. He recognized the fourth one as one of the men that was in the mausoleum cave with Levi Bancasee earlier that morning.

"I know you, you are Barcaba!" said Judas, "You were at the mausoleum with Levi earlier this morning. What do you want with me?"

Barcaba shouted, "I'll ask the questions here! What were you doing at Herod Antipas' Palace? Why were you talking to General Pantera for so long? And what were you taking to Caiaphas about also? Don't deny it, we saw you though the window. We have been following you." Drawing his weapon from its sheath he shouted, "Speak, before I run this dagger through you."

"I was trying to get Jesus of Nazareth released," Judas answered. "Let me go, I have an order from Pantera to have Jesus released into my custody. I have to go now before it's too late, let me go!" The other men were still holding his arms.

"Let me see the pardon?" demanded Barcaba, "I want to see what kind of deal you made to have Jesus released. Did you give up Barabbas or Levi? Or did you give up the whole revolutionary movement? Speak or I'll cut your throat right here!"

"I gave up nothing! I just asked for Jesus' release and General Pantera granted it to me. I just left Caiaphas because I wanted to return the thirty pieces of silver I was paid for Jesus."

"Looking through Judas' pockets, Levi was saying, "I don't believe that you would turn down any money, and I don't believe that Pantera would be so generous as to let one of his most famous prisoners go just like that." Sticking the point of his dagger under Judas' lower jaw he demanded, "Confess! Who did you give up?"

Barcaba retrieved that pardon from Judas' pocket and began to read. "Ah, here it is, men, listen to this." He began to read the pardon. "This will introduce Judas Iscariot Pantera, my son. He is to be given immediate custody of Jesus the Nazarene. They are to be given an escort back to Herod's Palace accompanied by as many Physicians that may be necessary to bring Jesus back to complete health."

He looked at Judas and then at the other men and said, "Did you hear that? Judas Pantera, the General's son at that! This imposter is not the son of Simon Josiah after all! He is the bastard son of our mortal enemy General Octavio Pantera!"

"He has to be a spy for the Romans," averred one of them.

"Yes, he has to be," the others chimed in.

"No, I am not a traitor," pleaded Judas. "I don't care about any liberation movement anymore. All I want is to have the Master released before it's too late. I beg you, please let me go before it's too late.

"You heard him men," prompted Barcaba, "He doesn't care about our movement anymore. Come on, let's take him to Gehenna, to the trash dump fires. I know how to get the truth out of him."

Judas tried to fight them off, but they were too many. He kept imploring to be let loose so he could free Jesus from the prison. His begging only increase the pleasure that these men were having in doing what they were doing.

They finally reached the edge of the large pit that served as the dumping ground for Jerusalem. This was where the town's trash, the dead vagrants, and dead beggars from the streets and the diseased dead where thrown and their bodies burned to ashes. It was a huge hole about sixty feet deep and about three hundred feet wide. Some of the town's people referred to it as Gehenna, meaning extreme torment. It was always smoldering and periodically it would burst into a full-fledged fire. The heat from it was almost unbearable at the edge where they stood.

They then tied a noose around Judas' neck. As Barcaba placed it around his neck he noticed the necklace that Judas was wearing. He took it from him saying, "You won't need this where you are going, you traitor!"

"No, please, give me back the necklace. Do what you want with me, but please, don't take the necklace. You don't know what it means to me, please I beg of you!"

Barcaba's responded by spitting on Judas' face. He put the necklace around his own neck, then made Judas stand on an old piece of tree stump next to a lifeless tree that was next to the edge of the smoldering dump. The rope around Judas' neck was thrown over a large limb that extended almost to the edge of the small fiery gorge.

The rope was pulled tight, so much that it made Judas stand on his tiptoes on the piece of rotting stump.

"Who did you turn in you traitor?" demanded Barcaba as he shook the stump back and forth a little with his foot in an attempt to scare a confession from Judas. The other three men stood there, snickering and giggling as if this was the most sadistic enjoyment they had experienced in sometime.

"In the name of our Lord God, I am telling you the truth. I did not give up anybody. Pantera just gave me the pardon for Jesus. I have to get the Master out of prison before it's too late."

Waving the pardon in front of Judas Barcaba said, "Do you see your pardon? I'll tell you what its good for, I'll show you!" With that he wadded it up and threw it into the fires in the gorge. The heat was so intense, that the pardon caught fire while in the air as it floated down. It was aflame before it was a tenth of the way to the bottom of the gorge. Judas began to cry, not for himself, but for the Master. How was he to save him now?

All of a sudden, although completely emotionally drained and at the point of a total breakdown, Judas stopped all outward expression of emotions and stared out to heaven. In an excited voice he asked them, "Did you hear that? Did you hear the Master?"

The tormentors just looked at each other and wondered what Judas was talking about. One of them answered, "No, we did not hear anything. What do you think you heard?"

"I distinctly heard the voice of the Master, Jesus of Nazareth, very clearly saying, 'Father, forgive them for they know not what they do." At that moment his tormentors could see total relief and contentment in Judas' face. The four men could not understand this strange thing that had come over Judas. Here he was, wholly at their pitiless mercy, and he cared nothing for what was about to happen to him. They continued to torment Judas for a while. Then, in total frustration that they could not get a confession out of him, Barcaba kicked the stump out from under him. During this time, they could barely hear Judas saying, "Jesus, my Lord and Savior, thank you for forgiving me of my sins, and for bringing me to everlasting life with You into Your Heavenly Kingdom as You promised. Judas hung on the limb and struggled until he gave up the spirit. It took a few minutes of gasping and choking before Judas succumbed to death.

They left him hanging there, as was the custom of the Romans when they hung someone. This was done so that the dogs could tear the body apart and eventually bring it down and devour it. It was the Roman's belief that if a body was not buried, the soul could not find its way into heaven. Some Jews were beginning to accept that same belief.

Meanwhile, General Pantera had prepared a feast in anticipation of Judas' return. He reasoned that by the time Jesus was released, and they could return, it would not be later then two o'clock or so in the afternoon. When it got to be past the hour, he became worried that something might have happened to Judas. He ordered a horse and with about ten of his soldiers he rode to the prison. When He got there, he dismounted and walked up to the guard and said, "Have you seen a man named Judas Iscariot?"

The guard, standing rigidly at attention shouted, "Yes Sire. He was here this morning about eleven o'clock."

"Did he return here around noon or shortly thereafter?" inquired Pantera.

"No Sire, I have been here without relief, and I have not seen him return."

General Pantera became very concerned about the whereabouts of Judas. With the urgency that Judas had to get Jesus released, he would not have gone anywhere else but here. Where could he have gone? As General Pantera mounted his horse again, and began to lead his troops away, he noticed a man acting strangely, trying to be as inconspicuous as possible. It was Barcaba who had come back to his post to keep watch over Barabbas. He kept hiding behind some outdoor columns at the building across from the prison entrance. General Pantera began to ride his horse in a walk in Barcaba's direction and the troops followed. Barcaba knew that if he made a run for it, he could not out run the horses. Besides, running would bring greater suspicion upon him, so he decided to stay and try to lie his way out of this situation.

As General Pantera and his escort reached him, Barcaba said, "How can a poor humble citizen help you, your magnificence?" Barcaba was attempting to hide his fear the best that he could.

"Have you been standing here long?" questioned General Pantera.

"I have been here since noon sire. I want to make sure those devils you have locked up get what is coming to them. You see, no one knows the time or place of their execution, so I stand here, waiting. This way I'll be sure not to miss out on the fun of seeing them get what they deserve. They are a despicable lot and should all be hung by the neck until their bones rot. "

Just at that moment Pantera noticed the necklace around his neck. When he saw it he shouted to his troops, "Seize him!" The troops dismounted and grabbed him by the arms and threw an arm hold around his neck. General Pantera, still on his horse, looked down on Barcaba and began talking very slowly and meticulously to Barcaba so there would be no misunderstanding,

"I know you have seen Judas Iscariot. There is not any need for you to lie to me." Pointing at his chest General Pantera added, "You are wearing his necklace." Barcaba started to talk and lie to him about having found the necklace, but Pantera kicked him in the face and then replied, "That is not possible. The owner of that necklace was at the Palace with me when you say you got here to this place. I am going to give you one last change to tell me what you have done with Judas, and to take me where ever you might have him." Barcaba had never seen eyes so full of vengeance like he was seeing now. General Pantera's eyes seemed to go right through him. His eyes alone put a degree of fear into Barcaba that he had never ever experience before.

He became so frightened that before he knew it he said, "Okay, I will take you to him. But I want you to know that I had nothing to do with it. I was only there after it all happened. It was someone else that did it, I was just watching from a distance."

With a rope tied around his neck, and his hands bound behind him, Barcaba ran in front of Pantera's horse as he took them to Gehenna. There they found the body of Judas still hanging from the dead tree limb. Although he had only been there a few hours, his face was burned to a point that it was almost unrecognizable. The heat generated by the fires below in the gorge had burned it. A few more hours and it would have been impossible to identify him.

Pantera was shock! He lost his composure and he cried for the first time in his life. He never in his entire life remembered crying for anything before, not even when he was a child. He kept thinking, "How could my God Apollo be so cruel as to give him a son and then in less then two or three hours, take him away from him." He had Judas' body taken down. They laid it on his cape and he knelt down besides Judas' body and grieved. In the background he could hear Barcaba pleading for his life, but rage overcame Pantera, so he ordered that Barcaba be stripped naked and hung in Judas' place. Before they did, Pantera took the necklace back, and placed it around Judas' neck once again.

General Pantera then took Judas' body and buried it in the cemetery reserved for noblemen. It was eight o'clock in the evening by the time all was finished.

Chapter 17
The Re-awakening of Judas' Spirit

Early the next morning Pantera was visiting Judas' grave. It was Friday morning about eight-thirty in the morning. At the same time Pontius Pilate came out to the balcony of the Palace overlooking the pavilion with Jesus in chains behind him. He said to the Jews that were mostly freedom fighters standing in the pavilion "Look, I am bringing him out to you to let you know once again that I find no basis for a charge against him."

Jesus was wearing a purple robe, and a crown of thorns from which He still bled. He also had horrendous lash marks from the savage whipping He endured. Looking at Jesus Pilate said, "Look, here He is. He is only a man. Why do you fear Him?" Pilate was hoping that by seeing the vicious punishment he had inflicted on Jesus, they would have pity on Him and ask for His release. But it was not to be. They continued shouting, "Crucify Him."

"Shall I crucify your King?" he said to the crowd, hoping to change their mind one last time. "Is this really what you want me to do?"

"We have no other King but Caesar," the chief priests answered. Finally in frustration, Pilate handed him over to the Sanhedrin to be crucified saying, "I wash my hands of this. Do with Him as you please."

Jesus was then made to carry His own heavy cross to a place called Golgotha which is Aramaic for the words "The place of the Skull." By this time, Jesus was devoid of all human strength, so He fell three times with His cross on His way to Golgotha. After the third time, the Roman Centurion in charge of the detail to crucify Jesus grabbed a bystander named Simon, a Cyrenian and made him help Jesus carry the cross the rest of the way to Golgotha. There they crucified him by hammering extra large nails into His wrists and feet. Extra large nails, at least one inch in diameter where needed because the Romans found that smaller nails would rip right out of human flesh and would not hold.

His cross was placed between to two thieves who were crucified with him. From the sixth hour after being crucified, to the ninth hour that Jesus hung on the cross, darkness came over the land. About the ninth hour Jesus cried out in a loud voice, "Eloi, Eloi, lama sabachthani?" Which means "My God, My God, why have you forsaken me?" Then when Jesus cried out again, He gave up His spirit.

At that very moment the curtain of the temple was torn in two from top to bottom. The earth shook and the rocks split. Some tombs broke open and the bodies of many holy people, including Judas, were raised up from their graves. Some were raise body and soul and were seen walking the streets and some only spiritually like Judas.

At the moment of Judas' spiritual resurrection, in a town called Cyprus in the country of Greece, a woman was cleaning the floor at her home when Judas appeared and stood at her doorway. Judas called to her saying, "Cassandra."

She turned around and saw that it was Judas. Surprised and full of joy at seeing him she said very happily, "Judas my friend!" She ran to embrace him but he pulled back.

"Cassandra, you must not touch me, for I have yet to be sanctified. Our Lord God has reserved a special place for all of His Apostles in His heavenly Kingdom as He promised us so many times when He walked with us."

Cassandra did not understand, but she did as he asked and held back. Judas continued. "Cassandra, I had to see you just one more time before I left this earth to join our Lord and Savior Jesus Christ. I wanted you to know that other then Jesus, Reuben and Leah, you have meant more to me than any other person I have ever known in the world. I also wanted you to know that I am finally at peace. I have found and accomplished my destiny. It was and continues to be to serve our Lord Jesus Christ. Believe me when I tell you Cassandra, He is the Son of God. It was my destiny to help fulfill Scripture.

Before my birth, the God of Abraham, selected me, to represent all of mankind, since Adam and Eve's time to those yet to be born in the future, in offering to Him in sacrifice, the Lamb of God as an atonement gift. Jesus Christ is that sacrificial lamb that was sacrificed so that all the sins of the world, since the beginning of time, and yet to come could be forgiven. As in the Old Testament, Jesus was the Lamb, and I was Abraham. You must believe in Him, for only through Him can you find peace and joy and live in His Kingdom in heaven. I am at peace now. I have never experienced so much joy and happiness.

Cassandra, I have even seen my family, I have finally joined my mother, my grandparents, and Reuben and Leah, and Simon Josiah. I have also seen your father and mother in Paradise too, and they wanted me to tell you that you have grown into a beautiful, God loving woman. You too will see them soon, when God calls you into his Heavenly Kingdom.

It is so beautiful here Cassandra, just as you and I imagined when we were children laying on the grassy knolls and looking up at the sky. It is much more than what anyone can really imagine. Greed, hate, rancor, lust, pain, suffering, wars, and talk of wars do not exist here. There is only unconditional love that flows through everything from God. It is as Jesus told us, God is love, and those living on earth that abide in love, also abide in God, and God in them. Please know that I will always have this devoted love for you and it will grow and grow until the end of time."

When he had finished saying those things, he ended by saying, "Goodbye Cassandra, we shall see each other again. Until that time, pray for all mankind, that they may experience the love and compassion of Jesus Christ." He turned and walked out of the door and slowly his apparition disappeared.

She could not believe what had just happened! "This is impossible," she told herself. Was she seeing things? Was it a daydream? Yet it seemed so real! She felt very weak, and almost fell as her leg strength gave way after that encounter. She had to sit down on a chair by the table near the door before she fell on the floor. Her mind was completely occupied thinking about what just had happened.

After a few minutes she had just about convinced herself that it was only a figment of her imagination. What else could it have been? Things like this just don't happen. She was finally beginning to come out of this rapture state, still not believing what she had seen with her own eyes. But just then, as she stretched her left arm out on the table, her elbow hit some object that made a rasping noise as she accidentally moved it with her arm. She looked down and to her surprise, and unexplainably, there on the table lay Judas' necklace along with a beautiful radiantly bunch of forget-me-nots flowers.

In total awe, she slowly picked up the necklace, stared at it for a while, and then she picked up the flowers and embraced them both next to her breast, then slowly slid off the chair onto her knees, looked up towards heaven and began to pray.

The End